TWELVE URNS

by

Kristy Gherlone

Twelve Urns
Copyright © 2016 by Kristy Gherlone

Cover image:
Shutterstock/christopherolland

Published by Piscataqua Press
An imprint of RiverRun Bookstore, Inc.
142 Fleet Street | Portsmouth, NH | 03801
www.riverrunbookstore.com
www.piscataquapress.com

ISBN: 978-1-944393-07-6

Printed in the United States of America

Dedication

For my loving husband, Chris. Thank you so much for all of your support. I hope you know how very much you mean to me. You make me a better person.

And for my children and grandson, who keep me endlessly entertained and bring me daily happiness.

PROLOGUE
Germany 1945

"**I** have brought what you've been looking for, sir. Magdalena has sent me."

From within the folds of his dingy coat, the thin nervous man produced a small wooden branch and shoved it through the open and rotting doorway of an abandoned farmhouse. His hand was shaking, making it jump up and down slightly as though it was dancing.

"Please, please take it quickly! I must get out of here," he begged. He did not like the feeling he had. The hand that held the object tingled and made his knees feel rubbery. Small beads of sweat started to fall onto his glasses, making it nearly impossible for him to see clearly. He wanted to throw the thing and run, but he had his orders.

In the far right corner of the dark and crumbling house, a man sat in the shadows. He rose slowly and stood, studying the deliveryman for just a moment before going into the light. Quivering, the thin man lowered his glasses slightly and squinted his eyes in an effort to see, yet too afraid to look. Curiosity got the better of him and he peered out through the tiny slits of his eyes.

Even though unshaven and stripped of his uniform, he was unmistakable. Instantly a warm wetness formed on the front of his pants and he nearly dropped his offering. He stepped back, arm still inside of the door, his heart pounding and feet threatening to flee.

"You vill solute me," the man within the room asserted calmly, almost whispering and with a thick German accent. He reached out and snatched the arm of the thin man, squeezing tightly until he let go of the branch and it landed neatly in his hand. With his teeth tightly clenched and a small, thin—lipped sneer registering on his lips, he dug in with his dirty fingernails until he drew blood, but then suddenly released the terrified man, sending him sprawling backward. The thin man regained his balance and raised his right arm.

"Heil Hitler!" he managed to squeak before scurrying and stumbling out of the doorway and out of sight.

Where was she? Why hadn't she brought it herself? So many questions, but the relief at having his charm back was overwhelming.

He placed it around his neck, tucking it securely inside of his jacket next to his heart. It wasn't a charm, really, but a piece of root from the mandrake tree she planted years before. Black as coal and oddly heavy for a piece of wood, it had kept them connected through the dream eyes all throughout his life.

The thought that the connection might have been lost filled him with despair. He had been frantically searching for it for days.

Visions began filling his head. His body convulsed as the images played across his mind. When they were done, he began to retch violently the spare contents of his stomach. He understood now. He understood everything. His skin crawled and suddenly he became aware of his own foul odor.

The war was lost and his officers were all dead. Even the promise of the future war did nothing to comfort him. He was going to miss her so.

The hopelessness overtook him. He reached down to capture the gun he'd placed moments before on a broken and dusty chair that had been left behind by the previous occupants. He turned it over and over in his hands. How many people had this gun killed? No, not people. Animals. Isn't that what she'd always called them? He wondered for just a moment when exactly he'd begun to hate them so. He wondered why she never hated him.

Even though he was well into the woods, he was not far enough away from the stacks to be away from the stench of the last ones. Their ashes rained down through a gaping hole in the dilapidated roof and settled like moths on his shoulders. He could see all of the faces. So many. Just not enough. He wanted them all. It was what she wanted. He would have given her anything. He could at least give her one more.

With a quavering hand, he tilted the gun upwards toward the side of his forehead and pulled the trigger. He was surprised at how little it hurt. His fleeting thoughts were of her. He always thought of her. She was in his soul.

CHAPTER ONE
Boston 2015

B astian sat facing away from the door in the small, orderly office. His tiny back was curved slightly as he bent over the blocks he was handling on the floor. He was a beautiful child. His hair was blonde and shiny; like pure white gold, and his eyes drew stares from everyone who had ever had the chance to be near him. They were blue, so blue. His mother, Greta, thought they looked just like a rare sapphire would, freshly plucked from the earth and seeing the sunlight for the first time. His angelic face revealed nothing of what was within.

Greta nervously checked her watch. She'd been waiting months to get this appointment, eager to find out what was wrong with her child. It figured that the doctor would be running behind, adding to her suspense. God knew that she'd been through this before; many times. Trips to the doctor and waiting in rooms full of sick, crabby people had become a fairly routine part of her life. It was a far cry from the life she had wanted.

Bastian had been the picture of health when he was born. He came out a hefty eight pounds, four ounces, and was just a bit over twenty-two inches long. He was pink and beautiful and when Greta held him to her breast that first time, he latched on with vigor. She felt so lucky. She doted over him and marveled at every milestone. He smiled at two months, rolled over at three, and began cooing at four. Then, it was as though an uninvited stranger had visited in the night, stolen her child, and left her with any empty shell.

She knew something had to be wrong. Mothers just know. He stopped looking at her. He stopped smiling. Bastian became an island unto himself. He cried all the time and Greta could do nothing to comfort him. It was as if he wanted nothing to do with her at all. She read every book she could get her hands on, trying to find something that would explain her son's odd behavior. She consulted with Bastian's pediatrician several times, but he kept assuring her that it was just a phase and that it would pass. Greta desperately wanted to believe that, and tried to continue life as usual, but it didn't pass, and as each month went on, it was clear to Greta that something was horribly wrong.

Finally, Bastian's pediatrician had to agree when Bastian failed to produce even one intelligible word by the age of three, and sent them to Children's Hospital in Boston to have a series of tests. This was supposed to be the day…the day that she would finally have a diagnosis for her son.

"Ms. Hall?" Greta jumped at the sound, already on edge, and looked towards the door. A smiling nurse wearing a colorful set of scrubs stood in the doorway. "The doctor is ready to see you."

A glum looking man carrying a large stack of files breezed in and placed the papers on his desk before turning to address Greta. He gave her a lopsided smile and held out his hand. "Good morning, Ms. Hall, I'm Dr. Goldenberg." Greta stood, smoothed her skirt, and was just getting ready to shake the doctor's hand when she heard a noise behind her. Startled, she turned to look. Bastian, who had been quietly playing until then, had gotten up from the floor, kicked most the blocks away and stood facing the doctor.

His tiny face contorted into something that resembled anger and repulsion, though Greta couldn't remember ever seeing him display either emotion. His eyes turned dark as he glared at the doctor. In his hand he held one of the larger sized blocks. Dr. Goldenberg bent down to Bastian's level and attempted a greeting, though he appeared confused by Bastian's reaction to his entrance.

Without warning, Bastian began shrieking. A slew of baby blather sputtered from his mouth, and he suddenly leapt towards the doctor before anyone could move. Bastian began beating Dr. Goldenberg savagely with the block, smashing at his stomach and legs, while repeating the same garbled jabber.

The doctor bent down even further in an attempt to shield his legs and restrain the child, but Bastian dropped his weapon, grabbed Dr. Goldenberg's hair and pulled hard so that the doctor's face met his. Sheer hatred was showing on his face and spewing from his mouth. He bit the doctor's nose hard. Blood began to spurt out, dripping onto his white coat, before quickly pooling on the floor. A scream welled up in Greta as she stood horrified, but it didn't come out.

Bastian managed to scratch at Dr. Goldenberg's eyes, though the terrified doctor did what he could to try and protect himself. He held his arms and hands across his face and tried backing away from the tiny offender.

The room suddenly became alive with activity. Nurses, other doctors, and orderlies rushed in, prompted by all of the noise. They took quick stock of what was happening and surrounded Bastian. It felt to Greta like she was watching a horror movie. She was paralyzed with fear. Her disbelief kept her from moving. It couldn't be real!

A nurse tried to grab the child, but only managed to get part of his shirt, which enraged him even more. He turned on her, kicking at her legs and spitting. Bastian, blood dripping from his chin and sticking to his teeth, looked like a rabid animal instead of a small boy.

Dr. Goldenberg held onto his nose, blood streaming through his fingers and running down his arms, as he hollered, "Get some sedation!! This child needs to be restrained!"

Greta briefly snapped out of it and attempted to stop Bastian, and then she fainted.

"Dr. Goldenberg is in surgery. His nose will have to be completely reconstructed." After waking from her brief fainting spell, Greta was brought down the hall to the office of Dr. Jackson, who was another specialist at the Boston hospital. A nurse relayed the most recent events to her, while she waited to be seen. "I don't think he'll be returning to work for some time."

Greta could tell that the nurse was still shaken up, and she didn't blame her. Her own head was throbbing and she was still trying to make sense of what had happened. She was confused, tired, and worried for her son.

The nurse explained that Dr. Jackson would be taking over her son's case while Dr. Goldenberg recovered. He had ordered that Bastian be kept in the hospital until they could come up with a reasonable plan for his therapy, and it was he who would be trying to explain her son's diagnosis to

Greta.

Finally, Dr. Jackson arrived, dismissed the nurse, and closed the door. "We have gone over the results of your son's tests, and it's our feeling that Bastian has autism. I'm not sure if you know anything about autism, Ms. Hall, but it's an illness that is on a spectrum scale." Dr. Jackson sat down tiredly, and peeked over his glasses quizzically, though it was obvious by his demeanor that he was still reeling from news of the attack.

"Yes, I did do some reading about autism. It was one of the illnesses I came across in a pediatric book. I did a little more research when Bastian seemed to regress, but he didn't seem to fit all of the characteristics. Are you sure?" Greta asked.

"Yes, we are sure, and until today, it was unclear just where Bastian was on that scale. It would have been impossible to know until we saw him and tested him more extensively. Some of our patients function at much higher levels, almost at the normal range, but unfortunately, some are what we would consider severely autistic. Based on the events of today, and after consulting with my colleagues, I'd have to classify Bastian in the latter category, I'm sorry to say."

Greta was crushed. Autism! From what she'd read, autism couldn't be cured. She closed her eyes with disappointment and wiped at her forehead with the cool, wet washcloth that was given to her after her fainting spell. Her mind raced, trying to remember all of the other stuff she had either heard or read about the illness.

Though Greta had labeled it in her own mind as a possibility, she'd really been hoping for a developmental delay instead. A diagnosis of autism would be something that would stay with Bastian forever. Speech problems, social issues...the list went on.

Maybe it was wishful thinking on her part, but she'd been hoping that whatever Bastian had would be an easy fix, and she'd be able to get on with her life without too much disruption. Given her profession, having a typical child would have been a struggle, but one with severe autism would be a big challenge.

She wrongfully assumed that Bastian would probably need speech therapy, maybe even some tutoring, but nothing as extensive as what the treatment for autism would be.

Until then, Bastian had never shown any aggression, only what appeared to be a silent and solitary existence, rarely even making eye contact with her. It made her worry, but through all of the months of meeting with doctors, and through all of the tests that were preformed, somehow she'd tricked herself into believing that the outcome would be something simple.

Earlier, while she'd been waiting in Dr. Goldenberg's office, she'd had hope, but with the horror of what had happened and the diagnosis of autism, Greta felt scared and defeated.

She couldn't get the images of blood out of her mind. Dr. Goldenberg's shrieks kept playing over in her head. Greta lowered her head into her hands, trying to steady herself and come to terms with what had happened.

"I know that you've been through a lot today, and it's understandable if you're feeling overwhelmed," Dr. Jackson soothed.

"That's just a little bit of an understatement, don't you think?" Greta asked thickly, looking up at the doctor. It was the worst thing she'd ever had to witness. Seeing Bastian like that made her feel like throwing up.

"Look, I don't know a whole lot about autism. All that I do know came from some pediatric books and some internet research that I did on the illness. What I have read indicated that children with autism cannot be cured, right?" she asked, hoping that he could dispel her worst fear.

"From what's been studied and published prior to the last ten years would, indeed, indicate that autism cannot be cured," Dr. Jackson admitted, "however, it does appear that as the number of diagnoses has risen, which by the way, is one in one hundred and fifty-six births, it's since been studied more extensively. It's now the opinion of several well esteemed psychiatrists and pediatricians that the illness is, if not curable, something that can be overcome," he offered, giving Greta a small bit of hope.

Well, if there wasn't a cure, Greta didn't see how an illness could be simply "overcome." It didn't make sense, but she was sure she'd be finding out all about it in the coming days. It was a lot to take in, and Greta was feeling a bit traumatized. She had plenty of questions, but just wanted the answer to one; the rest she could sort out later. She really needed to know if what happened was something that was typical of autistic behavior, and if it would be something that she would have to worry about repeatedly. She didn't like to think about the possibility that he might attack someone else.

"What I need you to explain is why my son, a normally quiet child, would lash out so suddenly today and in such a vicious way?" Greta's voice quavered a little, but she continued. "He's never done anything like this before, and I just can't understand why it happened. What would make a child with autism attack someone like that?"

"It's not uncommon for children with autism to have times in which they lash out at others for no apparent reason," Dr. Jackson explained. "In studies, it has been shown that any change in a child's routine, loud noises, or the introduction of new people can sometimes trigger episodes of violence. It is our thought that the stress of being at this new place, coupled with the introduction of a new doctor, may have triggered Bastian's episode. What's important now is that we get Bastian the right treatment and therapy so that these episodes won't happen again," he stated with finality.

He placed Bastian's file onto his desk and paged his nurse. "First, I will take you to see Bastian, and then I'll have my nurse, Jane, meet with you to explain what we need to do next. If you have any more questions, please do not hesitate to ask. I will also have her prepare a pamphlet of information, along with a couple of books on the subject for you to take with you and look over during Bastian's stay here." The doctor rose and smiled reassuringly. "We'll be in touch. Try not to worry."

Yeah right, Greta thought. She reached for her pocketbook, thanked the doctor and started for the door, but paused. "If Bastian already has a diagnosis, and you know what triggered his episode, then why is it necessary that he stay here?" Greta inquired, grasping for any kind of reassurance that the doctor could give to her before leaving.

What she was really worried about, if she were being completely honest with herself, was that they were keeping him because they thought he might have another episode soon. The thought sickened her.

Greta, who had never been truly scared of anything, was

now afraid of her son. Though he'd never done anything to hurt her before, after what she'd witnessed, she just couldn't be so sure that he wouldn't. What if she got him home and he attacked her?

The doctor placed a comforting hand on her shoulder. "Again, try not to worry Ms. Hall. We work with many children who have autism. We know, for the most part, how to manage the illness. His stay here is really just precautionary. We'd like to monitor him for a few days and set up treatment before his release. Before his discharge I'll personally make sure that everything is in place for when you both go home," he told Greta lightly, but then in a more serious tone, "We want to make sure the episode that Bastian had is not repeated. While we have seen attacks before, I do have to say that none of them were quite this serious. I don't want to make you feel worse than you already do, but Bastian has probably caused permanent damage to Dr. Goldenberg's face. If that had been a schoolmate of Bastian's, the outcome could've been much worse."

Greta lowered her head and shut her eyes to block out the image of something like that happening.

"Let me take you to see him and we'll do our best to make sure he is safe and comfortable for the evening," Dr. Jackson promised as he led her out the door.

Any comfort that Greta had been feeling left her. The doctor was right. Even though Bastian's behavior today was horrifying to say the least, and as hard as it was to imagine, it could have been worse.

"Please send Dr. Goldenberg my apologies," Greta told Dr. Jackson as she left. She knew it wasn't enough, but it was all she could offer.

❖

It was a good feeling to be speeding down Route 1, top down on her aging Cabrio, music full blast, enjoying the warm sun and the smell of summer. Kelly Eaton liked Boston, though not as much as her home in Maine.

Her long, blonde hair flew behind her as she sped down the road, and Kelly knew she made more than a few heads turn her way, though that was not at all what she was looking for. Too much attention only embarrassed her.

She'd been feeling a bit lonely, and had been spending time with a guy she'd met in class. He was not the type of guy she usually went for. He certainly wasn't like her old high school crush that she couldn't stop thinking about, but she welcomed the company and was excited to be meeting him for dinner and drinks at the Kowloon. Chinese food was high up on the list of Kelly's favorites, and she couldn't think of a better way to spend the evening.

Shit! Her phone was vibrating. It was a good thing it did vibrate, because she would never have heard it over the pulse of her techno music, or her own voice singing along with the lyrics.

"You better not be canceling, I'm almost at the restaurant!" Kelly uttered into the mouthpiece. She tried balancing both phone and steering wheel, while veering in and out of traffic at the same time.

"Is this Miss Eaton?" a professional, clipped voice asked.

Damn, she should have screened. Probably a telemarketer, she thought as she reached to turn down the music. "Yes this is Kelly Eaton." She breathed a little sigh, waiting for some kind of sales pitch.

"Miss Eaton its Jane. Jane Tuttle. I'm the nurse at Children's, the one that works for Dr. Jackson."

"Oh, hello Jane," Kelly answered, relieved. She'd spoken with her before when she'd referred a couple of clients to her. "What can I do for you?"

"Well, Dr. Jackson asked that I give you a call. We have an especially difficult case, and he suggested that you'd be the best person to handle this one."

Kelly was thrilled. Since she had moved to Boston almost four years ago to attend college, she'd been helping to fund her education by working with children who had autism. It was totally unrelated to her field of study, but the pay was great, though not enough to make a living on, and she loved working with kids.

Her real passion was language. It didn't matter what the language was. If Kelly heard it, she could pick it up very quickly, and she was proud to admit that she was fluent in three different languages, and spoke passably in two others.

She didn't stop there. There were always twists to any language. Different dialects within a language used by some of the older populations that, having been passed down in some generations, were now forgotten by most, but still used in isolated regions. That was a particular fascination for Kelly, though just a hobby.

She couldn't imagine a need in her field of interpretation for such small groups of people, but if she could find one in German that she could actually crack, then it would make for an excellent senior thesis.

She and her professor had begun work last year researching the different forms of German, which was his native language. It was frustrating, to say the least. There was very little written on the subject, and it was impossible to find anyone in their area, or even living at all, who could be of much help.

At the end of the semester, Kelly had all but given up, and had decided that she would do her thesis on the tribal people of Africa and the different languages spoken within the central and eastern parts of the continent. It had been done before with so many people traveling to Africa and the research being done that the information was easily accessible and would probably seem boorish. She'd already been studying the Nilo-Saharan region, which in itself had one hundred and forty languages spoken. However, her professor hinted that there was a possibility that after the summer break he might come up with something, and asked her to be patient.

In high school, her guidance counselor let her take dual language classes each year, and after graduation, she'd been readily accepted into Northeastern, where she was actively pursuing a degree in language interpretation. Not that she wasn't good enough to become an interpreter now, but these days you had to have a degree. You needed an expensive piece of paper or no one would even consider you.

With the prospect of a new client and the money that would bring in, she could relax a little bit. Her previous client had just aged out of the program, leaving her unemployed for the time being, without enough income to support herself.

"Just give me the number and I'll get back to you tomorrow morning," Kelly affirmed, as she scanned the parking lot for Greg's Jeep. "I'll definitely take the case."

"Like I mentioned, it's an especially difficult one. This little guy is showing some serious aggression, so please do call me first thing in the morning," Jane pleaded. "You may decide that you don't want the job."

Kelly was nonplussed. "Definitely, first thing. And don't worry, I've had a lot of experience. I'm sure it'll work out fine." Kelly pulled into the spot next to Greg's and quickly jotted down the number that Jane gave her.

Kelly thought she heard the nurse sigh a little as she was hanging up the phone. She wouldn't let it put a damper on her evening. She was hoping to have some fun! Whether the little angel was difficult or not, it didn't matter. She needed the money and she'd have to take the case, no matter what.

A small sob escaped Greta as she entered the room and saw Bastian lying in a hospital bed with his feet and arms held by restraints. He was sleeping peacefully, with the help of the medication that was running into his arm.

To Greta it seemed unbelievable that this same child, her child, had gone so crazy just an hour before. His little face was so serene in sleep. His blond hair had been brushed back from his forehead, giving him the look of a perfect angel.

A drop of blood, which had escaped the nurses cleaning, lay dried on Bastian's cheek next to his ear. Greta immediately went to the sink and got a wet paper towel to wipe it. She didn't want any reminders of what had happened. She bent over to plant a small kiss on his forehead. His eyes fluttered, but he did not awaken. A tear escaped Greta's eye and landed on Bastian's nose, which she also wiped away.

As Greta sat in the chair next to Bastian's bed, she

listened to the quiet blips of the monitors to which Bastian was connected. She was so tired, but the events of the day kept playing out in her mind, though she willed them to go away.

She kept wondering if this was somehow her fault. Could she have done something while she was pregnant that would make Bastian autistic? Maybe it was all of the chemicals that she worked with on a daily basis at the lab. Maybe it was genetic.

She made an attempt to read a magazine left on the nightstand by one of the nurses, but she just couldn't seem to concentrate. She searched back through her mind, trying to figure out how she got to this point. This wasn't at all how she expected her life to turn out.

When she was young, Greta's mother had been very hard on her. She rarely made time for her or for fun. Her job as a lawyer for the District Attorney's office always came first. Responsibilities and chores were doled out to Greta on a daily basis. Her mother was an old-fashioned woman who had immigrated from Germany years before and stood by her notion that German girls did not grow up to be good German women without a lot of hard work. She didn't seem to understand that they were no longer in Germany and that things were different in the States.

Greta made a resolution at a very young age that when she was an adult, she would live by her own rules. No one was going to tell her what to do or what to be. She dreamed up the most fascinating lives with the help of her favorite movies and television programs.

However, she adored her father. While he was also from Germany, his mother was Jewish. Despite the difficult times they went through during World War II, he was more easy going. He took Greta with him most Saturday afternoons to the park, where they would try out some of his experiments on the expansive grassy lawn.

A very creative scientist, her father worked in a lab testing bombs for the military. Greta was fascinated by it the first time he had shown her what could happen if you put together two separate chemicals. She was hooked, but her mother strongly discouraged it, and finally put a stop to the Saturday experiments, telling both of them that it was too dangerous.

If she couldn't become a scientist, then she would be an actress, a model, or at the very least a writer. She would let the dishes pile up in the sink and she would never, ever scrub the floors with ammonia.

At the age of sixteen when she had gotten her license, she escaped as much as she could from the disapproving looks and the never-ending lectures from her mother.

Living in New England never failed to excite Greta. Its changing seasons and weather offered a wide array of both color and diversity. In less than an hour, a person could go from quiet green hills, with crystal clear streaming waters, to the fast paced bustle of the city. Greta especially loved visiting Boston, where the choice of restaurants, historic sites, and waterfront areas always gave her a thrill.

She grew up in a large town in New Hampshire, which under the thumb of her mother had seemed dull and boring, but when she was old enough to drive, she discovered the advantages of being able to skip from one place to another and still make curfew. The restaurants and exciting nightlife lured her in, and she was forever chasing the next adventure.

However, being in Boston at the hospital, it felt to Greta

like the equivalent of visiting McDonald's as a child, and then working there as a young adult. The magic was just gone. It all came down to duty and responsibility. Her last thought before her eyes became heavy and she dropped off to sleep was how much she hated her mother for being right. It really did all come down to duty and responsibility. She was an adult, and a mother.

"Ms. Hall?" A nurse had come in and was standing at the end of Bastian's bed when Greta awoke. "I'm Jane. Dr. Jackson has assigned me to your case. I'm very sorry to disturb you since you're finally getting some rest, but we have some things to go over, and I was wondering if you would come with me."

Greta didn't know how long she had been asleep. An hour? Maybe two. She looked over at Bastian who was still sleeping soundly.

"Don't worry about him. We'll have someone keep a close eye on him," the nurse explained, noticing Greta's reluctance at leaving him. Greta gave her son a wistful glance, and followed the nurse out the door.

The hospital smelled sterile, which she supposed all hospitals did, as she plodded tiredly along after the nurse. The floors gleamed with cleanliness and wax, and something about that made her miserable. Jane's office was slightly homier, but no matter how she had decorated it, it still held that odor, like stale bleach and wet cotton. Jane stared patiently at Greta as she settled herself in.

"I'm sure that your head must be swimming with all kinds of worries and questions. I can't even imagine what you're going through, though I have been with many parents as they were given the diagnosis of autism. It's never easy. I'd like to give you some reassurance that we'll do everything we can to make your job as Bastian's parent easier," Jane offered kindly.

If Greta could be grateful for anything, it was that she'd chosen this hospital for Bastian's treatment. Everyone was really trying to be so understanding and helpful, despite what her child had done to one of their doctors.

"The typical treatment for children who have autism begins at the age of about 18 to 19 months, or usually about the time they are diagnosed. We like to get them started as soon as possible," Jane explained. "So, typically speaking, at three, Bastian is a little far behind. He'll need speech and physical therapy, which will help him to communicate better, and develop the fine and gross motor movements that children with autism typically lag in." She went on with the efficiency of a person very well versed in the subject. "But the most important piece of Bastian's therapy, however, will be the introduction and work of an early interventionist," she concluded, and waited for Greta to respond.

Whatever therapy was needed, of course Greta would agree to it. She'd have to. She had excellent insurance, and even if she didn't, she would have spent all of the money she had inherited from her parents and managed to save over the years for the purpose of seeing her son get well. It was her responsibility, she thought dully.

While she had heard of the speech and physical therapy before, she had never heard of early interventionists. She had no idea of where to find one.

"As far as the speech and physical therapy, I'm sure I would have no trouble finding either of those, but I've never heard of an early interventionist, I wouldn't even know where to begin to look," Greta revealed. "What exactly does an interventionist do?" she asked.

"Actually, Ms. Hall, you won't need to worry about any of those things. The hospital has planned to set everything in place for you before you leave," Jane answered reassuringly. "All of Bastian's therapy will be done right in your home, so you see, it'll be a bit more convenient for you. As for the early interventionist, I've already taken the liberty of calling someone who is highly qualified. She's a great interventionist who has had excellent results with some of her other clients. She will be coaching your son on many aspects of his life, from the development of language, to simple life skills."

Greta nodded, taking it all in, though her heart was sinking. It did sound like a lot, and it sounded very intrusive. She wondered if she'd have the time to do everything that needed to be done with her work schedule. It was really getting busy lately, and her boss wasn't that great about allowing time off.

"Kelly, Bastian's interventionist, will be visiting your home on a regular basis and working with your son there. We find this treatment, while intrusive for the family, to be the most effective for the child," Jane continued, confirming Greta's own thoughts.

She didn't have any family close by, so the realization of what she was facing seemed overwhelming. She didn't have a lot of friends either, and therefore didn't entertain a lot of company. What Jane had suggested was going to be tough for her. She would have to allow strangers into her home to do what she was neither trained, nor equipped to do. She would also be giving up some of the control on how her son was raised. Yet the idea that she wouldn't be completely alone in all of this was somewhat appealing.

Kristy Gherlone

While she didn't know a lot about autism, she did know that she loved her son, no matter what he had. She would do everything she possibly could to get him on the right track, and if that meant making some sacrifices, then she'd have to do it. Her boss would have to deal with it too. She knew she was needed there, so he couldn't just fire her. She hoped. "When can we begin?"

CHAPTER TWO

As Greta unlocked the front door to her small but immaculate Cape style house in Brighton, Massachusetts, Bastian zinged past her and dropped to the living room floor, immediately beginning to line up the blocks he'd left there days before.

The house smelled musty as houses usually did when not inhabited for a few days, and Greta, already exhausted from the last two days spent at the hospital, knew that she'd have some work to do before the meeting with Bastian's new team of specialists.

She didn't know why it was important for her to make a good impression. She'd always been a decent housekeeper, but she wasn't used to strange people coming into her home. It made her feel vulnerable...open to scrutiny.

It never really occurred to her until that point that she was a single mom. A statistic. With all of those people coming in to work with Bastian, maybe they'd find her unfit. Maybe they would see all of it as her fault.

Dr. Jackson assured her that there wasn't anything she could have done to prevent Bastian's autism; that it was in no way her fault. In spite of that, she couldn't help but feel that she could have done more. Perhaps the doctor had been wrong and some of the chemicals that she'd worked with had caused this. How could he be so sure that they didn't?

Labels of caution were plastered all over pretty much everything she used, and though she was always careful, following every precaution, they were very dangerous.

Either way, she couldn't help but feel that she should've been more aggressive in the beginning, pushed the issue as soon as she started to notice that something was wrong. But how could she have known? She'd never really been around children in her whole life.

It did make her wonder, though, where autism came from. When she'd been a kid in school, there wasn't any such thing that she could remember. She'd never even heard of it until just a few years ago when it started making the headlines.

There were kids in her school who had diabetes, and she saw them eating special snacks and juice throughout the day. She'd seen kids that were confined to wheelchairs, and knew of children with retardation who went to special schools.

Recently, she'd heard theories about autism. People blamed it on the immunizations, or diet, or possibly the environment. Whatever it was, and wherever it came from, she couldn't help but feel cheated that her son had it.

Greta never thought she'd even have children. Always trying to do the opposite of what her mother did, she'd decided a long time ago that she didn't want the responsibility. She'd never even babysat like some of her friends had done.

She liked children well enough; it wasn't that. It was just that she'd been determined to live free from responsibility and duty.

Greta couldn't help feeling like a burden to her mother when she was growing up. She knew that her mother loved her in her own way, but she always came second to her work.

Laughter and fun were rare occurrences with Greta's mom. She always took a serious and focused approach to anything she had to deal with, parenting included.

It probably didn't help that her parents had her late in life, as if she were an afterthought. Her mom expected a lot from her. The house always had to be in order; not just picked up, but clean to the point of being almost sterile. She also insisted on complete quiet, definitely prescribing to the myth that children should be seen and not heard. She banished Greta to her room often, while she worked.

Her dad had been gregarious and charming, while her mom was prone to seclusion and suspicion. They hosted and attended many social functions, at the insistence of her father, and if he had one flaw, it was that he spent more time worrying about what others thought of them, and worked hard at maintaining the image of a perfect family.

Everyone expected that the only child of two very accomplished people would follow in their footsteps, and Greta's parents let her know that they would accept nothing less. She'd spent a lot of time in her teen years rebelling against them. There were many heated arguments, threats, and punishments.

Greta would skip curfew, staying out until dawn drinking with friends, and had run away on more than one occasion. The summer before her junior year, her mother had told her that they were sending her to Germany to live with her grandparents to avoid any further embarrassment she might cause them. She was packed up and left at the airport gate without so much as a goodbye from her mother, but with a reluctant and tearful hug from her dad.

She'd spent the worst year of her life there, and promised

her parents that if they would let her come home, she'd do what they expected. Her dad lobbied hard to get her back, and she was finally allowed to come home.

That time away, though difficult, had been great for her relationship with her dad. Fearing that she might be sent away again, he took Greta under his wing, and got her a part time job at his lab, teaching her his trade.

At first, she'd only been allowed to do light cleaning around the lab, but eventually he gave her more responsibility, letting her test certain chemicals. She discovered that she was skilled at being able to tell the difference between usable components and junk.

She studied hard and went to college, forgetting the troubled years of her teens. She excelled, obtained a doctorate, and landed a fantastic job working for a government lab. She felt content with her life, most of the time, but she always felt like she was missing something.

She dated very little, even though she'd inherited her mother's natural blonde hair and delicate features. She was always getting asked out, but the few times she accepted, she spent most of the time worrying if they would be truly compatible. She wanted someone who shared all, or most of her interests, and that was tough to find.

The men she did go out with seemed threatened by her intelligence and the undeniable abilities she had in her field. She'd proven herself to be the best in her area of expertise and they couldn't handle that. She'd all but given up when she met Luke.

He was an older, dazzling, very charming scientist who had been in charge of her particular lab. He and her boss, Jack Neddick, were old friends and college roommates, back in the day. He'd drop in from time to time to see him and to admire her work and monitor the work of her colleagues. He asked her out, they had dinner, dinner led to more.

She'd found out that she was pregnant on her fortieth birthday. To say that Luke was upset about it was an understatement. He was adamant that he didn't want the baby, taking a job clear across the country to get away from it.

Greta decided that abortion was really the only option. She didn't want to raise a child alone, but when she got to the doctor's office and saw the little blip on the monitor confirming the pregnancy, she'd felt a fluttering inside of her, and the strongest urge to protect that tiny life at all costs.

Her mother, and even her dad, considered this new turn of events as the ultimate act of defiance. Pregnancy out of wedlock was the worst thing she could have done to them.

They stopped talking to her. Her father died of a massive heart attack just a month before Bastian was born. Greta's mother followed shortly after, following a brief battle with cancer.

Greta was sure it was the shame, not the illnesses that killed her parents. They died of the shame she had brought to them.

Though they cast her out before they'd died, the deaths of her parents only cemented in Greta the feelings of abandonment and of being truly alone in the world.

Her beautiful son had filled the empty void in her life, and quiet as he was, gave her some much-needed company. She had been determined to fill his life with laughter and fun, to break the cycle that her mother and her mother before her bestowed upon her. It was with such cruel irony that Bastian seemed incapable of either.

As for Bastian, it was as if he'd never left home at all, as if nothing had ever happened. She watched him for a moment. He studied each block closely, placed it on the floor and then, oh so carefully, put the next one in line with the first. He muttered to himself as he worked, in that strange babbling baby language of his.

She hoped that whatever it was that the interventionist did would break him of that habit and get him to play with other children. Help him to communicate with her in a way that she could understand.

It didn't seem to matter to him that he was now home after being away for the last few days. He'd just picked up where he left off before Greta had taken him to his appointment. But Greta felt it. She was tired and had so much to do. Greta left Bastian to his blocks, and sorted the mail and wondered if she would be strong enough to handle all of this on her own.

Disastrous. That's how Kelly's evening had really gone. Greg told her as soon as they were seated that he'd decided that maybe they should just be friends. He'd just gotten word that his ex-girlfriend was coming back to Boston, and he wanted to see if there was still something between them. He hoped Kelly would understand that he didn't want to start anything he couldn't finish, if she knew what he meant. So much for having someone to hang out with for the summer! Well, at least she'd have a new client to keep her busy, she thought.

She'd spent the rest of the evening drinking way too

much, and then ended up having to have Greg drive her back to her apartment.

She invited him up, but he declined. She woke up feeling embarrassed and stupid.

She'd made her call to Jane first thing, as promised, and was going to try and get a little more sleep.

She had a throbbing headache. Where was that water bottle? Water and ibuprofen: the only known cure for a hangover. That and sleep. She was just drifting back off when the phone jolted her awake again.

"Hello?" she rasped.

"Is this Kelly?" a man inquired brightly.

"Professor Stein?" Kelly questioned, surprised, though she knew the answer. He was the only one she knew who had such a distinct accent. But why would he be calling her during summer break?

"Yes, Kelly! How's your summer wearing along?" he asked.

A bad time to ask. She almost felt ashamed of herself and a little embarrassed at being caught so off guard.

"Oh! Well, it's going fine," she lied. Although they had gotten fairly close with all of the work they had done together, Kelly never shared much of her personal life with him.

"How was your trip to Germany?" Kelly inquired about the professor's recent trip to see his aging mother, who still lived there.

"Well, actually that is what I was calling about," he confessed. "I've brought my mother back to live with me. She's getting along in years, and with no family close by, I thought the safest place for her would be here with me. She doesn't know anyone here but me, so I was hoping to introduce you. Do you think you could make some time to stop by and meet her?"

Kelly was a little intrigued by the idea, but couldn't imagine what Professor Stein's mother and she could possibly have in common.

Still, it would be awesome to have someone to talk with that spoke fluent German. It would be a good chance for her to practice, and maybe pick up a little more of the language from a native speaker.

"Well, of course. I'd love to," Kelly answered. "I do have a busy week coming up, as I have picked up a new client. I'm actually going to meet him and his family in a couple of days."

"Oh, that's good news, Kelly," Professor Stein exclaimed. "I was wondering if you would be able to find another student. I'm so glad things are working out for you. Whenever you have the time would be great. I believe I may have something interesting to share with you, and if it works out the way I hope it will, I'm sure you will be quite thrilled," the professor offered, piquing her interest even further.

"Okay, well I can't wait. I'll call you sometime this week to make the arrangements."

"Fine. Fine. I'll let her know," he stated happily before hanging up.

Kelly thought about Professor Stein's call as she showered. She couldn't help but think that there was more to his call than he'd shared.

❖

"What a beautiful child you have." Kelly whispered softly as she peered into the crib at Bastian. He was sleeping peacefully, clutching a worn yellow blanket. His eyelids fluttered sporadically, caught up in some kind of dream.

Greta smiled and reached her hand in to rub Bastian's back gently. He'd been sleeping for nearly an hour, and she didn't mind waking him. She wanted him to meet Kelly as soon as possible.

He was definitely getting worse. The first day home from the hospital had been uneventful, but he'd taken to biting and hitting her over the last couple of days without warning. She'd simply be wiping his face and he would lash out. The first time, he bit her so hard, he drew blood.

His babbling was also getting worse. He seemed to be carrying on conversations with some unseen person, not only when he played with his blocks, but at other times too.

Bastian rolled over and stretched before opening his eyes slightly. It took a moment for him to focus, his eyes roaming about, until they found Greta, but then quickly looked away.

"Bastian, someone's here to see you," Greta announced gently as she smiled at him.

For a moment she worried that he'd be frightened and angry. She certainly wouldn't want to wake up and find a stranger looking at her. She'd been so guarded since bringing him home from the hospital, waiting for anything new to trigger another outburst.

Bastian peered at Kelly with still sleepy eyes and stood shakily, still hanging onto the blanket. He seemed to consider her with mistrust for just a moment. His eyes darted about her, landing briefly on hers, but then he looked away quickly as he often did with Greta. Then his eyes sought Kelly's once again and instead of looking away, he suddenly smiled widely.

Greta was shocked! She couldn't remember the last time Bastian smiled. He reached up and offered his blanket to Kelly. Greta's heart overflowed with sudden joy, but then a small part of her was jealous. She quickly tried to squash the feeling. It didn't matter to whom he responded, as long as he responded to someone. She'd just have to be patient and hope that someday he'd come back to her.

Greta set them up in the sunny, but tiny kitchen. Having gone out the day before to purchase the special chair the team needed for him, she had attached it to the table, and Bastian sat squirming as Kelly worked with him.

She left them to their work, not wanting to interfere, and started cleaning up her room, which hadn't been done in so long, she couldn't remember when. She had a hard time concentrating though, and after a while, she went to check in on their progress.

"Book," Kelly stated clearly, holding a copy of "*There Is a Monster in My Room*" next to her face for Bastian to see.

It seemed as though strapping Bastian into the chair was a good idea, as it appeared to keep him focused on his work. He wasn't screaming to get out, and was actually paying attention to Kelly. The first couple of minutes that he'd been in the chair, it was all she could do to keep him from almost hanging himself by trying to jump out of the seat, and she'd gotten scratched badly in the process.

She was supposed to gradually increase the amount of time he would sit each time she worked with him, but for the time being, she told Greta that they'd aim for half an hour.

Almost to the minute, he began to scream, wanting to get down, but Kelly had him sit a moment longer. Testing his limits, Greta was sure.

His eyes wandered, looking everywhere but at Kelly's face. Typical behavior for an autistic child, Kelly assured Greta.

"The key is to get him to make as much eye contact as possible," Kelly informed her, noticing that Greta stood silently watching them interact.

She unwrapped a large piece of bubble gum and put it in her mouth. "With enough trickery it'll soon become second nature."

Kelly blew a gigantic bubble. Bastian couldn't seem to help his curiosity as he watched, transfixed as the bubble grew larger, his attention drawn to Kelly's face, which was exactly where she'd wanted it.

Kelly popped the bubble loudly. Then as Bastian looked at her mouth, she pronounced the word again. "Book". She held it next to where the bubble had just popped. Bastian looked at the book, and then reached for it, snatching it away from Kelly. He studied it closely, opening the cover.

"Ba," he beamed.

Kelly smiled at him reassuringly. "That's right. Book," she confirmed.

Greta did all she could to keep from leaping with joy at the almost word. She didn't want to do anything that would distract him.

Bastian looked back up at Kelly's mouth and made similar chewing motions with his mouth as if trying to coax her to make another bubble.

Kelly began chewing quickly then produced another larger bubble and popped it.

"Pop!" she exclaimed.

This brought a shy smile to Bastian's face, but then he

quickly looked away. He struggled hard to get out of his seat.

"Okay, okay," Kelly conceded.

While Kelly leaned over to undo his straps, Bastian suddenly reached up and grabbed hold of one of the braids that she'd worn in her hair. Greta held her breath, ready to spring in case he should do something awful, but Bastian held it gently in his fingers, studying it carefully with his eyes before letting it drop. He looked directly into Kelly's eyes and smiled.

"Good job for today, Bastian," Kelly beamed at him. She was happy with his accomplishments so far. He was adorable and incredibly smart for a kid that was so far behind in his therapy.

He tried wiggling the rest of the way out of his chair, so Kelly obliged by helping him down. He raced off into the living room where he plopped himself down to play with the blocks. It was clear that he was done.

"But tomorrow we start the real work," Kelly announced, more for Greta's benefit.

Kelly was seemingly forgotten as Bastian began to methodically line up his blocks in careful rows. He chanted as he did this in his baby babble.

Greta and Kelly leaned against the doorway to the living room casually as Bastian played.

"Why do you suppose he does that?" Greta wondered aloud, looking toward her son.

"Nobody really knows why they insist on lining things up like that, but pretty much all of the kids I've worked with have done very similar things. It seems to be one of the MO's of autism. The objects in which they line up differ...Sometimes its blocks and sometimes cars. They seem to take comfort in putting things into a linear pattern," Kelly continued, "but as for the babbling, only they know what they're saying." She laughed, as just then Bastian appeared to be making two of the blocks have an imaginary conversation.

Greta smiled too, but Kelly could see the worry on her face and wanted to put her at ease.

"One of the most important things I can do for you is to set up a Picture Exchange Communications Systems book, or as we say, a PECS book. It's a book that has small pictures that we take of items Bastian sees every day and things he likes to eat, or play with. We'll cut and laminate the pictures, and attach them to the pages in the book with Velcro. Once he becomes used to the book, he'll be able look through and take out one of the pictures and give it to you in exchange for the item."

Greta thought about that for a moment, "It sounds interesting, but isn't the idea to get Bastian to start talking?" Greta had waited so long to communicate with her son and she didn't want anything further from holding him back.

Kelly knew from experience that a parent's main goal was to get the child talking as soon as possible. Kelly would have liked to reassure Greta that Bastian would eventually learn to speak, but she couldn't. The truth was that some children never became verbal, and sometimes a number of children who did learn to speak didn't really understand what they were saying. They were only able to parrot back what was told to them.

This was the hardest part of her job, Kelly thought. Every parent wanted a guarantee, and with autism, no one could offer that.

"What you'll see as time goes on, is that we'll be using a number of tools to draw out communication. As well as the PECS, we'll also be using sign language. We'll use every available method we have, but for the most part, it'll be up to Bastian," Kelly stated.

The suggestion of sign language made Greta uncomfortable. She didn't know a single sign. She'd never had any reason to learn, and wouldn't have a lot of time with her demanding job. She didn't want to be the only one in the process that couldn't communicate with Bastian.

Kelly saw the worry creasing Greta's forehead again.

"The signs we use will be very simple and easy to learn. I will say this: I've worked with a lot of children over the last couple of years, and I've never seen anyone respond as quickly as Bastian has. I have no doubt that in a very short time you and Bastian will be communicating regularly."

Kelly would have liked to stay and make Greta more at ease, but she had promised to meet Professor Stein in his office. She was more than a little curious as to what he had for her.

"Okay, well if you're all set for today, I'll see you tomorrow, and we can start working on the book I was telling you about," Kelly added, as she grabbed her briefcase full of toys.

Greta had been so optimistic watching Bastian's progress as he worked with Kelly, but knew that unlike her lab, she couldn't control any of the variables in Bastian's case. Kelly was right. It would be up to him. Watching him as Kelly headed for the door made her feel hope for the first time in a while.

"Thank you so much Kelly, and if there's anything I can do to make this easier for you, please let me know."

Kelly reached into her briefcase, pulled out a book, and handed it to Greta.

"Well, if you want, you can start learning this," Kelly joked.

'*The Joy of Signing.*'

Kelly pulled her car into the lot at the University easily. She never would have been able to find a spot like that in September. The campus was fairly empty this time of year, though there were a few summer students lounging on the perfectly groomed lawns, at least making a show of studying.

Professor Stein asked that she meet him there so they could drive to his house together, and as she headed up the deserted stone stairway that led to the west wing of the building, Kelly couldn't help but feel the familiar pull in her gut, similar to what she got on the first day of school. Nervous excitement mixed with a tad of unease. Something about the smell of the wood floor wax and shellac brought back memories of her middle school gymnasium.

She walked down the familiar hallway that led to his tiny, cluttered office, and as she rounded the corner, she spotted him just locking the door.

"Kelly!" the professor greeted her pleasantly. His thinning hair was scattered and his glasses were slightly askew, making him appear a bit flustered compared to the usually composed state with which Kelly was accustomed. "Perfect timing. You look well. The summer is agreeing with you," he told her as he gave her a quick hug.

"You do too," Kelly lied. He looked tired, she

thought...perhaps a little older since returning from his vacation.

"Well, let's not dally. Mother is waiting. I can fill you in on the way there," Professor Stein claimed as he ushered Kelly out to his car.

A half hour later found them driving slowly through the old, quaint neighborhoods that became the suburbs of Boston. Kelly loved driving out that way. The historic homes with lavish woodwork and lawns holding hundred-year-old oak trees made her wish that she could have seen it all back in the time before the city had grown around it. It was a beautiful place, but it wasn't Maine, and nothing would quite measure up to the beauty of her home state.

Professor Stein had been telling her about his visit to see his mother in Germany as they drove on, explaining the difficulties he had faced after arriving there.

"Well, you see the problem is that I just can't leave her alone for more than an hour at a time," Professor Stein continued, changing the topic to his current situation. "I wanted her with me so that I could keep an eye on her, but she gets into trouble the moment I step away."

So far, from what Kelly gathered, bringing his mother home with him had turned out to be a little more than the professor had bargained for.

Apparently, Professor Stein's mother, Helga, wandered outside and locked herself out of the house. It had taken the professor the better part of an hour to find her. He'd been frantic and was just about to call the police when he finally located her sitting patiently on the back steps. It was chilly that day and she had nothing on but a thin nightdress.

Kelly felt sorry for her and hated to think of what would've happened if that had been during the brutal winters they usually endured. Also, from what he'd been saying, she'd burned herself on the stove, not yet familiar with the modern efficiencies of a kitchen in the States.

As Professor Stein told Kelly about his trip to Germany and the horrible state that his mother's house had been in, Kelly could imagine how awful he must've felt at being oblivious to her situation. He had no way of knowing how she'd been living, as she'd never mentioned any of her troubles.

It had taken him the better part of a week just to try to make it somewhat less hazardous, but he had failed. Books, papers, and clothing were piled up in every corner of her house, and she refused to throw any of it away.

She'd been living without electricity, and couldn't seem to remember how or when she had last paid the bill. She resisted any attempt at his trying to organize her house.

"If she'd had someone close by that I could've asked to check on her periodically, it never would have gotten that bad. I couldn't tell from her letters that anything was amiss. It wasn't until I left her to attend church on the Sunday before I was supposed to leave that she fell, and I decided I couldn't leave her there alone. It took a lot of coaxing to get her to come here with me. I had to threaten to put her in a nursing facility," he admitted regretfully.

Kelly felt bad for him. She knew that it was a possibility for her someday to deal with the same scenario concerning her own parents. With the rising cost of health care and the outrageous prices of nursing homes, she didn't doubt that she'd either be faced with caring for them herself or helping to pay the cost of someone else doing it.

"Well, if there's anything I can do, please let me know." Kelly patted her professor on the shoulder sympathetically.

"I feel I owe you so much for all of the time you put into my language studies."

It was true. Kelly would not have been so far ahead without the significant help Professor Stein had given her. She couldn't even count the number of nights he'd stayed late to help her with a test, or even just to listen to her complaints.

"Well, now that you mention it, and I must admit that I feel rather like a heel for not having brought it up in the first place, but you see, I need to be sure first that mother likes you, and I, well, I am a bit like her, I admit, and not very good at asking for..." Professor Stein sighed, stumbling on his words.

He decidedly pulled the car over to the side of the road and looked at Kelly apologetically.

"I'm going to need someone to watch her, especially on the nights that I have to stay late at the University, and I can't think of anyone else I'd rather have do it than you." He posed this as more of a question than a statement.

Kelly was honored that he'd ask. Professor Stein, while a fantastic teacher and a wonderful friend to her, had been reserved up until then about sharing much of his personal life with her. She knew that it must be very hard for him to have to ask her for help.

"Before you say yes, or no, if that's what the case may be, there's some things that you should really know about her," he cautioned.

Kelly nodded, urging him on.

"Mother's had a difficult life, especially in her younger years. Now, I'm not going to go into all of the details, but I will say that the trials she has been through in her life have made her very wary of strangers," he continued, "She's very set in her ways. Stubborn to the point of her own detriment, and will never ask for help of any kind."

Kelly laughed a bit, inwardly thinking that Professor Stein's mother sounded like some of the students she'd had in the past.

"When I told you that I had something of interest for you, I may have been premature. I was hoping that once I got my mother here with me, she might start opening up a little bit more, and possibly share something that I have been wondering about for a very long time. Unfortunately, my attempts at trying to get her to talk about it have been met with the same stubborn refusal that I've always gotten from her." The professor looked at Kelly sheepishly.

Kelly could see that what Professor Stein had to tell her must be very hard for him, but she was too intrigued to stop him.

"You see, when I was a young boy, mother had a visitor. It was a rare occurrence that we would have guests, but especially someone I didn't know. She asked me to go outside and play, but I was curious since I had never met this lady before, so I spied at the window." The professor paused, seemingly unsure if he should continue or not, but Kelly urged him to continue. He decided it couldn't do any harm.

"After the lady and my mother were seated at the table, and of course the customary tea was poured, my mother did the strangest thing...she began to speak to this lady in a language that I'd never heard before. As you can imagine, I was quite surprised. I didn't know that my mother knew anything but German. After they'd talked for some time, the lady began to raise her voice, not quite to shouting, but clearly angry. She got up, leaned in close to my mother, and began shaking a finger in her face. My mother just sat there wringing her hands with a look of worry on her face. She kept shaking her head no, and finally the lady got up and prepared to leave."

Kelly couldn't contain her interest. "What do you think the lady could've said that would have your mother so worried?" she asked, now quite involved in the professor's story.

Professor Stein adjusted his position to face Kelly, "I'm not sure, but as the lady was leaving she uttered a phrase, which I didn't understand, but remembered, or at least I think I remember. It was something to the effect of *'Siedemen Kommendie'.* Then she walked back to my mother and put her finger to my mother's lip and whispered something else that I couldn't hear."

Kelly thought about this for a moment. Automatically, her brain tried to translate the first phrase into something she could recognize, but came up short. She was sure it was of German descent, but couldn't decipher it. "So you don't know what it was she said?" she asked her professor.

"I'm afraid I don't. I tried asking my mother about the strange conversation she'd had with the lady but she got angry with me. She told me to forget what I'd heard and never speak of it again. Then she grumbled something that I'll never forget. She said, *'Die torichten wird sterben.'*"

Kelly immediately got chills, "The foolish will die," she translated the phrase.

Professor Stein removed his glasses and rubbed at his eyes. He was obviously tired, but pressed on.

"I haven't been completely honest with you," he admitted. Professor Stein, seeing Kelly's obvious confusion explained further, "I must confess that since that time I witnessed the conversation between my mother and the lady I have thought of it often. I believe it was the catapult that had us packing our possessions that very night so we could catch a boat to the United States. We were unsuccessful, of course. Papa had not had time to obtain the necessary papers for travel. I was very young, but I remember quite well the fear in my mother's eyes; the absolute desperation in her voice that night pleading with the dock officials to let us go. The day after the visit from my mother's mysterious guest, she lost her voice and has not spoken a word since," the professor stated resolutely.

Kelly was dumbfounded. Professor Stein never told her that his mother was mute. "Then how's it possible that you've managed to stay in touch with her through the years?" Kelly couldn't help but ask.

"At first it was difficult. Through letters, mostly. After the death of my father, I went to stay with her for a time and managed to get her a captioned phone, for all the good it did her. She barely ever used it, preferring her letters to keep in touch with me," he told her.

Kelly could imagine how hard it must've been for her professor to leave his mother like that. He would've had to take her at her word when she told him that she was doing fine. When speaking with someone you can pick up on nuances, subtleties in a voice that would often give a clue as to how the speaker was actually feeling, regardless of what they actually said. The written word in text does not paint much of a picture into what is actually going on, especially if the writer wanted to hide something.

"In all of my years of research, and in all of the years I've worked as a translator, I haven't come across anything resembling the language my mother spoke that day. I'm not sure who the strange visitor was, but I'm sure that whatever happened that day is somehow the cause of my mother becoming mute."

Kelly couldn't imagine how a visitor could possibly be the cause of someone becoming a mute. Though it could be considered a coincidence that she lost her voice the very next day, there would have to be some kind of medical explanation, and asked her professor if she had been evaluated.

"She refused to be seen by any doctor. She began writing everything she wanted to say, which was very little after that. When I got a bit older I questioned her once again about the day the guest came, but she held fast that she wouldn't discuss it. So, I guess when I suggested to you last year that you do your thesis on German dialects I was hoping that perhaps you might uncover something I hadn't. Then I might be able to gain some insight into my mother's predicament."

"Professor Stein, while I appreciate your vote of confidence in my research abilities, it's doubtful that if you've never been able to figure out what language they were speaking, I'd be able to." Kelly chuckled a little but was secretly flattered that her professor obviously found her so capable.

"You've been at this for many years, and I've only just begun, so I'm not really sure how I can be of help, except to look after your mother, which of course I'll do," she replied to his earlier question. She was a bit disappointed that she wouldn't be able to learn much more German from Professor Stein's mother, knowing then that she couldn't speak. However, she couldn't help but feel a tingle of excitement at finding herself in the middle of a real life mystery of sorts.

"Kelly, you're a fantastic interventionist. If this wasn't true, so many families and doctors wouldn't recommend you. You've made quite a name for yourself in that profession, though I know you'd rather focus on your language studies. You've made remarkable progress with your students. You've gotten children to speak that otherwise wouldn't have been able to. You've gotten them to interact socially and to be able to attend school with their peers. It's my hope, that perhaps with a little bit of sly work from you, you can get my mother to open up to you. Get her to talk about what happened that day back in Germany," he presented hopefully.

To Kelly, this felt like a lot to hope for. Yes, she had made progress with the kids she had worked with, but Helga Stein wasn't a child. And if Professor Stein was any indication, not stupid either.

"With my mother refusing medical treatment and her age, I really don't expect her to live a long time. It's very important to me that before she dies someone is able to solve this mystery once and for all. I don't expect miracles, I assure you. I know a lot will depend on my mother. I'm only asking that you give it a try, please."

At that, Kelly was sure that no matter what, she would give it her best shot. She'd never seen her professor so vulnerable, and it made her uneasy.

"Of course," she told him, smiling sympathetically. "I'll do what I can, as I've told you before. I feel I owe you so much, but I'll tell you the same thing I tell all of the parents that I work with, that I can't make any promises. You were right in saying that a lot of this will depend solely on your mother. She may not even like me!" Kelly joked.

"There's only one way to find out," Professor Stein chuckled. He started the car once again and merged onto the road.

CHAPTER THREE
Austria 1896

The first time Adolph saw Magdalena, he was a small child. He had been sent outside of his home to play in the cool spring air. Bundled up in the itchy wool coat and hat Mama made him wear, he sat on the steps, licking an icicle that had fallen from the house. He heard a noise and turned to look. A woman stood in the snow outside of the house next door. He was tentative as she called to him from across the yard, holding a cookie in her hand.

She was beautiful, with long, reddish blonde curls flowing down her back. Even from a distance, he could see her blue eyes. The snow reflected on them and made them appear like some of the jewels he had seen in Mama's special box. Her dress was like none he had ever seen before. It was long to the ground, and seemingly made of shimmering gold. He could see her bare feet that peeked out the bottom, and her toenails were decorated with silver jewels.

She was speaking to him. It sounded strange. He did not understand her words, but she wanted him to come closer, that much he knew. He was hungry and wanted the cookie, so he got up from the steps and walked to the edge of his yard.

Kristy Gherlone

A dog, large and growling, ran toward her from across the icy road and bared its teeth. It wanted the cookie also.

Skinny and starving, its bones were visible through tight yellow fur, and its tongue hung from its large gaping mouth, dripping with white foam.

The dog was almost to her, and for a moment, he feared the cookie would be lost, but the dog, close enough to drool on her feet suddenly stopped.

It yelped and began to whine, then dropped to the ground. The dog rolled onto its back in a submissive pose, eyes pleading and wet with sudden fear. Magdalena looked over toward Adolph to see if he was watching. A small smile played on her lips. She placed the cookie on the stairs and turned toward the dog, which was writhing at her feet, quite seemingly in pain.

She uttered a few words in a strange language Adolph was not familiar with and pointed a crooked finger over the dog, swirling it around and around, as though she were stirring coffee. Its belly began to swell. Bigger and bigger it grew. Adolph's eyes widened as he tried to get a better look. He was fascinated. The dog's gut was so tight with pressure that the tiny hairs lining its belly jutted out like a porcupine. Blood began to trickle in small lines that looked like tiny red rivers.

Magdalena extracted a shiny object from her pocket. A knife? A letter opener like Papa had on his desk? He couldn't see it clearly. He craned his neck, but he was too far away. He wanted to see, so he went closer to watch.

Magdalena bent over and suddenly jabbed the object into the lower half of the dog's stomach. It made a whooshing sound, like air letting out of a balloon. The dog made a small guttural sound. Its face registered both surprise and fear before it fell silent as she cut it up to its neck. It was still twitching, legs kicking wildly in the air as dark red blood flowed out and stained the snow.

She squatted over the dog and placed her hands within the cut. Adolph could hear its ribs cracking as she spread the dog's body wider. He was mesmerized.

She grabbed hold of something inside the dog and tugged slightly. He stepped closer still, almost to her then, but just out of reach. He felt tingly. The tiny hairs on his neck tickled him. It was frightening, but it excited him too. Magdalena stood up. She had something in her hands.

Closer. Closer. He was right next to her then and could see that Magdalena held a small, squirming puppy. It was beautiful. He'd always wanted a puppy. Papa vowed that he would never have one. 'An unnecessary burden' he had proclaimed.

She placed it in his arms, and it began to lick his face. Magdalena patted his head, her hands still wet with blood. "*Gudkinsič*", she said. He didn't know that word, but she was smiling at him.

He carried the puppy the last few feet to her house and snatched the cookie from the stairs, quickly shoving it into his mouth. She laughed, and opened her door for him to go in. "Happy Birthday," she offered in his language. He didn't know how she knew.

Magdalena could sometimes see events in the future. Sometimes she could see them clearly, and other times it was harder, as though she was looking through a thick fog.

She told him that he would have many followers, beginning with her, and laughed as she threw her head back, making her golden hair cascade down her back. It sounded like music to him.

She made Adolph feel good. Made him feel special. Papa never had time for him, and Mama was too busy with her social functions and trying to please Papa. He did all he could to sneak away to Magdalena's house as much as possible.

At home he was often left in the care of the family nurse. He hated her. He hated her for many reasons: for spending more time with the other children, for making him do her chores while she sat reading to them, but most of all he hated her because she was a Jew. Magdalena pointed out that to be a Jew was very bad. He was very glad that he wasn't one of those, whatever it meant.

One night at bath time, Nurse unclothed and got into the tub with Adolph as he took his evening bath. She didn't have one in her quarters, and though she'd done this with all of the children, and had many times before with Adolph, it felt different that time. It disgusted him, but he was also strangely excited. Though her breasts were as small as plums, they dipped in and out of the water as she washed him, making the brown parts shiny with wetness. He felt funny down there, where the pee came out.

He reached out to touch her nipple, curious, but she slapped his face hard. He wanted to cry, but he wouldn't give her the satisfaction. Furious, he leaned over and bit one of her breasts hard enough to draw blood.

She jumped up angrily and, dripping wet, yanked him out of the tub and threw him into his room, where she locked the door. There wouldn't be any *kuchen,* which was his favorite desert, before bed that night.

He told this to Magdalena, not daring to tell Papa that the Jew had slapped him. He was worried that he'd be the one who was punished.

Magdalena unclothed and led him upstairs.

"Let us wash that Jew off from you," she coaxed as she drew a bath in her big, white porcelain tub, before getting in herself and settling across from him. She told him that he could touch hers if he would like to. He did. The next day, Nurse was gone. No one knew what happened to her.

Adolph's mother died not long after Nurse went missing. Magdalena went to Papa and offered to take over some of the duties. That began a most unusual and unpredictable upbringing.

It was plain for anyone to see that Dolphie, as she took to calling him, was her favorite child. She spent most of her time working with him and teaching him many things, but she could also be very strict with him.

She'd make him get up early to do his exercises, and to take his dose of the medicine to cure his tapeworms.

"You are far too skinny and small, my little Dolphie," she warned, doling out generous portions of the bitter liquid. He hated it, but if he could take it without making a face, she would reward him with special time, maybe even let him sleep in her bed.

Magdalena made him take only ice cold baths, and would make him stay outside in winter without a coat or shoes. She told him that she was making him stronger.

If he could endure it without complaint for whatever time she had decided, she would give him extra dinner and sweets.

She taught him how to dissect animals, and to identify the bloody parts inside. If he could do it without retching, she would let him skip a dose of the worm medicine.

They would take long walks in the forest each day after school, and Magdalena would share secrets with him. She

Kristy Gherlone

would only share the secrets in her language, which Adolph was learning rather quickly. Adolph's brothers and sisters were not allowed to learn, and it made them angry. Adolph loved that he had something that they didn't.

Mostly Magdalena shared secrets about the Jews, telling him about how, in a vision, she'd seen that they would gather together in armies and begin killing the Aryans and the Germans. That frightened Adolph, because he knew that a lot of what Magdalena predicted often came true.

She gave him a special necklace made of wood, and told him that if he always wore it, he'd always be safe. She would keep him safe.

She was the one who told him that he would soon be an only child, and she'd be able to spend more time with just him. He knew he should be sad about that, but the thought of having Magdalena all to himself was pleasing.

One by one, his brothers and sisters fell ill with the fever and died. Magdalena told him that it was because of the Jews; that they were unclean and spread diseases amongst them.

He was terrified to go to school for fear that he'd fall ill as well, but Magdalena made him a potion to keep him safe from the sicknesses of the Jews.

Sometimes, if she had to be busy doing a task for Papa, he'd ask Magdalena if he could play with some children from his school. She didn't impose too many rules on him, but the one she made him abide by was that he was only allowed to play with children that looked like she did.

"If you must play, Dolphie, then at least select children with light hair and blue eyes. You are not to play with Jews," she told him. "I don't trust that you would recognize one of them on your own," she concluded with a firmness in her voice. By then he knew not to disobey. He'd made that mistake only once.

When he was quite young, he and Magdalena had been shopping at a local market. He'd grown very bored, as she had been taking too long in picking out a selection of meat for dinner. He began playing hide and seek with another child as Magdalena was occupied with the sales clerk. It didn't feel wrong to him. It was just another child to play with. When Magdalena finished her business and saw what he'd been up to, she grabbed him by the arm and dragged him outside. He'd never seen her so angry. It frightened him and he wet his pants.

"You will not play with those filthy little creatures!" she scolded him. "If you can't learn to tell the difference between a human and a pig, then I shall make markers for them to wear so it will be easy for you to identify. From now on you are only allowed to play with children who have light hair and blue eyes."

Adolph cried all the way home. Not for being scolded but for being stupid. Magdalena often told him that to be stupid was almost as bad as being a Jew.

When he grew a bit older, they would share a bed more and more at night when Papa would go away on business. When Magdalena slept, she'd often dream. Her dreams sometimes came into his head and he could see images flashing before him.

In one vivid dream, a young Magdalena, just twelve years old with ribbons in her hair, was coming home from feeding the chickens out in the field. Her father had to go away to work, and had to Magdalena's pleasure, given her the responsibility of feeding the animals.. She'd been so happy, so proud.

When she went into the house, her cheeks glowing with the chilly air, a man was there with her mother. She recognized him as the man who had come a few days before asking Papa for work. Papa told him that he didn't have any to offer.

The man had yelled at Papa and called him a liar. Papa chased him off with the ax he kept in the house to chop wood. The man was a Jew. She remembered him saying that when he was arguing with Papa, he'd claimed, "I am just an honest Jew looking to make a decent day's wage." He smelled very bad and Magdalena was glad when he left. The greasy smell of him stuck in her nose until she used some smelling soaps to get rid of it.

At first she didn't know what was happening. He was straddling her mother on the floor. Her dress was pulled up to cover her face, but Magdalena could hear her mother sobbing. The man was making noise and was moving up and down, while grabbing at her mother's breasts. His dirty face became contorted as he cried out.

Then the man looked up and saw Magdalena. His eyes focused on her. He got up onto his knees with his pants still down around his ankles.

Magdalena's mother cried as she pulled her dress back down. Adolph could see that her mother's face was bloody and could feel that Magdalena was suddenly very frightened and torn. She wanted to run, but wanted to go to her mother. Before she could decide, the Jew lashed out and grabbed her arm. Magdalena's mother tried to stop him but he punched her violently back to the floor and she fell silent.

The man leaned out suddenly and grasped a fistful of Magdalena's hair. He pulled her to the floor. His crooked smile showed that he was missing teeth. The ones that remained were stained yellow and brown. He mashed his lips into her hers. His breath smelled like rotting meat. Magdalena began to vomit and he slapped her.

He pulled up her dress, yanked her legs apart, and stuck one of his dirty fingers into the folds of her most private area. It hurt and she began to cry. She tried to get up, but he punched her hard enough to make her numb.

He dangled his male part in front of her face and told her to put it in her mouth. She turned her head but he punched her again and again until she did.

The horrible smell of him and the thrusting hit her gag reflex and she vomited once again. He took it out and paused just a moment over her before he shoved his manhood within her.

Magdalena and her mother were tied up and kept as prisoners in their own house. It seemed to be a long time that they were there. Adolph could see the clock on the wall striking twelve four times in that image. The Jew left for a short time, but came back with three others.

They took turns raping Magdalena and her mother repeatedly. The pain Magdalena felt between her legs made her dizzy. She felt bruised from the inside out and could barely walk to use the bucket they allowed the girls to use as a toilet.

She had bruises and bite marks all over her body. They had left no part of her untouched, and she knew that her mother was faring the same, though they wouldn't allow them to speak to each other. When their eyes met, her mother's held shame and defeat. She looked away.

The men ate all of the food they could find in the house, laughing as they went through the cupboards, spilling out whatever they did not fancy.

They ate messily, greedily shoving the food into their mouths and making a mess on the floors. To Magdalena they resembled the pigs out in the pen, and when they didn't offer the girls any of the food, Magdalena grew weak with hunger and fatigue.

Adolph all at once became aware of a sound that had been in the background of that vision. It was there all along, but it was so persistent that it became just a hum as the violence continued around them. It was a baby. He could hear a baby crying. It wouldn't stop. He could feel the pain that it caused Magdalena. She loved that baby as if it were her own. It was her baby sister; her only sibling.

Magdalena's mother pleaded with them to let her feed it. She begged them, as she wailed, to be allowed to go to the cow barn for milk.

Viciously, one of the Jews grabbed at her breast and squeezed it hard until a small amount of milk oozed out. He called her a lying whore and accused her of trying to use her own baby's suffering as a means of escape.

He slapped her across the face and then laughed as he leaned his head down to suck on the breast noisily before offering it to the others. They all took turns on the nipples, making a game of it until they were dry.

One of the Jews went to the baby and snatched it violently from its crib. Her diaper hung soaking from her little frame, as it hadn't been changed in a long time.

Her little eyes were swollen and her face was blotched red from all of the crying.

At first it appeared as though he would oblige the sobbing mother. He began to hand the baby to her. She quieted just a bit at seeing her mother, but then the Jew suddenly veered off, sneering, and opened up the cast iron door to the wood stove, which was red with fire.

Magdalena's mother shrieked and tried to grab at his pant legs. Magdalena went flailing at him in an attempt to pull her sister out of danger, but he threw the child in and closed the door tight. The baby cried out just once more before she was silenced forever.

Something happened to Magdalena in that moment. He couldn't see it clearly in the image. It may have been something that couldn't be seen.

The hate that had been welling up inside of Magdalena suddenly burst from her, swirling all around her. It was a hate so strong it felt like fire. She stood in the corner of the room with her fists in tight balls, her eyes blazing with rage. Adolph felt this hate. He'd never felt anything like it before. It filled him.

The room suddenly felt strange. It became hard to breathe as the temperature dropped quickly. Adolph could feel Magdalena's heart race and see her breath come out in quick gasps, smoky with the cold. He saw something reflecting on her breath. It was a form of some kind, but he couldn't put his finger on it, it was too fleeting. Whatever it was grew larger and expanded outward, hovering all around her, like a black wind, making her hair blow back before projecting itself away from her and towards the mesmerized men.

The Jews' faces turned from wonder to fear. They shielded their eyes with their hands and then they were suddenly ablaze. The black wind had enveloped them and the pressure in the room was such that Adolph felt as though he himself would ignite with the force. The fire was so hot that the Jews' hair melted into their skin, and sweat tinged red with blood rained down onto the floor from their anguished faces.

Magdalena didn't move as they ran around trying to find some comfort, some kind of escape, but instead, fueled the flames.

Adolph woke up writhing and with a fever. Magdalena was pressing a cool compress to his head as he woke. She was speaking softly to him.

"Sometimes evil can be born from hatred if the hate is strong enough. But not everything born evil is hated."

There were many things that he didn't understand, but Magdalena would only show him what she wanted to. He knew that she kept a lot to herself.

As he grew older, he had the strongest urges to paint. Magdalena encouraged him, even taking him to a small art store in town where she traded some of her jewels for paint and an easel. Papa would not give him permission to enroll in the art class he'd wanted to attend, so Magdalena took him there in secret.

He knew that her visions had shown her something important about his painting. Something that even she couldn't explain. It was something in the future, but too far out for her to see clearly. She just knew that it was important. He knew not to question her.

On one chilly night as they were heading home after class, Papa saw them. He'd been furious for the defiance, and he and Magdalena began arguing. Papa reached out to slap Magdalena but she stopped him. He saw his Papa cringe and reach up to rub his temple. The last image Adolph had of his father was as he fell to the ground, bloody tears seeping out of his eyes.

Since it was just the two of them then, she allowed him

to paint as much as he wanted. Strange images passed from his mind to the canvas night after night. Sometimes he'd wake from sleeping to find himself at the easel, sleep-painting. He would study the paintings, trying to figure out in his awake mind what his sleeping mind was painting.

Though he would never admit to it, some of the paintings frightened him. In one painting in particular, there was a city, but none like he had ever seen. The buildings were strange and metallic, with no visible skyline. It looked cold and septic. The painting chilled him. The objects he painted were nothing he could even recognize. Nonetheless, Magdalena encouraged him, almost willed him to paint, and when he slept at night, sometimes she showed him what to paint through his dreams.

Adolph came to realize, however, that when she was done with something, she was done. There was no use in arguing with her. She set the rules.

He'd come home from school, the last day of the school year in his sixteenth year. He had been slightly giddy because he'd just received his papers to be drafted into the Austrian army. He was sure that Magdalena would be very proud of him.

He was inclined all of a sudden to paint her. They'd been sharing a bed every night for quite some time, but she'd never let him touch her in the way his young male body longed to. Sometimes it was torture trying to fall asleep next to her, with her sweet flowery smell, and body close to his. He felt so restless and out of control that he would rub himself for relief while she slept next to him.

She'd been out in the garden that day, loosely clad in a white cotton dress. The sunlight caught her hair and made it shimmer as she tiptoed around the beans and cucumbers, as she plucked off the beetles that started infesting that year.

He was so stricken with her beauty that he ran inside quickly to gather his painting supplies, feeling as though if he didn't paint her that very moment, he'd never get the chance again.

He'd been so engrossed in his painting that he didn't realize that she'd finished in the garden and was walking towards him. He was aroused from painting the outline of her breasts, and when she demanded, smirking, to know what he was doing, he sheepishly showed her. He was embarrassed for having been caught with such an obvious bulge in the front of his pants, and was sure she'd be mad at him for his predicament.

She playfully wrenched the painting from the easel and ran with it, and he tried to snatch it back to avoid further embarrassment. She was laughing and made quite a game of it, but suddenly stopped.

"You are done painting," she murmured huskily, eying his bulge. "I told you weeks ago that you were done." Growing more serious, "You have too many more things that you need to be focusing on and yet you defy me." She smiled.

"Painting me is an idle waste of your valuable time; however, I have to admit that I am quite flattered. I believe you have painted what you were supposed to and now it's done," she stated firmly as she began to walk away. "I managed to sell the last of your paintings today, Dolphie, and now it is finished. Time to move on to other things," she informed, casting her words carelessly over her shoulder.

Adolph didn't understand and his temper flared. "You had no business selling my paintings!" he shouted, suddenly furious that she wouldn't consult him. "Why would you do it?" he demanded.

When he'd tried to sell some of his earliest paintings at market, he'd gone home discouraged when no one would buy them. More than one person laughed at him that day, and an old lady, who had been a vendor next to him, even had the audacity to tell him that he should try selling rocks instead. "You would make more money," she snickered, but Magdalena told him that someday people would pay ten years' earnings for even a small glimpse of his work.

"A peach just picked from the tree needs time to ripen, Dolphie. You must be patient. For a peach ripening on a sill is much more coveted than one eaten in haste. It's bitter. It needs time to sweeten."

He'd gotten it into his head that if everything she told him were true, and so far it had been, then it was better to hold on to the paintings and make the money himself someday.

Realizing that wouldn't happen, he became angry. He'd grown fond of his work. He spent so much time on them that it seemed criminal to him just to sell them off so quickly. They'd been hanging in his room. How dare she do such a thing?

Adolph was so angry that he wished to strike her. He ran after her and lashed out to do just that, but she caught his hand and put it on her breast, under the top of her dress.

At first he was confused, and still angry, but the feel of her hard nipple in his fingers aroused him anew and his manhood swelled once again. He longed to kiss her, and leaned forward to find her lips meeting his, the same hungry need in her that he felt. It was so delicious and pleasing. He'd been thinking about this moment for a long time. His anger was all but gone.

He drank in her taste and scent. Magdalena reached down and unbuttoned his trousers, and they fell around his ankles. She placed her hand around his hardness and began to rub it roughly. He leaned into her, a low moan escaping his lips. How he'd longed for her touch; for just such a moment. He felt like he would fall apart in her fingers.

Just when he was about to let himself go, at the very moment that it felt like every fiber in his body was centered at his throbbing member, and pleasure so great that his body was heaving with it, she whacked him hard across the face with her free hand. Hard enough to leave a welt. He cried out, but oddly it was with pleasure as well as with pain. His manhood spurted its juices into her hand. He was ashamed and dazed from the blow, but oddly aroused again.

"I know how it feels to be angry. I know what it feels like to want something so badly that you'd be willing to hurt the ones you love to get it," Magdalena told him softly, "but you must trust me, always trust me. You have many lessons yet to learn, but I think I've been foolish in letting this one wait so long." Her voice was low and seductive.

"I think your desire is causing you some frustration towards me. Anger is a good thing, but it must be directed at the right people." Magdalena's eyes grew dark. "If you ever think about striking me again, you won't be thinking of anything again."

Magdalena was still holding him in her hand, and gave him a tight squeeze, making Adolph squirm.

In her eyes, he saw a reflection, and it stilled him. Frightening as it was, he couldn't look away. Armies of people, arms outstretched in front of them chanting. They had bands of red around their green, coated arms.

"I want you to remember that without me, you are nothing at all, just an ordinary boy, *nichts (nothing)*, but with me, you will be led to a greatness that far exceeds anything you could ever imagine. You will be revered, loved, worshipped, respected, and yes, even feared. Money is nothing compared to the power you'll have." Her tirade finished, she softened and released her hold.

Adolph was beside himself with shame and fear. How could he have even thought of hurting her? He loved her more than he loved anyone. She was all he could think of. Magdalena had never been that angry with him before. The look in her eyes showed him that he wouldn't care to ever make her that angry again. He pulled up his trousers and apologized to her.

Magdalena kissed his forehead and took him by the hand. A smile played on her lips as she led him into the house and upstairs to the bedroom.

"Let's work out some of that frustration. I need you focused on the work ahead," she cooed seductively while removing her gown, "for in just a few short weeks, you and I will be leaving Austria so you may serve as you are supposed to, and there will be little time for this."

He decided to wait to tell her that he had just joined the Austrian army. He didn't want to spoil her mood.

A strong image came to him that night as he lay in bed next to her. Magdalena's father was on a big stage. The people gathered there were watching him intently.

Magdalena was in the front row of the auditorium, smiling. People all around her were clapping. He was in a uniform of sorts. It was hard to see clearly in that image through the smoky fog that was whispering all around him.

No, not a uniform. A cloak? A Cape? Yes, it was a cape. He had a wand in his hand. He was making magic. Magdalena's father was a magician!

The audience couldn't see what Magdalena could. The light radiating about her father was deceiving them. Making them see things that were not actually there. Magdalena was mesmerized. How was he doing that? People were throwing coins and other valuables onto the stage in appreciation.

The image of Magdalena switched to another time, not long from that event. She was hiding in her room holding a candle to see the pages of a book. Her father's magic book! There was a symbol on the cover. Magdalena had shown him that symbol before. It was called the blood flag. The sign of the sun, as she called it.

Her father had gone into her room to kiss her goodnight, and saw that she had it. Adolph watched as he snatched the book from her violently, making her jump back against the wall. He looked angry, but also afraid. His weathered, tired face was pinched with grief. "You must never, ever touch this book again. Do you understand me?" he raged.

She was frightened at being caught, but then angry with her father for not allowing her to continue reading it. "I want to be like you. I want learn how to make the magic!" Magdalena cried, indignantly.

"This is MY book. It wasn't meant to be used by.." He fumbled with his words, still shouting, then softened, "I'm sorry, Magdalena. I cannot teach you, nor can I permit you to learn," Magdalena's father told her.

"Why, Papa? It isn't fair!" Magdalena cried.

"Your mother and I couldn't agree on whether or not you should be told about the aura. She was very worried that if you were told, you wouldn't be able to keep it a secret and that we wouldn't be able to keep you safe. Neither of us could have predicted what was to happen..." His voice caught, on the verge of tears. He turned away as if he were going to leave.

"Please Papa. It's okay. Please tell me!" Magdalena begged.

He hesitated at the door, caught in an inner turmoil.

"Papa, please," Magdalena asked again softly, sensing that he was losing his resolve. She had been right.

Magdalena's father pulled a chair close to her bed and sat down with the weariness of a defeated man. He looked at her in anguish. He hesitated, not sure of how to begin with what clearly needed to be explained.

"For as long as I can remember, certain members of our family have had a special being inside of us. Something that made us different from all of the others. Nobody knows where it came from; we have just always called it the aura. It's something that can be called forth in times of trial, and we always believed that it was a great gift."

"For centuries, people in and around our village would call upon us to help them achieve certain things, using our aura, and in turn, would provide to us food and other necessities. It became a way for us to make a living, and others, like myself, could use the aura for entertaining for profit. When an aura presents, a mandrake tree is planted in celebration. We've always called it the tree of luck. It brings the one who planted it good fortune throughout their life, and helps to bind them to their aura. The connection between tree and aura is very strong. If the person planting the seed has a good understanding of what they want to achieve in their life, then the tree helps them to get that. It hears a person's innermost thoughts and desires."

"Do I have a tree Papa? Did you plant one for me?" Magdalena interrupted excitedly.

Magdalena's Papa shook his head sadly, "You must let me finish now, princess, and then perhaps you'll understand."

Magdalena quieted, anxious to learn more of the tree. She should have one! Her aura had come!

"Pieces are cut from the tree and given to people you love. Every time you need help, a piece may be cut and ground into tea. It helps strengthen the aura. When the pieces are given and worn close to the skin, perhaps fashioned into a necklace or carved into a bracelet, it keeps you connected through the dream eyes. It can even connect one who has the aura to one who doesn't. Your mother is not of our people, and refuses to believe such superstitions. She won't use the mandrake root." His voice broke and he began to weep.

Adolph saw Magdalena reach out to her father and rub his head for comfort, but it didn't feel like comfort to him. He could feel that it wasn't one of empathy.

"If your mother would just have worn the root I had given to her from my tree, it would have kept her safe. She could have called to me! We could have avoided what happened. None of this would have ever.." He cried openly then, and it took a few moments to collect himself. When he was able to speak, he began again with his story.

"Everyone loved our people. They respected us. Parades were held each year in our honor. We never made any attempt to hide what we were. There had never been a reason to. However, one year, just after my tenth birthday, the elders hired a young man from a neighboring village to come in and help with the fields. He knew about us and was very fascinated by our aura. He would spend much of his time asking questions, instead of doing the work he was hired to do."

"He fell in love with a girl who was far too young for him; so young that her aura hadn't yet shown itself. Her parents told the man to stay away from her and asked him to leave the village. He left unwillingly and angrily, but snuck back late one evening and climbed up a tree to her room. He put a pillow over her mouth and ripped the mandrake root from her neck, thus severing the connection she had with her family."

"He did unspeakable things to her, and during the course of the night and the violence that the little girl suffered, her aura presented itself. It came forth, much like yours did, and it wasn't of the good light." He paused again, waiting to see Magdalena's reaction.

He hated to speak to her about any of that. He was fearful that in the telling of the little girl from his village, it would remind Magdalena of her own time of violence, but her expression was only of keen interest.

"Go ahead, Papa," she told him reassuringly, "I want to hear the rest," she urged.

"When the girl's parents awoke the next day, they found a terrifying scene. The floors, the bed, and even the walls in the girl's room were all covered in blood. They were frantic, trying to find her, and thought her dead. The entire village was called to search for what they feared would be her body. It took many hours, but she was eventually found alive."

"She was at the river bank. She'd found the seed for her mandrake tree in the special book her parents saved for her, and planted it. There was nothing anyone could do."

"Lying next to where she sat was not only the body of her attacker, but the bodies of several of the men from the village from which he came."

Adolph could feel Magdalena's pleasure. They should be dead. She was glad for the girl.

"From that day on, the girl's aura could not be tamed. It swirled blackly all around her, reinforcing her own hate, and nurturing her vicious thoughts. It helped to fuel her anger, causing the deaths of many more. She gave the pieces of her tree to those who would help her. She hadn't given them in love, but in spite. The people from the neighboring villages began to fear us and stayed away. We became poverty-stricken. People not of the aura began calling us witches and burned many of our houses, trying to force us to move away."

"It was decided that the girl must be killed in order for the rest of us to get back into the good graces of our neighbors," he continued.

"There was much discussion about how to go about killing her. By our own law, when someone dies, they are to be burned and the ashes placed into an urn. In doing this it releases the spirit, catapulting it into the next century. They may live again, for a time. However, the elders decided that the girl would be killed and buried deeply into the ground so that her spirit couldn't escape and live again to bring such shame to our people. This caused an upheaval in our community. Some people thought that she should be allowed to live again as perhaps she might come back with the good light. Other people were in agreement that she should be buried. Though the arguments went on for days, the matter couldn't be decided unanimously."

"Did they kill the girl Papa? It wasn't her fault. It wouldn't be fair!" Magdalena cried.

"I'll tell you Magdalena. You must let me finish. This is very hard for me," he shushed her.

"Some people not of the aura were invited to sit in on the discussions out of good faith, to show that we were trying to make amends. Their fears about us, already rooted in them, only aided them in using the information against us. They descended upon us when we were at our weakest. So hungry and skinny from lack of food, we were unable to fight. Though our auras gave us a good planting that year, we didn't have the strength left to harvest the crops. They killed the girl first, in her sleep, and then as many more as they could capture. They buried our people deeply into the ground where we couldn't find them. The ones who managed to get away took what they could of their possessions and some seeds of the mandrake trees and fled."

"The ones who were spared met one final time. It was decided that the ones with the aura could use it, but only in secret. I broke that promise by making the magic, but I had no choice, Magdalena. My aura alone can't break the drought this year and I've already cut most of my tree during the trials in my life. I have to save what I have left. I don't have another to plant."

Magdalena gave her Papa a look of disappointment. He assumed that it was because he went against the promise, and added, "We needed the money. I should never have brought you there, then you never would have known," her Papa told her remorsefully.

Magdalena started to protest, but her Papa shushed her again with a wave of his hand.

"The Aura people will never again plant the seeds of the

mandrake tree. The aura must die out, Magdalena. We all knew that what happened with that girl could happen again and we would all be at risk. We also knew that a tree planted was a marker for who we were, and it would show the ones who would harm us where to find us."

"But that's not fair Papa! If we're special, we should be able to use it. I should have a tree! I want my tree!" Magdalena pouted righteously.

Magdalena's papa shook his head. "We also came to one last decision, Magdalena," he told her, slowly. "We decided that if anyone of our people bore a child whose aura didn't present in the good light, they would have to be killed."

Adolph could feel Magdalena's shock. He watched her jump up and back away from her father in fear.

"I'm not going to hurt you, Magdalena. I could never..." Fresh tears welled in his eyes as he stood and went to her, hugging her tightly. "I know what I promised, but you are my daughter and it's not your fault. I can't punish you for something that isn't your fault."

"Maybe if you teach me some of this magic, then my aura will be good? It could be good! After all, Papa, the only time it was bad was that time with the Jews." Adolph could feel Magdalena's pain still raw with remembrance.

"When someone is touched with such violence, the aura is born of a bad influence. When a tree is planted, it won't be a good presence. When you feed the aura the teas from the roots and it grows stronger, it will cause much destruction," Magdalena's father told her.

"It won't. I promise. I could make it do good things," Magdalena swore.

"While you have shown us a great deal of restraint, it's much too dangerous for me to allow you to coax your aura even further by planting your tree. You will not have a tree. The seeds have been destroyed. Your aura will be weak and will eventually leave you. Without the tree, it will surely starve. It's the only way to keep us safe. The book won't help you without the aura, so you must stay away from it."

Magdalena began to protest, but could see that it wouldn't be any use. Papa had made his decision, and there were no seeds to plant. Adolph could taste the disappointment in Magdalena. It tasted bitter, like poison, on the back of his throat.

"I'm sorry. I hope you can understand," he stated with finality. Magdalena didn't protest further, and considering the matter closed, he gave her one last mournful look before leaving her, book clutched tightly under his arm.

She must have the book! The urge was too strong. She wanted a tree! Adolph felt this pull in his gut, a feeling of want and longing.

Adolph saw her as she waited for her father to leave the next morning. She stood at the window holding the curtain back just enough to see him, but not enough for him to see her.

Magdalena's mother was in the kitchen making *brot*. Her belly was large and round.

Magdalena snuck out of the house and went into the cow barn by the field. She'd seen her father take the book there.

She went straight to the high shelf above the first stall, where her Papa kept his important papers, and found it easily. She sat and read until it was too dark to see the pages any longer.

She learned many things that day. If she had a tree and fed her aura the tea ground from its roots, she would be able to manipulate others. She would be able to make them do what she wanted, to see what she wanted them to see. If she fed it regularly, like a baby, it would become strong and healthy and give her what she wanted most in life.

She also learned that what her Papa had said was true, that sometimes a person's aura could come forth before its time due to an act of violence against the host. In doing this, it would present itself in a bad light and could be used for purposes that had never been intended...for hurting people and for righting the wrong done to them. However, if it were coaxed out with a series of teachings, and a tree was planted with good intentions, then the aura would be of a good light, meant for blessing the host with talents, knowledge, and helpful visions. Couldn't she have both?

She would teach herself, she decided. She didn't need her Papa or anyone else to help her. She *would* have both.

Adolph saw Magdalena reaching to put the book back up in the hayloft where she had retrieved it. She didn't want to get caught reading it and risk having it hidden permanently.

Something fell out and dropped to the dirt floor. Hidden in the folds of the book there had been a tiny seed wrapped in paper. The beautiful handwriting on the pouch bore her name. Her seed! Papa lied to her! Adolph could feel Magdalena's anger, but also her delighted relief.

The book cautioned that she shouldn't plant the seed until she had a firm understanding of what she'd like to achieve in her lifetime, for this would set the tone of her aura. It also had warned that she should use it sparingly. A tree was meant to last a lifetime, but it was not an endless commodity.

Did she not wish for something so badly it consumed her every waking thought and invaded her dreams?

Clutching the seed, Magdalena skipped out of the barn happily. She knew her father would be furious if he caught her. She should plant it now, before he got home and saw that it was missing.

Magdalena did understand what it was that she wanted. She'd wanted it since the horrible time with the Jews.

She looked for a shovel, eager to begin. She found what she needed in the tool shed and planted her tree amongst the other trees in the orchard, hoping to conceal it.

She'd just finished putting the tools away when her mother's screams sent her running toward the house. The baby was being born. Her mother didn't want her to fetch the doctor. She didn't want anyone to know.

The baby came out quickly and covered in messy goo. Her mother handed the screaming, blood soaked child to Magdalena without even looking at it.

"Get rid of it," she cried, shrinking back away from it as though it were a snake instead of a child. "I don't want to see it."

Magdalena wrapped the wiggling baby tightly in a cloth and brought it outside. She wanted to smother it with her own hands.

She didn't want to look because she was afraid that if she did, she would see the Jews. She did look, though. Her curiosity was too great. Its tiny black eyes blinked up at her, and Adolph was surprised that she felt not hate for this child, but something else. Adolph was not permitted to see the rest of this image. Magdalena had awoken him.

"Sometimes evil can be born from hate if the hate is strong enough. But not everything born evil is hated," she told him again, as she had when he'd witnessed the first horrible vision.

He laid awake, staring at the ceiling and wondered about this child. This Jew baby. He hoped that she killed it. The less Jews there were in the world, the better. Even a half Jew should not be allowed to live. He hated them as much as she did.

Still sleepy and not quite midnight, Adolph drifted back to sleep and saw an image of Magdalena in the yard by the apple trees. The seed she'd planted had begun to sprout before her eyes. It grew bigger and bigger until it became clear to her that it wouldn't be concealed. Though he could feel her apprehension at her father finding out, Adolph could feel the satisfaction it gave her too. It made her feel powerful. He could feel her power. She could move mountains if she wanted.

Her father came home and saw what she'd done. He dropped to his knees and frantically tried to pull it up, but it had already started to branch and was firmly rooted. He was in such a state of despair that he got up and began to shake Magdalena violently.

"You don't know what you've done! You are such a foolish girl!" he wailed. "Oh! What've you done?" He dropped to his knees once again, and holding his head in his hands, began to rock back and forth, sobbing. "What did you wish for Magdalena? You must tell me!" he cried.

"You know what I wished for papa. They must pay," she told him, satisfied that she had done it. There wouldn't be anything he could do about it.

"I held you in my arms when you were just a baby. Perfect in every way. I had such hopes for you. They ruined it for me, and for you. You were changed Magdalena, and you'll never change back. You've been touched by evil, and therefore everything you touch will always be evil," he told her.

Looking the most wretched that she'd ever seen him, his face streamed with tears, his eyes became frantic. He snatched her arm and began dragging her towards the house, yelling for his wife to start packing. They must get out of there quickly before they were found, but there was nothing to be done. His wife was too weak from just giving birth. She couldn't summon the strength to get out of bed. They'd have to wait and hope that they had time to get away.

Magdalena went to the barn in the night, unable to keep away from the book. She wanted to learn everything she could.

A noise outside pulled her out of her studies. It sounded like arguing; men's voices in anger.

She heard a popping sound, and suddenly there was an orange light coming through the slats in the barn walls. She opened the door and was engulfed by smoke. Her house was burning. Her parents would surely perish.

Adolph felt in Magdalena not sadness, but relief. The book was now hers, and she'd always have her aura to care for her.

Chapter Four

Present Day

Greta lay awake, staring into the dark long after she should have been asleep. She'd been up way too late as it was, going over the sign language book that Kelly had given her a few months before.

She hadn't had much time to look at it, and when she did, she couldn't seem to concentrate, though she knew she should buckle down and learn.

Bastian was making progress, though it had nothing to do with her, she thought regretfully.

She'd been so busy at work lately. The pressure the government had been putting on her to get her current job done quickly left her little time to spend with her son, and feeling tired and crabby when she did.

Bastian's team would be coming in the morning to check on his progress and to do another evaluation, and she'd be tired again. If she could just sleep! Sleep and not worry so much, though the reason for her lack of sleep that night really didn't have much to do with work or the sign language book. It had to do with Kelly.

She'd been having conflicting feelings towards her. On the one hand, she was grateful that Kelly was willing to work with Bastian at all. People willing to work with kids like him were scarce. She certainly wouldn't have the patience to do a job like that.

Bastian was her son, so she supposed her patience where he was concerned was average, but she doubted that she'd be able to work with anyone else's child. She doubted that she could feel that same affection, or control the frustration she felt more and more.

Day after day, Kelly came and performed the same repetitive routine, sometimes rewarded with a smile and a hug, sometimes getting bitten or screeched at. Greta knew it had to be very difficult and frustrating for Kelly, yet she always seemed to be genuinely happy to see Bastian, and always left with a smile.

Bastian adored Kelly. He responded to her. They seemed to have a connection that Greta only wished she could have with her son. Sometimes after she left, Greta would try some of the things that Kelly had been working on with him, but he didn't seem as interested as when Kelly did them.

Her biggest problem was that she still couldn't understand him, therefore she was often unable to give him what he asked for. It usually ended up with Bastian screaming, and Greta giving him everything she could think of to make him stop.

If she were being honest, she'd also have to admit that she gave in to him too quickly, almost never forcing him to do what he was supposed to be doing, for fear that he might hurt her.

She was hoping that learning some signs, as Kelly had suggested, would allow her to at least partly be able to communicate with him, but it was clear that she either lacked the skills or desire to learn the damn signs. Language wasn't her talent, so trying to mimic the illustrations in the book made her look like she was swatting at bugs instead of communicating. She looked and felt ridiculous.

Kelly seemed to have an intuition when it came to Bastian. Something that told her exactly what he wanted, and therefore she was able to produce it with very little effort. Bastian was always so proud of himself when he could express a desire and have it met. He liked being understood. He smiled at Kelly and hugged her a lot more often than Greta, and it hurt. Feelings of jealousy were not too familiar to her. She was hoping that she could hide her feelings. That they wouldn't get in the way of the progress that he was making.

In another week, Bastian would be starting nursery school, attending three out of the five days. With him going on Monday, Wednesday, and Friday, it meant having even less time to spend with him, as her day off had always been Wednesdays. She worried that this was going to push him even further away from her. With all of the people coming in and out of her house, offering suggestions and making changes to her routines, it already felt as though she'd completely lost control of her life and of being a mother to Bastian.

It felt like she was just another member of his team, and not his favorite, at that. She knew that it was important to put her jealousy aside and continue to reinforce Kelly's efforts, but it was hard.

Paula, the case manager for Bastian's team, was pushing hard for the nursery school piece to Bastian's program, but Greta was extremely worried for the other children at the school. She liked Paula's professionalism and knowledge, and she trusted what she said, but if Bastian hurt one of those children, as he had with Dr.

Goldenberg and often did to Kelly and herself, Greta wouldn't be able to forgive herself.

When she'd mentioned her concerns, Kelly told her that she would be accompanying Bastian to the school to minimize the chances of anything going wrong, but Greta worried that it was going to push Bastian even closer to Kelly and further away from her. In the beginning, she hoped that Kelly would be able to bring her son back to her. That she'd be able to one day have a normal relationship with him, but lately it seemed as though it was only pushing her even farther out of his life.

Giving up on sleep, Greta decided to get up and start getting ready for the day ahead. She wanted to get the house clean, and also make her guests some refreshments.

She thought about making an apple torte. Her mother's recipe for apple torte was the best she'd ever tasted, and she was pretty sure it would make an impression. She wondered briefly if Kelly could cook as well, but then scolded herself for her uncharitable thinking. She had made a vow to do better.

She checked to make sure she had all of the ingredients before doing a quick look in on Bastian. She was happy to see that he was still asleep, and hoped she'd have time to finish everything before he woke up. It was doubtful, but she could hope!

His brow furrowed as he whimpered softly in his sleep. Probably a bad dream, she decided, and went to cover him with the blankets he'd kicked off during the night. He stirred slightly and began to mumble what sounded to her like the word, 'cart'. Probably a word he heard while working with Kelly.

It had only been a few months since Kelly had started

working with Bastian, and maybe her expectations were too high, but she'd thought that his language skills would be a little farther along by then. He hadn't gained much in the way of any real language skills, and Greta was beginning to worry that he may never learn to speak.

Bastian awoke and stood abruptly, immediately screaming to get out. He began shaking the bars of his crib and jumping up and down. So much for the torte!

Greta chuckled, "Okay, little impatient one, give me a moment."

She stepped away for just a second to grab a fresh diaper, and Bastian climbed up and over the bars, landing with a thud on his head. Greta rushed to him, horrified, but he was off and running, seemingly unscathed by the incident.

Greta chased after him, trying to make sure he was truly unhurt, and found him in the library, which surprised her.

The library was one of the reasons that she'd bought that house out of the ten or so she'd looked at. She'd been an avid reader her whole life, and had amassed a huge collection of books. The high ceilings with wall-to-wall bookshelves seemed perfect for her.

There was also enough room for her comfortable leather furniture, and for the beautiful pedestal globe she'd placed in the center of the room. As far as she knew, Bastian had never even been in there, preferring the living room where his blocks and other toys were. Nonetheless, that was where she found him, and he was spinning her globe. Greta watched silently from the doorway so she wouldn't disturb his sudden new interest.

Bastian spun the globe quickly, using both hands to make it faster. Greta feared that he was going to break it and was about to redirect him, as Kelly often did when he was doing something he shouldn't, but he suddenly stopped.

He pointed at the globe with his tiny finger.

"Afica," he concluded nonchalantly. Greta was stunned and thought that she hadn't heard him correctly, but as she got closer she saw that he was right. His finger was pointed directly at Africa.

He spun it once more and stopped. "'Stralia." Again he was correct. Australia! Greta was shocked, but overjoyed! Was he actually talking; using real words?

How could he possibly know that? She scanned her brain for any possible reason, time, or place that Bastian might have learned about geography and was coming up short, not to mention that he had never spoken a recognizable word until just then.

She watched him again as he found Asia, and again as he found Europe, speaking each continent in the best way he could. Greta got goose bumps...the little hairs on the back of her neck were prickling.

She saw him spin once more. He seemed to be struggling to find something, as at first he spun the globe one way, then much slower, turned the globe around and around, and spun it in the opposite direction.

Abruptly, Bastian stopped spinning. Greta could see that he'd found North America. His head moved in quick back and forth motions, and she could see that his eyes were frantically roaming all over, slanting slightly as they strained to see more clearly the tiny print. She was waiting to see if he'd be able to put the two words together. The other continents were just one word.

Bastian became still and seemed to focus in on something. He studied the map for just a moment longer before raising his finger. He pointed. "New Yuck City," he claimed and smiled brightly.

He turned to look at Greta, and declared again with a certain confidence, "New Yuck City."

Her excitement suddenly dimmed as she could see that he had, in fact, been hurt in his fall. To her shock, she saw blood trickling from a deep gash on his forehead. Scooping him up quickly, she rushed him out to the car.

After spending the last few months looking after Helga for Professor Stein, Kelly decided that he'd done her quite a favor. She adored Helga, though in the beginning she hadn't been so sure.

During their first meeting, Helga was cordial enough and had been a good, but stiff hostess. She offered Kelly some type of German cake that she'd made after figuring out the oven, surprising her son immensely, and freshly brewed tea. Then she scooted herself, clad in her sensible brown German shoes, into her room and promptly shut the door tight.

Kelly laughed. Helga had left her and the professor to entertain themselves.

Professor Stein, chuckling, excused himself. He knocked on his mother's door and pointed out that it wasn't good practice to leave an unmarried male and female unchaperoned, knowing that good old-fashioned manners would bring her back out. He was right. No idle tongues would be wagging in the neighborhood that night, after all. Kelly was greatly amused with the old—fashioned thought.

Once she'd settled, reluctantly, back at the table with Kelly and her son, Kelly asked Helga some polite questions to which Helga answered with her pen and pad in the briefest possible sentences. It wasn't until Kelly began talking about the work that she was doing with the children that Helga began to open up a little.

It turned out that she loved children, and would've had more, if she'd been able. This was a piece of information that Professor Stein hadn't mentioned to her. She'd been an only child herself, and hoped for a large family one day, but it wasn't to be.

Kelly found her to be quite smart and warm, and Helga seemed to enjoy the company. Professor Stein suggested a game of *Tausend Kilometer,* and then a German form of the American Scrabble game, to help improve Kelly's German vocabulary, which sent them all into fits of laughter when Kelly thought she was spelling *schwul* (humid, soggy) but forgot the umlaut over the u, which turned the word into gay, homosexual. They all had so much fun, in fact, that Kelly stayed for dinner, which she and Helga prepared together.

It was becoming second nature for Kelly to arrive at the professor's house, greet Helga with a kiss, and sit down to read all of the things Helga wanted to tell Kelly, but could only write.

She wrote about the plants she wanted to put in the garden, about shopping lists. She would pepper Kelly with questions about her love life (her nonexistent love life, Kelly kept reminding her), and her desires and dreams. It pushed Kelly to think about things that she hadn't really thought of for a long time, and made her wonder, when she got to be Helga's age, what her life would be like. What would she be looking back on?

It also made her wonder how many of Helga's dreams

came true and how many regrets or disappointments she might have suffered.

The few attempts Kelly made at trying to get Helga to open up about her life in Germany yielded only bits about when her son was growing up. Kelly didn't want to push too much too soon, so she settled for their leisurely morning walks and afternoon teas followed by her German lessons, which Helga insisted upon for Kelly's benefit.

Kelly didn't realize just how much she missed her own family until she started spending so much time with Helga. Her grandmother had passed away a few years ago, but Kelly still thought of her often. They were very close when Kelly was growing up, and she had many fond memories of baking with her in her cozy, warm kitchen.

Being with Helga in the professor's kitchen sometimes made her heart ache, thinking about her loss, but she was grateful that she seemed to be finding an unexpected surrogate in Helga.

She'd been so busy lately with Bastian and looking after Helga that she really hadn't had the time to check in with her own parents. Maybe she'd give them a call when she was finished with Bastian's meeting. Maybe she would plan a short trip to Maine, she thought, as she drove on towards Greta's house.

Greta's cheeks still burned slightly with embarrassment as she and Bastian pulled into the driveway after a lengthy trip to the ER. An hour's wait to see the doctor, and she'd been treated like nothing more than an overly concerned new mother. They'd sent her on her way with a chuckle and a Band-Aid for Bastian's head.

She wasn't stupid, for goodness sake. She had a doctorate. Bastian was her son. If anything happened to him, she'd have only herself to blame, she thought indignantly.

She spied the cars in her driveway and instantly remembered the meeting. Drat! She would be woefully unprepared when she had such high hopes of looking like she had it together. Well, there wasn't anything she could do about it. At least she would get the chance to ask if anyone had any insight into Bastian's new development, she thought as she opened up her door and went to explain their tardiness.

A half-hour into the meeting, Greta finally had the chance to ask about Bastian's behavior that morning. She explained in detail what had happened. Everyone had smiles of relief as she told them about his new language skills, but Kelly was the first to speak up.

"Oh! I was wondering what his talent would be!" she exclaimed, startling everyone with her sudden outburst.

Greta and the team gaped at Kelly. She blushed, feeling foolish for her impulsiveness and began to explain.

"Well, during my work with autistic kids, it has been my experience to find that a lot of them possess skills that are above the norm for even intelligent adults. Some were brilliant in math, while others mastered the piano, or violin. I even worked with a little boy who was such a great artist, they chose one of his paintings to be commissioned at the Museum of Modern Art," Kelly apprised.

The discovered talents of those students held some fascination for Kelly, though not as much as foreign languages did. It seemed, from some of the research that she'd done and her experience, that some children with autism could be considered geniuses.

Kelly saw her fellow team members squirming uncomfortably and knew she probably shouldn't have spoken up. She hated that her mouth seemed to separate from her brain on occasion. She did have a talent for blurting things out, but it was interesting that sometimes while working with a child who had autism, she could begin to see a certain brilliance develop. Just like most of them had blonde hair and blue eyes, they all could be pretty intelligent too. It was almost as if they were all broken off from the same DNA branch. She couldn't help but say something.

Paula spoke up, admonishing Kelly with a scathing look.

"Greta, while what Kelly mentioned is true to some extent, not all children with autism display the true gift of being a prodigy," she confided softly, placing a hand on Greta's arm. "It's perhaps a bit premature to explain exactly what happened today. Children with autism routinely become magpies, if you will; often imitating exactly what they've heard in the same tones they heard it in." Paula raised her eyebrow knowingly at Kelly before continuing. "I worked with a family once who was overjoyed that their son seemingly learned to talk in just a matter of days of working with his aide. In those few days, his vocabulary had grown from just a single word to the ability of making complete sentences. They called me in so that I could observe his progress and to see if I could offer any more tools to speed up the process, but upon further examination by the team, and myself, we determined that the child was unable to identify the things that he was speaking of. He might say, 'I want some animal crackers,' only to push them away, and point to an apple instead. He could say all of the animals but when given cue cards to look at, he would point at the zebra, but say school." She paused and waited to make sure everyone was still with her.

Kelly rolled her eyes. Of course everyone was listening. Paula was in her element. She was the team leader and made sure to point that out whenever she could. To her, Kelly was nothing more than a peon. Gretchen, Kathy, and Greta all nodded in approval, probably riveted by every word. Paula really knew how to command an audience with her superior attitude. Kelly wanted to cut in, but held her tongue as Paula prattled on.

"Words are just words unless there is something there to put meaning behind them, and that child was only imitating the words he heard from his aide and repeating them. It's more than likely that Bastian saw a television show about the continents and he was merely imitating," she finished smugly, and gave Kelly another look.

Kelly never cared for Paula. She had a very condescending way about her that always made Kelly feel like an idiot, though she knew she wasn't. With all of her degrees, Kelly found Paula to be lacking in two very important things necessary for this job: common sense, and a love for children. Information learned from books was great, but actually spending time with the students and getting to know them beyond what was written was the best resource Kelly had in learning about them. They were individuals, not research specimens. Kelly had clients, more often than not, display significant brilliance in a particular area, and intended to say so.

"While I agree with Paula to some extent," Kelly began, shooting a look of her own to Paula, "it's been my experience that more than half of the children that I've worked with have been prodigies in one thing or another. I must admit that I always find it exciting when and if the gift presents itself. Now, it could be that Bastian was imitating something that he heard, but from what you told me happened this morning, I don't see how it's possible that he could have correctly identified the continents by pointing on a globe merely by imitation," Kelly stated, looking at Greta for verification.

Greta was confused by the whole topic. In the research she'd done on her own concerning autism, she had read that a number of children with autism did display some amazing gifts, on occasion, but with just a slightly higher incidence than typical children.

She had no reason to believe up to that point that Bastian would be special. If anything at all, she was ashamed to admit, she thought of Bastian as severely behind, almost bordering on retarded. However, she couldn't deny that he'd identified most of the continents and New York City all on his own. She knew in her heart that Paula's explanation just didn't hold true in their case. As Kelly had pointed out, it would be difficult to imitate something to that extent.

A small part of her felt a bit of excitement that he could possibly be a savant, while another just hoped for normalcy. Wasn't it enough that the poor kid was already going to be set apart from his peers? Scenes from the movie '*Little Man Tate*' ran through her head. She looked towards Bastian who was seemingly unaware that they were talking about him, or even there with him, for that matter.

"If, in fact, Bastian did turn out to be a savant, do you think it would be best to encourage him, or try to keep him

Kristy Gherlone

at an age appropriate pace?" Greta directed her question at Paula, which disappointed Kelly some. It didn't surprise her, but it stung just the same.

"I think at this point, we should all just try our best to keep Bastian on task with the plan we have in place," Paula answered. Kelly shook her head in disagreement.

"And I think that if someone has a child who possesses a natural talent in anything, we would be doing a disservice by trying to squash it. Think of all of the geniuses in the world that have been major contributors in the advancement of medicine, computer technology, and oh, I don't know, a lot of things. Think of Jonathan Keeley! He was responsible for the discovery of ten new species of plants in the rain forest that have been directly linked to the cure of five major illnesses."

"I would just like us all," Paula gave Kelly a warning look, "to keep on task for now and see how it goes. If Bastian advances further and shows any other behavior that would suggest he was functioning at the genius level, then it'll be up to you, Greta, to decide if you would like to get him tested or not. There's a school for gifted children with autism. The Weisenhoff School. I've heard they can do some pretty amazing things with these kids. But for now, I think we've gotten ahead of ourselves."

Paula was the one to wrap up the meeting, promising Greta that they would meet again soon, encouraging her to call if there were any problems with the introduction of nursery school. She bent down and patted Bastian on the head on the way to the door but he didn't even look up from his blocks. Kelly got a great deal of smug satisfaction when she got a hug.

As Kelly reached her car, Paula confronted her. "If you

disagree with me at a team meeting, the time for discussing it wouldn't be in front of our client's parent."

Kelly knew that Paula was furious with her, but was betting it didn't have anything to do with making Greta uncomfortable. It had to do with her own embarrassment. She didn't give a crap about Bastian, or his long—term results. She only cared about being right and sounding smart. However, Kelly knew that she'd treaded on dangerous ground. Paula outranked her, and she shouldn't have disagreed with her in front of a parent.

If she wanted to push the issue, Kelly could be out of a job, and this was more than just a job to her. She loved working with Bastian, and even if she didn't, she needed the money.

"I only want what's best for Bastian, and I'd like to encourage him to become the person that he's meant to be, not someone that we alter to suit society," Kelly confessed quietly. "Why shouldn't Bastian have every opportunity in life, even if it sets him apart from his peers?"

"I think you may be in the wrong business, Kelly, because our job isn't to create geniuses. Our job is to take these children and try very hard to get them to fit into society where they'll be able to function as normally as possible with as few obstacles as possible." She threw her briefcase into her car, slammed the door and turned to face Kelly again.

"Jonathan Keeley indeed! Everyone knows about Jonathan Keely, everyone knows about Caleb Schneider too, the famous autistic basketball star. 'Isn't it great that kids with autism can beat the odds and impress a nation with their talents?'" She sneered. "You always see stuff like that plastered all over the news. Who you failed to mention though, was Alex Manning..." Paula offered, lowering her voice.

"I'd forgotten about Alex," Kelly murmured. She was beginning to see where Paula was going with her tirade, and it made her angry.

"I'm sure you have. No one talks about Alex anymore since his arrest for creating that bomb that killed twenty kids at the Jewish arts center, and you didn't mention Corey Thomas either. The famous Corey Thomas who was responsible for the deaths of hundreds of children when he conned a pilot flying a 737 into letting him take the controls...just for a second because he was only seven and already oh so talented in aviation, having flown his daddy's plane. He killed all of those kids at the Kesher School and everyone on board that plane!" Paula wrenched open the driver's side to her car and stood glaring.

"We'd all like to think that the parents we work with only want what's best for their kids, but sometimes that's just not the case. Sometimes the very people who are supposed to be helping these kids end up trying to capitalize on them. They convince the parents that it would be a crime to let their talents go to waste. They make promises of fame and fortune, and then these parents let them take their children away to be studied, to be tested, and pushed to the very limits that often make them snap. You've been at this long enough to know these children are prone to violence, and that violence is often prompted by pushing them too hard."

"Well, you can't think that I would try to do that!" Kelly exclaimed.

"I'm not suggesting that you were, Kelly. However, sometimes the best intentions can end poorly. If Bastian were to have a gift for geography, cartography, or anything else, I'm telling you, the best thing you could do for him and his mom would be to ignore it and stick with his plan."

Kelly shook her head in frustration. "I have been sticking to the plan. Bastian is making excellent progress. I'm sorry, but I just don't see the harm in helping him to achieve loftier goals than tying his own shoes. Besides, he hardly shows any violence anymore. Well, not too much anyway, and not all kids with autism end up like Alex or Corey. Besides, you were the one to bring up the Weisenhoff School," Kelly pointed out.

Paula sighed as she fished her keys out of her purse. "I've seen you work, Kelly, and I know that the very thing that makes you good at what you do is also your downfall. You get too close; too attached. I have seen this in you before, but never like this. You are too attached to Bastian, and if you can't rein it in, it's going to end poorly for everyone. His violent outbursts may be less right now, but I can assure you, if you push him...if Greta starts pushing him, he could snap and someone could get hurt. I suggested that school because they seem to be the best at channeling some of the violent outbursts by giving other ways to express all of that energy they seem to possess. Please think about that the next time you work with him." With that, Paula got into her car and drove away.

Kelly knew, on some level, that what Paula said was right. Sometimes these kids could be violent. Sometimes, like Corey Thomas, they could even be deadly, but this was Bastian! While it was true that she hadn't been able to completely stop the biting and hitting, she was usually able to redirect him before it got out of hand. She was encouraged to see that a child who wasn't prone to showing

Kristy Gherlone

emotion could feel bad about hurting her when he did. She could see it in his eyes. He would always give her a hug after, or touch her cheek. She sensed that he genuinely cared for her.

She didn't care what any of the so-called professionals claimed. If Bastian did have some special talents, then she would do all she could to help him develop them. Nothing he'd shown her had led her to believe that his behavior was anything but typical for a child with autism. She could definitely handle him.

CHAPTER FIVE

"**H**i Greta, it's Kelly. I have a favor to ask you. I was wondering if you'd mind if I brought someone along today when I come to work with Bastian." Kelly was due to work with Bastian in an hour, and it was really last minute, but she had no choice, though she knew she could get in trouble for even asking.

Greta hesitated. She wasn't really up for company, but if it meant that Kelly wouldn't be able to come if she told her no, then she really didn't have a choice. "I guess it's alright. Who is it?"

"It's my professor's mother, the one from Germany. She doesn't have anyone to stay with her today and I don't feel comfortable leaving her alone."

"Oh yeah, I remember you mentioning her before. Yeah, I guess she can come, but she'll probably be bored."

"I doubt that. She loves kids! Are you sure you don't mind?" Kelly hated that she was even in that position. It was most definitely against company policy to bring someone completely unrelated to Bastian's team with her to a session, but she didn't know what else to do. Paula would have a fit and it would give her something else to lecture Kelly about, but Professor Stein had a meeting during her scheduled time with Bastian, and she couldn't leave Helga home alone for that long.

Kristy Gherlone

"No, I don't mind. As a matter of fact, it might be nice to have someone to talk with while you work with Bastian," Greta answered graciously.

"Ok great! See you soon!"

Kelly and Helga had been spending a lot of time together, and even if Professor Stein hadn't asked her to, she would have felt obliged to take Helga along with her. She'd been noticing lately that Helga not only seemed tired, but a little down too. Maybe it was the dwindling daylight hours, but Kelly thought that Helga should get out a little more.

She was quiet as they drove on towards Greta's. She'd been trying to get Helga interested in some of the local activities that the community had for seniors, but she politely declined. She suspected that Helga might be embarrassed by her inability to communicate normally. Kelly tried telling her that many people her age were hard of hearing and probably wouldn't even notice, but Helga always gave the excuse that she was tired and quite happy at home.

She was pretty sure Helga wasn't going to open up to her in the mental state that she seemed to be in. Kelly still hadn't had much luck in getting Helga to share anything about her past life beyond being a wife and mother. Kelly knew, fond of her as she was, that Helga really could benefit from being with people closer to her own age. While she was feeling bad about breaking policy, if she were being truthful, she had been looking for the chance to be able to introduce Helga to Greta.

Both being of German descent, and Greta having lived there for a while, should give them a bit of common ground and something to talk about. Perhaps if they started talking about the "old country" as Helga referred to it, it would compel her to give up some information.

Helga knew that she was a foreign language major, and about her interest in learning about languages that weren't used anymore, but the few questions that she dared ask were dismissed immediately. Subject closed. Kelly, unable to curb her curiosity any longer, came right out and asked her if she was aware of any other languages that were spoken in Germany when Professor Stein was young, but she immediately bristled and clammed up.

Kelly feared that she'd asked too much. Helga was definitely suspicious and quickly changed the subject, asking Kelly about her love life, which she knew by then was a foolproof way to get Kelly to shut up. Kelly had to laugh because it had been mentioned more than once that at Kelly's age, Helga was already married and had a child. Kelly knew that Helga thought that she should give up her career and get married. So, Kelly got to return the cold shoulder. Subject closed. The truth be told, she would love to get married, but with Bastian, her schoolwork, and looking after Helga, she felt like she'd never have the time to date again!

"Hi Greta, thanks again for having us." Kelly shuffled past Greta with her briefcase and a reluctant Helga in tow.

"It's no problem, really." Greta smiled and turned towards Helga. "Would you like to come in and sit in the living room with me?" Helga smiled shyly and followed her in.

Confident that Helga and Greta were comfortable with one another, and seated in the living room with freshly made tea and cake, Kelly began her work at the table with Bastian.

He was doing very well and Kelly was proud of herself.

While he had not begun talking in earnest yet, continents excluded, he'd picked up on the sign language rather quickly. Unfortunately, the picture exchange book idea failed. Kelly knew that this was the one thing Greta was hoping would work, but she hadn't really given it much of an effort beyond the first few days. Bastian wanted to sign to his mother, but her skills were sorely lacking and she didn't need Kelly to tell her that a little studying would go a long way.

She'd sensed on more than one occasion that Greta had grown a bit jealous of her. It was nothing new, really. It had happened before with some of her other clients.

The children she worked with saw her so much, and got so much one-on-one time, that they became just as attached to her as she did to them. She got all of the hugs, all of the good work, but turned over to the parents at the end of the session, all of the negative behaviors started coming out again. It was hard to explain to parents that it was actually a good thing. It meant that they felt more comfortable with them. It was a trust thing. Not the case with Kelly and Bastian though. He didn't seem to have any qualms about acting out in front of her.

She liked all of her students, but for some reason Bastian had really stolen her heart. His sweet little face and eagerness to please her made her smile. Even when he was being naughty, she did all she could not to laugh at his adorable face. She looked forward to the days that she got to work with him, though with some of her other students that had not always been the case.

She enjoyed their table time and their walks. Kelly supposed that it would be really hard to have her own child someday and have him only want to hug a stranger. She was sure it would be devastating.

As much as she loved working with autistic children, she could only hope that she'd have a 'typical' child…if she ever had time to meet anyone and settle down. She chuckled at that thought, thinking how much Helga would love that!

Greta told Kelly that since the day in the library, Bastian hadn't spoken another word. Kelly decided to bring along some tools that should either confirm or deny what happened that day. She reached into her bag of tricks, as she liked to call it, and pulled out a folded map.

Bastian, having been given some animal crackers to snack on, since he'd been especially attentive during his session, was lining them up in order instead of eating them as he should.

He didn't seem to notice Kelly as she carefully unfolded the map of the world. Lost in the methodical pattern, Bastian began to scream when Kelly told him that snack time was done. She began to scoop up the snack, but Bastian pulled them from her, carefully putting them back in the order that he had them in.

Kelly touched Bastian's chin lightly and gently pulled his face towards her so that he could see that she needed his attention.

"Snack time done," Kelly explained matter-of-factly, but he didn't need any further coaxing. He'd spotted the map.

He pulled it towards him, and brushed the crackers away, some of them falling to the floor. His eyes lit up and his chubby fingers moved all over the map. He stopped moving and pointed a tiny finger.

"New Yuck City," he offered, looking at Kelly with a small, giddy smile. He seemed very proud of himself, but Kelly got a tingly feeling, causing her to shiver a little. He was pointing at New York City. It was undeniable.

Not wanting to base her opinion too quickly on one attempt, she reached into her bag a second time and pulled out a different map, an older map not quite set up in the same way as the one Bastian was using.

She quickly exchanged the maps so that Bastian couldn't protest too loudly. It worked. He roamed again with his eyes and fingers. It took a bit longer that time, but he found what he was looking for.

"New Yuck City," he stated again looking at Kelly. Instead of smiling as he had before, he grabbed at some of the crackers that avoided the floor and carefully chose a lion, pushing the rest away.

He placed it on the spot where he was pointing. Kelly started to think that maybe he was using the cracker to try to communicate about the zoo in New York City. Maybe that was how he knew. He probably watched a children's show about the zoo there.

The thought process didn't last long as Kelly was startled to see a look come over Bastian's face that she hadn't yet seen. It almost looked to her like he was angry...furious, for that matter.

Before she could react in any way, Bastian brought his tiny fist down hard on the cracker, completely crushing it into the map.

He looked at Kelly, and for the first time since she had started working with him, he began to laugh. A good, hearty laugh that was just a bit too cynical for his age, or for Kelly's comfort.

"What a goof!" she scoffed, trying to sound light hearted, though his behavior had her a bit unhinged. "Don't you crush your crackers on my map!" She laughed, rustled his hair, and made a show of dusting off the map.

Bastian giggled at her and pushed himself back, indicating that he was done with his session whether she was or not.

Kelly released Bastian from his chair. As per routine, he zinged past her into the living room and flopped onto the floor to line up his blocks.

Helga stopped writing in her tablet for a moment to smile at Bastian as Greta inquired about his session.

"Umm, well..." Kelly didn't quite know what to say. She decided at that moment that she'd need to study him further before saying anything that would make Greta worry even more than she already did. "It was good," she concluded and then changed the subject to ask how the two ladies had gotten along. She half listened and half paid attention to Bastian to see if he would do anything else weird as they described their visit.

Convinced that Bastian was back to his semi—normal state, Kelly told Helga that it was time to go. Helga stood, waving away Kelly's attempt to help her and began to write in her note pad. If nothing else, at least she'd been able to give Helga a few hours away from home and something else to think about. She looked happy and relaxed as she handed Greta a thank you note.

"You're welcome, Helga, and thank you Kelly, for bringing Helga with you today," Greta exclaimed as they started towards the door. "It was really nice catching up with what has been going on in Germany. I hadn't realized how much I missed hearing about it until she came today," she admitted, looking genuinely pleased.

It was a relief that they got along so well, but Kelly was still thinking about her session with Bastian. He seemed fine, but she was still a little disturbed by his behavior. While autistic kids were known to be quirky, he'd gone beyond the norm. She gave him one last look before turning to leave.

Helga reached out to shake Greta's hand, but something back in the living room suddenly caught her attention. Her eyes narrowed with confusion as she walked past Greta's outstretched hand and back into the living room. Both Greta and Kelly were baffled and followed her back.

Helga stopped when she reached Bastian and stood quietly over him as he manipulated his blocks on the floor. He was babbling again. The look on Helga's face registered shock and disbelief. Kelly could see Helga staring at Bastian, her eyes suddenly widening in fright. She clutched at her throat, "*Wie kann das sein?* (How can this be?)" Her words came out raspy from years of being idle. She looked towards Kelly desperately, shocked.

Kelly was stunned. She'd never heard Helga speak a single word until just then, and from what Professor Stein had told her, hadn't spoken since that day they had the strange visitor.

"I'm sorry." Greta apologized with confusion, "I don't remember much German at all. My parents refused to speak it at home and I didn't keep up with my studies when I returned to the States."

"I thought she was mute?" Greta turned away from Helga, raised her eyebrows and mouthed the question to Kelly.

Kelly didn't know what had happened. How could what be? She stood there, unsure of how to respond. All she could do was shrug her shoulders.

Greta stood looking at Kelly and then turned back to

Helga. Perhaps Bastian's behavior was what had her so upset. She felt she should explain.

"This is just something he does all the time. Nothing to be concerned about." She was embarrassed for herself and her son. She knew his behavior was odd, but until then had never really had anyone witness it outside of Bastian's team. Her cheeks were starting to turn pink, but Helga dismissed her worry with a quick wave of her hand. She looked to Kelly.

"*Ubersetzen bitte,*" she told Kelly, making no attempt at writing in her tablet. It wasn't a question but a desperate plea. She needed Kelly to translate.

Without waiting for an answer, Helga's voice became strong as she began firing German at Kelly. Kelly worked as fast as she could to keep up with the translation. What she did understand, she didn't really understand. What Helga was saying didn't make any sense.

Kelly addressed Greta with an apologetic expression at what was asked of her, but out of respect for Helga, and because of the pleading look Helga was giving her, she felt that she owed it to her to make the translation.

"Helga would like to know how long Bastian has been speaking this language," she asked with an embarrassed shrug.

Greta was completely confused. Bastian was babbling. All babies babbled. Surely she must know that. Perhaps the poor lady was having some kind of episode, some kind of lapse in her thinking.

"Kelly, you know as well as I do that he is just babbling, can't she see that? Surely she must remember this from when her son was small?" She didn't know whether to giggle or cry.

Kelly saw Helga begin to shake her head, and thinking she didn't understand, wanted to explain in a way that wouldn't offend her. She explained in German that it was just baby babble (*baby-geplapper*) but Helga began to shake her head vigorously.

She lowered herself gingerly onto the floor with Bastian. Her old knees made slight popping sounds as she descended. Her face creased with concern as she began to listen to his babbling once again.

Kelly noticed the alarm on Greta's face as Helga put herself within Bastian's reach. She knew all too well about what happened at the doctor's office when someone new was introduced too quickly.

Greta moved closer to grab Bastian should he try something, but he seemed unaware of what was going on around him. He was unfazed by Helga. He barely gave her a glance as he continued with his play.

It was when Helga began speaking to Bastian that he stopped lining up his blocks to listen. She was speaking to him not in English, not in German, but in a language Kelly had never heard before. She felt completely confused, but also a bit tingly and excited. Could this be the language Professor Stein had been talking about? Her mind was spinning. Why had she just begun talking now? And why to Bastian?

As Kelly listened, she was sure that she couldn't detect the language's origin. It did appear to have some German roots by the sound and accent, but she couldn't recognize any of the words.

Bastian looked up from his blocks and directly into Helga's eyes, stunning both Greta and Kelly at once. Eye contact was so rare for him, and literally unheard of with a stranger. Helga had really gotten his attention.

He picked up one of the blocks and Greta bent next to him, ready to pounce should he strike, but much to her utter amazement, Bastian began to speak back to Helga, moving the block up and down as he did like someone would if they were using their hands to speak. It was a quick interaction, but what Bastian said to her was very clearly posed as a question. There was a small uptick at the end of his words and a questioning look on his face. Whatever he'd asked of Helga, whatever he'd said, had her completely unglued. His language, this supposed babble of his, had indeed begun to sound very much like the language that Helga was speaking.

Helga reached for Kelly, a look of panic and fear on her face. Though normally shy about asking for help, she grabbed at Kelly's arm to assist her in getting off the floor. Kelly obliged and as soon as her feet were under her, she immediately headed for the door. Her face was pinched with fright.

She paused quickly at the door, "*Gott mit dir sein* (God be with you)," she said to Greta, and rushed out towards the car, leaving Kelly stunned.

"What did she just say to me?" asked Greta, visibly confused. She wanted to know just as much as Kelly what had taken place.

Kelly was confused herself, but quickly composed herself and felt compelled to make some kind of an excuse for Helga. Until she could figure out what happened, there was no sense in alarming Greta. She calmed herself outwardly and called over her shoulder to Greta as she followed Helga to the car.

"I'll call you later. Nothing to worry about, I'm sure."

Kelly waited until Helga's door closed before adding a bit more quietly so as not to offend, "You know how old people are. They get a bit confused at times."

Eager to get Helga alone so she could ask her some questions, Kelly called out to Greta as she stood, still stunned. "I should get her home to rest. Thanks for having her today. I'm sure she enjoyed it very much." Then she promptly shut her car door and backed out of the driveway.

Greta paused at the door. So odd, she thought. She'd had such a nice conversation with Helga just a few moments before. There was nothing to indicate that the woman had been delusional in any way. She seemed normal enough, very pleasant in fact. 'Ah well,' she thought as she closed the door. 'You just never can tell.' But as she turned around she suddenly gasped. Bastian wasn't on the floor where he'd been just moments before.

She quickly scanned the room and found him at the window. He was waving! One tiny hand was holding the curtain back and the other hailing goodbye.

"The foolish will die," he hissed, and let the curtain fall back into place before turning around to face Greta.

Greta wasn't sure at first if she heard Bastian correctly. She was suddenly chilled. What an odd thing for a toddler to say. Especially since up until then, all she'd managed to get out of him were a few continents and a city of all things.

Greta dropped to her knees so that she was at eye level with him. For the first time since he was an infant, he looked directly into her eyes. As she looked closer, it was almost as if he was looking through her, not at her. He had such an odd expression on his face. It wasn't her Bastian.

"What did you just say, Bastian?" she asked slowly, almost as a whisper. She prayed that he would please just answer back with his usual babble. She'd been waiting for months for him to talk, but this was too much. Too much too soon. And too weird.

"I said the foolish will die, mother," he answered casually, "are you going to be foolish when the time comes? I think you will," he answered for her, and then he was there again. His eyes wandered away from her as he dropped back to the floor with his blocks.

Greta's breath caught in her throat. What in the hell just happened? Whatever it was, she was grateful that it seemed to be gone for the time being.

Later that evening, Bastian began speaking to her as though he'd always been able. The language part of his brain had opened up; seemingly unlocked. With his barrier gone, Greta knew that she should feel happy. She wouldn't have any more trouble communicating with her son, but something about it just didn't seem right.

Kelly and Helga traveled in silence as they exited the cul-de-sac road that Greta lived on. Kelly saw that Helga was still trembling slightly from her encounter with Bastian, and though her hands were folded in her lap, she kept rubbing them back and forth nervously as she stared out the window.

Kelly couldn't imagine why Helga would have said, "God be with you," to Greta.

The curiosity about the language, and why Helga had suddenly tossed her silence aside to speak to a toddler was killing Kelly, but she was reluctant to start questioning Helga in the state she was in. However, she felt that she must say something, though she wasn't really sure of what.

"Helga," she began, but the elder woman silenced her with a quick wave of her hand.

"I know you have much questions," Helga began slowly and in broken English, surprising Kelly once again, "but I feel it not be right for me to speak with you without first having discussed dis with my son. He has right, I guess, to hear what I have to say first hand. I know what you two have been up to. I am old, not dumb. I know that he has asked you to try and get some information from me about something he saw when he was boy," she told Kelly, raising her eyebrows with an air of righteousness. Kelly felt like a kid that had been caught stealing cookies. Had she really been that obvious?

"Until now, entire conversation would have been, how you say dis? *Sinnlos?*"

"Pointless," Kelly translated easily for her.

"I not going to speak more of it now, but I have request for you," she turned and looked very somberly at Kelly. "I am beg to you. Stop going to that house. Stop your work with that child. Immediately."

Kelly couldn't imagine what was going on in Helga's head at that moment. Bastian was a small child with an illness, how could she not see how innocent he was? How much he needed his therapy to get well? She'd spent hours telling Helga about the work she was doing, and how much each of her students had improved with the help of an early interventionist. Helga was acting as if Kelly could be in some kind of danger in continuing her work with him, and in Kelly's opinion, was acting a bit delusional, which worried her.

Maybe she should pull off at the nearest gas station so

she could make a private call to Professor Stein and ask what she should do. Maybe she should bring Helga to a hospital for an evaluation.

"Helga, I'm not sure at all what you think happened back there, or what you thought about Bastian, but I'm telling you that I'm perfectly safe working with him. I've been with him for a while now, and what you saw today is a pretty typical day for him. Actually, he did really well for having a stranger in his house, which would usually send him into a tizzy. He needs me. The money I make working with these kids helps to pay my college loans. I can't just stop working with him. You and I talked about this. Routine and continuity are the most important things when working with the autistic," she noted with finality, though she didn't even know why she was bothering to explain anything to her at that moment.

"Kelly, please try to understand, there is more to dis than you know. I just cannot share with you now."

Kelly was convinced that something was quite obviously wrong with Helga. There had to be. She thought she'd done a pretty good job in explaining autistic behavior to Helga to prepare her for the visit, but maybe the differences between typical children and one with autism were too much for her.

It was better if she just got her home to rest. She was betting that after a good night's sleep, everything would appear different in the morning.

CHAPTER SIX

I
t had been three days since Kelly had dropped Helga off at home and explained to Professor Stein what had happened. He'd been as stunned as she was to learn that his mother had begun speaking again. He wouldn't have known right off if Kelly hadn't told him, because as soon as Helga got home, she went straight to her room and locked the door without a word to either of them.

Kelly had been grateful for the chance to talk to the professor without offending Helga, and he listened quietly, growing concerned when she told him what she'd said to Greta before leaving. He promised that once he had it sorted out, he would give her a call and fill her in. In the meantime, he told her to take some time off to enjoy what was left of the summer.

Kelly decided to take him up on the offer, racing home and throwing a quick bag of her stuff together. She wasn't scheduled to see Bastian again for a couple of days, and since she had been missing her parents horribly, she made a solid decision to try and forget everything, at least for a little while, and spend the weekend with them.

The waning summer smells were a comfort to Kelly as she headed north toward Maine. The salty sea air mixed with pine and tired maple leaves made her long for her high school days when she had nothing better to do than throw on a pair of shorts, pick up some friends, and head to the beach for the day.

As much as she'd grown to love Helga and Bastian, the weight of all the responsibility was getting to her. She was young. Much too young to worry about so many other people all of the time.

Bastian would be starting school soon, as would she, she thought with a hint of remorse. There would be little time for visiting anyone once her fall schedule started, though as she neared home, something made her want to quit everything and just stay home in the comfort of her parents. She hadn't realized how homesick she had been.

It would be nice to sit down to her mom's cooking and be able to sleep in, just knowing that her parents were right there if she needed them. The old house, with its familiar smell of good cooking and her mother's perfume, would be just the thing to get her back on track. A little refresher.

She couldn't explain it, but she'd been feeling a little spooked lately, as if her sense of safety had been shaken just a bit. It was nothing that she could really put her finger on…she just had the feeling like something was wrong, but couldn't define what it was. Something was out of balance, or maybe something bad was going to happen. She was probably just being foolish, but never in her life had she felt so off.

Kelly pulled up to the old red farm house that she had lived in almost her whole life, and nearly bolted out of the car when her mom came outside to greet her. After giving her a long overdue hug, her mom held her at arm's length.

"Kelly, you look really tired. Are you getting enough sleep? Are you taking your vitamins?" Kelly's mom interrogated worriedly.

"I'm getting as much as an almost senior with two jobs can get I suppose, and yes, I'm taking my vitamins," Kelly answered, hoping that would be the end of it.

"You are way too young to be looking this tired, not that you're not still beautiful," she added quickly, patting Kelly's cheek tenderly. "You always look beautiful, but do you think that maybe you have taken on too much? Maybe you should quit one of your jobs and just focus on your schoolwork. Graduation is not that far away, you know," she told her, taking her suitcase from her with a look of concern, and letting her in first.

Kelly didn't want to be hurtful by reminding her that working through college hadn't exactly been her idea. She needed to pay her own way, and had ever since she'd been accepted to Northeastern. Her parents didn't have a lot of money, and weren't able to contribute anything to her education.

"Nah. I'll be fine, mom. I'm okay. I am tired, but I think it was the drive more than anything else. It's nothing your yummy meatloaf and a good night's sleep won't cure. You did make meatloaf didn't you?" Kelly gave her mom a look of mock desperation.

"Of course! It's your favorite. Dad is doing up the potatoes now. Are you starving or can you hold off for a bit?"

"I can wait. How have you guys been?" Kelly asked, giving her dad a generous hug and peck on the cheek.

"Well, your mother has been bugging me to remodel the entire house, but other than that, okay. How's my girl?" he asked with a laugh.

"I'm good." Kelly's mom scoffed, so she added, "Really. I'm good. Just busy. Mom thinks I've taken on too much, but really I'm enjoying my work." Kelly relayed all of the

Kristy Gherlone

happenings of late with Helga, (leaving out the language, of course), and her work with Bastian.

"Helga sounds like a wonderful person. Anyone who takes such good care of our baby deserves my support," her dad concluded, setting a plate in front of Kelly. "And Bastian sounds really cute. I can't wait for the grandkids!" he teased.

"Now you sound like Helga." Kelly rolled her eyes.

"Are you dating anyone?" Kelly's mom asked between bites of food. And there it was. Kelly knew she'd ask. She always asked. Really, she was worse than Helga!

"No. I don't have time," Kelly proclaimed, averting her eyes to her plate.

"See? She doesn't have time. She's taken on too much," Kelly's mom clucked, shooting her husband an I told you so look.

"I'll meet somebody when the time is right. Don't you think I should graduate first? You were always the one who told me that a girl should make her own way; earn her own money and never rely on a man?" Kelly knew it was a gut shot, but it was, in fact, what her mom had always told her.

"Did you say that?" her dad asked, staring at his wife in stunned amazement.

"I just meant that…well what I meant was that…in this day and age and all…" her mom blushed scarlet. The truth was that her mom never worked. Kelly loved her, but didn't have a lot of respect for her as she watched her dad struggling to make ends meet on his own salary alone.

Kelly achieved what she had hoped for. Her mom's silence while she ate. She loved her very much, but boy! What a pain in the ass she could be sometimes!

It did miff her though that everyone seemed to have an

opinion on what she should do with her life. Helga and her mom wanted her to marry and settle down. Her dad wanted her to focus on school, and Greta wanted her to cure her son. Well, at least it felt that way to her sometimes.

Everything she'd achieved, she was proud to say, she had done on her own. She needed the outside work so she wouldn't be saddled with student loans when she finished school, like her dad had been. Plus, it was hard to explain to them how attached to Bastian she had become.

As difficult as he could be sometimes, he was making strides. It was really rewarding for her to see how far he'd come. She had every intention of seeing it through and even started making plans to push him a little harder, just to see how smart he really was. Paula would be pissed, but so what? In another year she would be free of her anyway and it wouldn't matter.

If she kept working with Bastian, maybe somehow he'd be able to overcome his autism and she might be able to help draw out some of the genius she knew was in there. She was not simply going to let that part go. If, in fact, Bastian was a savant, it would be criminal not to help him bring that out. He deserved every opportunity, whether or not it made Greta's life harder.

She felt closer to him than she had with any of her other students in the past. She felt a sense of urgency in working with him that she had never felt before. Maybe that was what was off. She knew that she should not get so attached to her students. It wasn't good for her and it wasn't good for Bastian. She would be leaving him, and it would be hard on both of them to say goodbye. Also, by allowing the special bond to continue, she was making it that much harder for anyone new to come in and work with him. He would expect the same kind of relationship, and it probably wouldn't happen.

She knew she should try to be a little more detached, but it was hard with him. She certainly couldn't just quit now. That would be devastating to his progress.

Kelly's dad, met with the same silence from her mom, addressed Kelly. "Are you in over your head Kell? You can always quit. I have some money…"

"It is not as easy as just quitting, mom." Kelly retorted, dismissing her dad and looking to her mom, which is where the conversation had come from in the first place. "These people are counting on me. You were the one who always told me to finish what I started. I can't just quit. Sometimes I'd like to, I guess, but just think…in less than a year, I will have my diploma, and hopefully I'll be working at my dream job."

"That's the spirit," Kelly's dad quipped, reaching over to rumple her hair.

Her mom, not wanting to end the conversation badly on her part, offered, "I heard that Jason Hardwick was in town. I saw his mother at the grocery store yesterday."

Kelly flushed scarlet. She always had a crush on Jason, and her mom knew it.

"Cool. Maybe I'll see him," she averted her eyes to avoid embarrassment. No matter how old she got, it seemed her mom still had the ability to make her feel like she was twelve again.

"Maybe," she smiled and raised her eyebrows at Kelly. "He's not seeing anyone. His mom told me that he's been busy too. Working in New York I guess."

Kelly helped her parents with the dishes, talked a little more about her work and Helga, but couldn't shake her restlessness. Perhaps it was a side effect of living in the city too long. "Maybe I will go out for a bit and see if I can find anyone around from school."

Her mom winked at her. "That sounds like a good idea. Not too late though, K?"

Kelly ended up driving around for a while. She wanted to see how much her old school had changed, and to see if there were any new shops in town. Bored, but not wanting to go home, she landed at the Crow's Nest, a local bar she'd been to before on her visits home. The thought of possibly seeing Jason again sent butterflies to her belly.

The parking lot was packed, and she almost decided to skip it and head home, but then figured a drink would probably help her to relax and forget her worries, at least temporarily.

"Holy shit! It's Kelly, everyone. Look!" Kelly was surprised to see one of her best friends from high school come running toward her. Giving her a big hug, she realized that she hadn't seen Maureen since Thanksgiving a couple of years ago.

Even with Facebook, Kelly was horrible about staying in touch with people. Everyone she wanted to stay in touch with was on her friends list, but she rarely went online.

"Where in the hell have you been?" Maureen admonished. "I haven't seen you in like forever!" Without waiting for Kelly to reply, she chattered on excitedly, pulling Kelly towards the back of the bar. "Everyone is here. They're gonna shit when they see you!"

Kelly was genuinely happy to find several of her classmates seated at one of the large tables in the back, but her cheeks automatically turned red when she saw Jason Hardwick sitting there. While she was hoping that he'd be there, she could never control her blushing, and it embarrassed her even more every time it happened. She knew it gave her away. He probably thought she was pathetic.

To her surprise, he got up and gave her a quick hug. "You look great. It's so good to see you again," he whispered in her ear, making her cheeks flame even hotter.

Three drinks later, Kelly was feeling a bit buzzed. She was also completely oblivious to the fact that she was ignoring everyone else while she sat in the corner talking with Jason.

It turned out he'd graduated the year before, and was working in New York City as an architect, doing exactly what his yearbook quote had hinted at. Kelly remembered it as being vaguely like, '*If I build it, will you come*?' or something clever like that, and he'd done it. Exactly what he'd set out to do.

He asked what she had been up to, but her goal had been to forget all of her worries for a while, so she kept the conversation light, merely touching on some of the highlights.

He'd been impressed to hear that she was working with autistic children, mentioning that he had been working with one for the last year on the design of the new Holocaust Museum. He remarked that the guy was a genius, only solidifying her theory on the subject.

She wasn't drunk, but she would be if she stayed, so she decided to head for home. She was ecstatic that Jason asked for her number. Not that she expected him to call, but it meant a lot after how head over heels she'd been for him in school. He was way out of her league, so she wouldn't get her hopes up.

The rest of the visit went smoothly. Her mom, sensing her annoyance, made an effort to rein in her questions and her criticisms. She didn't even ask if she'd seen Jason. Kelly enjoyed the time away from responsibility, and almost hated to leave, but on Sunday, it was time to head back.

She got a nervous feeling again as she packed up her stuff. Maybe it was her thyroid. She should probably get it checked out. Yeah, when she had time, she thought.

With promises to visit again soon, and a tearful goodbye, Kelly headed back to Boston.

CHAPTER SEVEN

G reta decided it was time to make a call to Children's Hospital in Boston and speak with Dr. Jackson. She was hoping that he might be able to explain some of Bastian's behavior. Fortunately, he was able to return her call that afternoon, and she explained to him what had been going on with Bastian since they had last spoken, and then recounted the events of the last few days.

While Dr. Jackson was relieved to hear that he had not repeated any violent behaviors, he, like Greta, grew concerned with his rapid language development and increasingly odd behavior. He suggested that she bring him in to be evaluated, stating that he may need to be put on some medication to even out his moods.

Greta was relieved. She half expected to be brushed off again, like she had been at the emergency room, and was glad that her worries were being addressed.

While she wasn't a strong advocate for medicating children, there had definitely been a change in Bastian's behavior, and it was somehow just as troubling as his outburst at the hospital. It was almost as if each day she awoke to find a different child in her son's bed; each day a few more pieces of her son missing, replaced with something else. She also felt that with school coming up soon, it would be best if she did all she could to make sure everyone involved would be safe.

Greta made the call to work to let them know that she wouldn't be going in. She got Bastian dressed and made the hospital trip in record time, but was informed that Dr. Jackson had an emergency, and that they would have a bit of a wait.

Bastian entertained himself by looking through a National Geographic Magazine. To Greta's surprise, he excitedly pointed out the different countries and began rattling off the populations of the regions within, which was definitely something new. She tried to maintain a cool composure, though on the inside she grew increasingly more uneasy with his apparent knowledge of such things.

Finally, both she and Bastian were ushered into Dr. Jackson's office. Since this would be the first time in many months that Bastian had seen Dr. Jackson, it was unclear if he would even remember meeting him.

It made Greta sad that the doctor distanced himself just a bit more than necessary, Greta felt, as he offered a hand to Greta, and then hesitantly to Bastian, checking for any signs of anger. She wondered if they would always be so guarded around her son.

Bastian stayed in the seat he had chosen, which was much too big for him, swinging his little legs back and forth as he sat next to Greta. He looked unconcerned and almost happy to be there. His eyes shone with curiosity as they roamed about the orderly room before they seemed to quiet and settle on Dr. Jackson.

Bastian was the first to speak. "Are you going to be my all the time doctor now instead of the man I hurt with my teeth?" he asked with a giggle.

Greta could see the surprise on Dr. Jackson's face. The last time he'd seen him, Bastian hadn't had any language skills whatsoever.

"I can be if you'd like that, Bastian," he told him earnestly, but shot Greta a look of concern.

"Yup. I like you a lot better. I don't feel angry when I look at you," Bastian chirped, and considering the matter settled, began to scan the room again for items of interest.

"Bastian, how would you like to go and play with Jane for a bit? I'd like to talk to your mom for a few minutes." Not waiting for a reply, he picked up the phone to page the nurse. She arrived in minutes, and escorted Bastian to the play area down the hall.

"I have to admit that I'm quite surprised to see how far Bastian's language skills have come along since the last time I saw him. I mean, we do hope for something like this when we set up the necessary therapies, but I've just never seen such quick results. I am, however, taken aback by the callousness of Bastian's demeanor, and I have to wonder if he is truly able to grasp the seriousness of what he did to Dr. Goldenberg."

Dr. Goldenberg, from what she'd been told, had yet to fully recover from his meeting with Bastian. While he'd been able to return to work, he would never look the same again. Dr. Jackson had informed Greta that while autism brought out some very odd behaviors from some children, it was a little more than that with Bastian. He seemed cold, and unfazed by his actions.

"That's why I called. I've been getting more worried every day. I'm happy that Bastian has begun talking. You can't even imagine my relief at that, but it just seems like it's all happening too fast, and the sentences that he chooses are very odd. It began with the globe..." Greta recounted the morning that Bastian began to identify the continents and finished with the experience from Kelly and Helga's visit.

The doctor listened quietly and attentively, jotting down notes as Greta went along.

When she finished, she felt foolish. Even to her own ears, the whole thing sounded strange.

"If you don't have any objections, I'd like to keep Bastian overnight. I'd like to do an MRI of his brain." Seeing the startled expression that Greta gave him, he went on, "I'm sure that we don't have anything to worry about here, but before I can determine positively if anything is amiss, I'd like to take a look. My guess is that we'll see some changes from the last one. Sometimes, something can trigger a certain area of the brain. Parts that were not functioning before can suddenly become alive with activity, setting off a chain reaction of development. It's really quite fascinating to see."

Greta hoped there wasn't more to it. If the doctor suspected a tumor or something even more horrific, she wished he'd just say so. Always wanting to be a step ahead, she'd like to know what she might be up against.

After agreeing to the stay, Greta went to sign the necessary paperwork and to phone her boss at work.

"Jack, it's Greta."

"Hey, we were just talking about you. How are things with Bastian?" he asked in mock concern, but Greta knew it was merely out of politeness. What he really wanted to ask was when she was coming back in.

"Well, they are keeping him overnight to run some tests, so it looks like I won't be able to make it in tomorrow either," she told him, and then paused, waiting for what surely would be an unpleasant protest. She'd been right.

"Damn it, Greta. I need you here! Haven't you hired a nanny yet? I can't keep putting off the Alpha One Team. They're really getting impatient," he raged, forcing her to hold the phone away from her ear.

"I can't just leave him Jack. He's my son. Even if I had a nanny, I'd still need to be here."

"Yeah, well they called again today. They want some results," he told her, as if that would make a difference.

Her work was very important to her, but Jack would just have to get used to the idea that Bastian came first. Anyway, she thought, it was partially his fault. He had been the one to introduce her to Luke!

"Look, I told you I didn't want to take this project, Jack. I have too much going on. Why can't you just give it to someone else, for Christ's sake? I'm doing the very best that I can!" The last thing she needed at a time like this was more pressure.

"I can't and you know it. They were very specific that you had to be the one to do this. Just get back here as soon as you can okay?" he ordered, hanging up his end without saying goodbye.

"Thanks for your understanding," Greta clucked sarcastically into the dead line before hanging up.

Greta could hear Bastian's screams as she neared his hospital room, making her run the last few steps.

She arrived to find a nurse struggling with him as she tried placing an IV into his arm. Bastian was kicking at her and spitting. With his eyes pinched shut, he shouted out the names of various US cities and the populations within as he lashed out randomly. His little foot made contact with the poor nurses chin a few times as she tried to settle him enough to get the needle into his arm. Greta would never get used to seeing her child that way, and could only hope it would be the last time.

At a loss for how to help, Greta climbed up on the bed with him and tried to hold him still, but it only seemed to upset him even more. He tore out strands of her hair, and dug at her bare arms.

Giving up, the nurse went in search of Dr. Jackson. Greta tried to soothe Bastian by rubbing his back and offering him a drink of water, but he wiggled out of her grasp and slapped the cup out of her hand, sending the water spraying all over the bed.

Greta forced him to settle by placing her legs over his and restraining his arms. When he'd relaxed a little either from fatigue or resolution, she tried the joint compressions that Kelly taught her. First she started with his fingers, taking each one in turn and pressing gently on the knuckles. She moved on to his hips and knees before finishing with his toes. He calmed until there were just a few residual jerky sniffs that told Greta the fit was over for the moment.

Eventually the nurse came back with another in tow. They brought a tiny plastic cup with some pink colored medication Dr. Jackson had ordered. It was supposed to make Bastian sleepy enough to allow them to place the IV. Surprisingly, he took it without complaint. He licked his lips after and set the cup down on the table next to his bed. It took only a little while before Bastian dropped off to sleep, which allowed the nurses to do their job.

A technician came and wheeled Bastian away for his MRI, and Greta went to the waiting area. Feeling sleepy herself, she nodded off, and was woken a short time later by Dr. Jackson.

"You can relax. We didn't find anything to worry about," he told her reassuringly, breezing in to deliver the findings.

"Thank God," Greta cried gratefully, releasing her breath.

"There were some changes from the last MRI, as I suspected, but thankfully they're all good. Bastian's parietal lobe is lighting up like a Christmas tree. The therapy he's been receiving has done your son wonders."

Knowing from her own science studies that the parietal lobe was responsible for speech and language, Greta breathed an audible sigh of relief, but it was short lived.

"I'd like to prescribe some medication for Bastian, however. His behavior, as you know, isn't quite what it should be, and this could be just the thing to help even out his moods. Fluoxetine, 30 mg once a day for 30 days, and then we'll see him again. I'll start him on it while he's here. If there are any nasty side effects, he'll be here and we'll be able to adjust the dose," he told her with practiced efficiency, as he scribbled on his prescription pad and handed it to Greta. "If the medication does work, some of the side effects will probably be visible right away. He could display fatigue and agitation, but the benefits might take a month or more to show, so it's important to keep him on it for at least a few months."

Greta just hoped that it wouldn't interfere with any of the progress he had been making. However, with the possibility of more normal behavior, she readily agreed to try it out.

After an uneventful night at the hospital with Bastian and new medication on board, Dr. Jackson released him early on Saturday morning. He told Greta to watch for any worrisome behavior, and to call him immediately if she had any concerns.

The sun shone brightly on what would be the last of the warm days of summer. Bastian was quiet as they drove towards home, which gave Greta time to formulate a plan for the days ahead. She knew that Bastian's school would be starting the following Monday. She was less worried knowing that the school he would be attending wasn't far from her work. If anything came up it would only take her minutes to get to him. She also felt better knowing that the staff they had on board at Kinder Care were trained specifically in autism, though they did accept normal children as well.

A few of the college professors and people who worked in the labs and other departments brought their children there. It had a good reputation, and she was very glad that Bastian had been accepted there without a long wait like some of the other places she'd inquired about.

Greta turned onto a side street that was a shortcut to getting home, and Bastian began fussing loudly in the back seat. It startled her out of her thoughts.

"What's the matter Bastian? We're almost home and then you can get out and play," she soothed.

Bastian began pointing and screeching excitedly. It took Greta a second to understand what all of the fuss was about. Something had certainly caught his attention. Bastian had spotted a yard sale in progress.

"Stop the car mommy. Stop the car now!" he demanded, finding his words.

Greta still wasn't used to her non-verbal son suddenly becoming so verbal. It was as unsettling as it was rewarding. She quickly checked him in the rear view mirror to make sure he was still properly seated in his excitement, and tried to maneuver her car around the others on the road.

"I want to go to that house." He pointed to the house with the yard sale. He tried to wiggle himself out of his car seat before Greta had the chance to stop. She eased the car over and in behind one of the many vehicles lined up along the road.

She could see many items littering the yard and driveway, but couldn't imagine why he'd be so interested in such a thing. They'd never been to a yard sale before. She didn't even think he knew what one was, though she did spy a collection of children's toys and books, and guessed it was what had caught his attention.

Secretly delighted that Bastian was showing some new interests, Greta decided to give in to his request. It was so rare that he asked for anything, and she was curious about what he wanted.

She barely finished unbuckling his seat belt when he raced out ahead of her, not even bothering to check if any cars were coming in either direction. Greta's breath caught as he ran across the road just ahead of her reach.

Grateful the road was clear, Greta caught up to Bastian as he was trotting up the driveway. "Don't you ever run out into the road like that again," Greta scolded. She tried taking Bastian's hand so he couldn't run off again, but he ripped his away and continued on, furiously making his way towards the back.

"Nice day for a yard sale huh?" one woman in a group of older ladies who were seated, knitting, asked of Greta. The others looked up and nodded their greeting to Greta before they went back to their work.

Kristy Gherlone

"Oh yes, lovely," she answered politely, keeping an eye on Bastian to see where he was headed. She was sure he would go straight for the toys, but instead, Bastian seemed intent on the garage, where a row of paintings had been set upright against the doors.

"Beautiful child. Is he yours?" the lady inquired.

"Yes, that is my son, Bastian," she answered, looking towards where he stood, so small, in among the other yard sale shoppers milling about. He'd stopped in front of one of the paintings, which was large and framed in graying wood and was of a crudely done city.

"Unusual name, but he sure is a handsome boy. Never seen another like him."

Greta could see that the older lady was having a hard time taking her eyes off Bastian, her knitting completely forgotten. She set it down and eased herself up from the folding chair, and limped a bit towards Greta.

"I'm Cora, by the way," the elder woman held out a shaky hand to Greta.

"Pleased to meet you. I'm Greta."

"Sure seems to like that painting. I miss my kids being that little. I had two of my own. Both boys too, but, and I probably shouldn't say this, not near as cute as your little guy. Both of them very different from each other. Oh it's funny the interests they take up isn't it?" the lady prattled on.

They both made their way over to Bastian. The painting had him completely mesmerized. His hands worked behind his back, trying not to touch, but then he gave in and gently ran his fingers up and down the rough texture of paint and canvas. Greta thought it was probably a tactile thing, as kids with autism often had tactile issues.

"Yes," Greta answered. "Until just recently all he wanted to do was play with his blocks. I can't imagine what he sees in that painting," she blurted, then blushed, thinking that she probably shouldn't have said that. What if she or someone she knew had painted it?

"Oh, I'm sorry," Greta stammered, embarrassed, "I just meant that out of all the toys you have here, I don't understand why he's so focused on that painting," she clarified, trying to redeem herself a bit.

"I know you didn't mean anything by it, but I wouldn't blame you if you did. Thing's as ugly as sin, truth be told. My husband was overseas for the war. Came back with it as a gift to me. Found it in some little shop in some town. I don't remember where exactly. Didn't have the heart to tell him I hated it, he was so proud of it. Never had a good eye for decorating, my poor sweet Rich. 'Leave the decorating to the women and the fixing to the men' I always said, but he had his way and hung it right over the fireplace, and that's where it stayed until he passed on last year. Figured it wouldn't hurt him any now to finally get rid of it. Offered it to my boys, but they didn't want it either," she admitted resolutely, then chuckled as she looked on at Bastian.

Bastian tried to pick up the painting but it was too wide for him to get his little arms around. He struggled with it, finally taking it by the top and dragging it quickly down the driveway, scratching up the frame in the process.

"Bastian, no!" Greta wailed, and ran to stop him.

"I'm so sorry," she apologized once again to Cora, as she tried to wrestle it away from Bastian. He began to shriek and held onto it tightly.

Greta saw that the frame was badly damaged. She would have to purchase it whether she wanted to or not.

Bastian flopped down and began to have a tantrum. He kicked his legs and grabbed at Greta to try to get the painting back from her.

"Don't worry a thing about it," Cora told Greta. "If he wants it so much, go on ahead and give it to him. No charge. Somehow I think my Rich would want him to have it," she concluded thoughtfully, as she looked briefly towards the sky, then back at Bastian.

"Are you sure?" Greta asked, wanting to make sure Cora held no lingering attachments to it, though she couldn't imagine why. It *was* ugly.

'Oh, the things we do for our kids' she thought to herself, laughing inwardly as she handed the painting back to Bastian after getting an enthusiastic nod from Cora. Bastian's tantrum ceased immediately.

Greta opened up her pocketbook. She wasn't about to walk away without giving something to the kind lady. She took out a couple of twenties and attempted to hand them to her, but Cora waved them away.

"Nonsense. You just put those right away. No charge is what I said and no charge is what it'll be." She smiled at Greta, but kept her eyes on Bastian.

"Thank you so much, that is very kind of you," Greta relented, feeling a bit like a heel.

"You just come back and visit me sometime. Bring Bastian, of course. That's all the thanks I'll need. Don't have any grandchildren close by. Would be nice to see a little one from time to time," Cora told Greta.

CHAPTER EIGHT

I t had been three days, and Kelly hadn't heard a word from her professor, and as much as she hated to admit it, it was killing her! She'd grown very close to Helga, and was genuinely worried for her. However, she didn't want to pry, and refused to give in to her curiosity and call. She decided instead to give Greta a call to make sure there hadn't been any change in Bastian's schedule for the week. There was no answer, which left Kelly with nothing better to do on the long drive back to Boston than think about the events of last week.

After she'd dropped Helga back at home with the professor, the day she'd gone with her to Greta's, Kelly went back to her apartment and researched autistic behaviors. In one of the articles she'd read it stated that sometimes children with autism could spontaneously start speaking. Not in the normal beginning stages, such as the "mama, dada" stuff, but in advanced words, as though they skipped over the rudimentary lessons, and went straight to where they should have been all along. The article went on to say that they appeared to store data for later use, with it sometimes coming out in pieces and at odd times until it all got placed where it should be, given the correct training.

As much as she hated it, Kelly was starting to think that perhaps Paula was right. Maybe Bastian wasn't a savant after all, but just a kid who had stored a lot of data for later use. Still, there was the map.

Something else in the back of Kelly's mind kept coming through. It was the conversation that Helga seemed to have with Bastian. It did indeed appear as though the two of them were having a real conversation. While she didn't understand any of it, nor had she ever heard anything like it before, when put all together in a conversation, and not in one-word spurts, like Bastian did while playing alone, it wasn't at all like babbling, she thought.

She tried to remember all of the times she'd heard Bastian doing that, and it occurred to her that all of the autistic children she had worked with babbled in that same way.

Finally arriving home, Kelly dropped her bag to the floor, threw her keys on the counter, and went immediately to check her messages. She was pleasantly surprised to see the light blinking on the phone, indicating that she indeed had a message. She pushed the button and was grateful to hear Professor Stein's voice.

"Hi Kelly, I hope you had a good few days off. I didn't want to disturb your vacation by phoning your cell. I'm hoping that you get this early enough on Sunday to be able to come for dinner."

Kelly quickly checked her watch and saw that it was five o'clock. It might not be too late, she thought. She hoped.

"My mother is insisting that you come over. I must apologize in advance. She's not herself right now, and has a pretty wild story to tell you. Please give me a call once you get in." The audible click told Kelly that the message had ended. She immediately picked up the phone and dialed Professor Stein's home number. Luckily, he answered.

"Hey there Professor Stein, it's Kelly. I hope I'm not calling in the middle of dinner?"

"No, no. We were actually waiting a bit to see if you were going to make it. Mother held off just long enough, it looks like. Come right over," he told her.

"Okay, good. I can be there in about a half hour," she told him.

Kelly arrived at Professor Stein's in good time, as the traffic was light, being a Sunday evening.

"Kelly, thanks for coming. You looked refreshed," the professor told her, planting a light kiss on her cheek as he took her sweater. He ushered her into the dining room where Helga was just setting out the tableware.

"Hi, Helga. I've missed you," Kelly greeted her with genuine happiness, relieved to see that Helga appeared to be doing okay.

Helga set the last knife in its place and gave Kelly a brief hug, "I miss you too, but I so happy you had chance to visit with your parents. Was it good visit?"

"Yes it was a good visit. Thanks for asking. I didn't realize how much I missed them until I got there," Kelly told her, following Helga into the kitchen to help gather the remaining items for dinner.

Kelly was dying to find out what happened that day with Bastian, and couldn't wait to hear the explanation for Helga's voice coming back, but she continued making small talk as they worked to get everything on the table.

A delicious dinner of baked chicken, squash, and potatoes out of the way, Helga retreated to the kitchen with the empty dishes, promising to return with dessert and coffee. She refused Kelly's offer of help, which left her and the professor a few moments to chat.

Kristy Gherlone

"I'm relieved that your mother seems to be doing much better than the last time I saw her," Kelly began, hoping to prompt the conversation that she had been waiting to have. The suspense was killing her, but she was trying so hard not to push. She knew from experience with the Steins that anything of importance wouldn't be discussed until dinner was finished and the coffee was in place.

"Yes, I have to admit that I've been quite worried about her. After you left her here the day you brought her to your client's house, she stayed in her room and refused to come out for many hours. I could hear her moving about, so I knew that she was relatively okay. I had just decided to go ahead and prepare dinner for us when she emerged," Professor Stein began. "She told me some pretty amazing stories that evening, and I'm still not sure if I can, or should, believe any of it. I have checked into some of it, and haven't been able to verify anything as of yet. One thing for sure, however, is that she was adamant that you be sufficiently warned about the dangers of working with your client, Bastian. Is that his name?"

"Yes. Bastian. And she said something similar to me, though I can't imagine what about him had her so spooked."

"I reiterated to my mother that you get the money to fund your college education by taking on kids like Bastian. I explained to her the importance of your work. She offered to fund the remainder of your expenses herself, out of her life savings. I'm not sure what to make of her aversion to that little boy, but I'm hoping that you can try to put her mind at ease. While she seems to be fine in every other aspect, I can't help but think that she could be getting some dementia," he whispered, as at that moment, Helga appeared from the kitchen with the tray of coffee and cake for everyone, to Kelly's relief.

After the coffee was poured and the slices of chocolate cake served, Helga finally sat down and began to speak with a bit of apprehension.

"Kelly, I not sure how to begin. I do not know of how much my son has already told to you. I guess I should start with what I think you find to be good news, as I know dis part will be helpful to your, oh how do you say this? *diplombareit?*" She looked toward her son for a better word.

"Thesis," he answered, making the translation seemingly without thought, though Kelly had already done so.

She was utterly confused. How could what happened with Bastian have anything to do with her thesis?

Helga began again, "I speak German, dis you know. English, I pick up both by looking at book and from having wonderful son who was very patient with his teachings to me. Though I could not speak in words, I began to understand what he says to me and was able to read and write it fairly well. What you do not know is that I also speak 'nother language." She sat hesitantly, as if proceeding with the topic was somehow painful. Kelly could tell that it was apparently very hard for Helga to talk about, but after pushing her plate away, with most of the cake still intact, she began again in halting English.

"I am from Aura people. Not a direct descendant, but relative just same. Enough so I am able to speak their language, which is language that has only been spoken by the Aura people for, *Jahrhunderte?*"

"Centuries," Kelly translated for her.

"When I began to speak language as little girl, it was only spoken by a few members of my own close family, and only handful of people that we knew of in total. As family lines become more diluted, the language acted like fire; burning furiously in the beginning but then dwindling down to a few flaming embers, until it was snuffed out completely. It was not something that we were supposed to pass on to anyone else. It was meant to die. Like our people someday."

Kelly, fully interested in the story, absently picked at her cake. The Aura people sounded mysterious and secretive.

"The language I speak is called *Tungri*. It is one that is as old as the Roman Empire itself, though I do not know exactly who our very first people were. Only that we each have something different, a being some would call it, inside of us."

Professor Stein, who had been listening quietly until that moment, suddenly looked towards his mother with surprise, and began to rise, casting an apologetic glance towards Kelly.

"Gerhard," Helga admonished, "please let me finish." She motioned for him to sit back down with a gentle wave of her hand, and though Kelly could see that it was hard for him, he nodded a hesitant approval and allowed her to go on as he settled back down.

Helga looked back towards Kelly again, "I know that my son thinks I have grown feeble in my old age. That I becoming sick in my brain." She glanced briefly at Professor Stein to find that his expression didn't discount her theory, but she continued anyway.

"I apologize ahead of time Kelly, as I am sure dis will be very difficult for you to comprehend, but there is no other way to show to you that what I say is truth."

Before Kelly had a chance to respond in any way, Helga closed her eyes. She felt the room begin to grow unusually warm. Uncomfortably warm.

The cotton shirt she was wearing grew damp under the arms and rivulets of water gathered between her breasts. She could see that Professor Stein was experiencing the same discomfort. He removed his sweater and dabbed at his forehead with one of the cloth napkins left from dinner.

Helga began to speak, but not in a way that Kelly could understand. She and the professor shared brief eye contact, both acknowledging that they were experiencing the same event.

A whisper of a wind suddenly blew through, making the napkins scatter and the candles whiff out, though the windows and doors to the house were closed.

Helga began to make a swirling motion with her pointer finger over her dessert plate, which had held an amount of uneaten chocolate cake, but now was a melted, sticky mess.

Something began to happen to the pooling chocolate. It started slowly at first. A light vibration turned into waves inside of the plate. Bubbles formed and popped, spitting miniscule dots of brown that peppered the rabbit-white tablecloth and everything in its reach. A tiny tornado of liquefied goo formed and spiraled around and around, throwing little darts of chocolate out of its mass here and there before pulling them back in again. It grew upward and into itself, stacking higher with each rotation.

Kelly could not look away, though she blinked several times to make sure her eyes were not playing tricks on her.

Helga's words became louder, mixing with a cacophony of ear splitting sounds that seemingly sprang up from every corner of the room as she moved her finger over and over again until she suddenly stopped.

Kelly jumped up from where she had been sitting, knocking over her chair.

"Oh my God! How did you do that?" she squealed.

There in Helga's plate sat a perfectly formed and intricate chocolate tree.

When Kelly was a little girl, her father's best friend, Nathan, or Uncle Nate, as she used to call him, used to get a kick out of entertaining her at family parties. He would pull coins from her hair or make a flower appear from inside of his hat. She truly believed that he had special powers.

Of course, when she got a bit older, she found out that he hid the coins up his sleeves, and was really just tricking her. She'd been disappointed that Uncle Nate wasn't really magic.

Her father had told her that while sometimes people are really good at producing illusions that could even fool adults, there really was no such thing as magic.

She wasn't a little girl anymore, but she'd gotten just as much excitement from watching Helga perform as she had her uncle all those years ago, but she was also baffled. Why would Helga insist that she go over there to witness a magic act? And it *was* a magic act. There was no other explanation.

She looked over at the professor to see if his expression would give anything away, but he appeared just as confused as she was, which was unsettling. Surely in his childhood, if Helga had such talent, she would've shown him at some point.

"That was very entertaining Helga," Kelly decided to say,

since no one else was saying anything. "It must've taken you a long time to learn how to do that." She picked up the chair and sat back down, awkwardly smiling at Helga, waiting for someone to tell her what all of this was about.

"I know dis would be hard for you, my dear Kelly. Is not trick. All of my people could do like dis, only sometimes much, much more. When we are more than just one, the power is very stronger. I could show to you more, but I see that your eyes do not let you believe just yet, however, you must listen to me. What I told to you was truth. You are in very bad danger when you work with that child."

Professor Stein, who until that moment seemed to be sitting in a stunned silence, finally got up.

"Mother, that's enough," he demanded, giving Helga a harsh glance before turning to Kelly. "I'm so sorry Kelly, I really don't know what to say. You must think that we've gone completely insane." His cheeks were aflame with embarrassment.

"No, no. Of course I don't think that." Kelly tried to sound reassuring though she still didn't know what was going on. She felt very uncomfortable. She didn't want to hurt either of their feelings by saying the wrong thing, but if she were being honest, it was all just a bit too weird for her.

"Helga, I promise you that Bastian is a very typical child with autism. He's very smart, and is learning more and more every day that I work with him. I probably should have done a better job explaining to you the differences between typical children and autistic. I know Bastian's behavior can seem weird at times, but I assure you that it's appropriate for his age and the length of time he has been in our program." Kelly could see by Helga's expression that she was already fixed in her opinion, not that it mattered. As fond of Helga as she'd become, it was really of no consequence whether or not she felt that she should be working with Bastian. The decision was hers, and she was going to continue her work despite anyone else's opinion. He needed her.

"Kelly, I grow to love you like daughter. Daughter I never had. I see that no matter what I tell to you, you vill not listen. Is okay. I understand. I see you love that little one. I may be too late already but I didn't know. How could I know? I should have listened." Helga looked towards the ceiling as if addressing someone from above and then put her hands over her face and rubbed tiredly at her eyes.

"Kelly, I don't expect for you to accept what I tell to you just yet. I want to teach to you my language. The language of Aura people. Let me teach you dis. My son told to me that it vill help you get good grade for your thesis and maybe you vill hear for yourself that what I say to you about Bastian is truth. If you know dis language and he speaks it again, you know for sure." Helga looked hopefully, almost desperately at Kelly.

She felt sorry for her. She really seemed to believe all of it and it had her upset. Kelly loved her too, and hated to see her this way.

"Helga, I'd be honored if you would teach me your language. It would mean a lot to me, and my thesis. I would like to know, though, if you are the last of your people to speak it, how do you think it's possible that a three-year-old could possibly know how to? How do you know that it was *Tungri* that he was speaking?" Kelly's brain had been swimming as Helga spoke, trying to put everything together and not doing a very good job of it. The magic...

the language... Bastian. None of it made any sense to her.

Helga hesitated a few moments, looking from Kelly to her son. She seemed to be trying to decide if she should answer Kelly's question or not. A look of resolution came over her face.

"I know that he knows. I know that he knows because my voice comes back to me. I also know because he asks me if I still have dis." Reaching into the pocket of her care worn sweater, Helga pulled out a neatly folded cloth handkerchief. She unwrapped it carefully, and there inside it was a tiny seed.

CHAPTER NINE

Sitting at the table watching Bastian master his latest puzzle, Kelly struggled to understand what all the fuss was about this beautiful child.

When she arrived for work, Greta met her at the door and filled her in on all of the latest...the hospital trip, the new medication, and the yard sale.

Kelly was miffed about the medication, though she knew she didn't have the right to be. Bastian wasn't her son, but if the goal was to get him as fully functioning as possible, then she didn't quite see how giving him a depression medication was going to help.

She'd done a bit of research on the drug when other clients of hers had been prescribed the same, and she wasn't happy with the possible side effects or the results. The benefits from taking it really didn't outweigh the risks.

The few clients she had that were on it were more tired, less able to concentrate, and less interested in their surroundings, which only exacerbated every characteristic of autism. She also found that the medication did very little in the way of controlling negative behaviors. Doctors would prescribe almost anything to keep the parents happy.

It surprised her that Greta went along with the medication. She knew from the start that Greta's goal was to help Bastian in any way possible, and get him to become verbal. Now that he was, it seemed like it scared Greta more than pleased her.

To Kelly, Bastian was a very attentive and eager student. Each time she'd worked with him, he'd been able to master something new, and showed her more and more affection. Yes, he was still showing some aggression, and it often took her quite a few tries of getting him to focus on her face to pull him out of it, but once the medication took hold in his system, she knew it could set him back.

"Want to see my picture?" Bastian asked suddenly, looking up from his puzzle. He didn't wait for her to answer, he just wiggled himself out of his chair, grabbed her hand and starting pulling her towards his room, which made her laugh.

"I'm surprised he even let you work with him today," Greta chuckled in mock annoyance. "He's been obsessed with that painting since I let him bring it home. The first night home with it, I found it in his bed after he'd fallen asleep."

"It's really ugly, but for some strange reason, he loves it." Greta whispered to Kelly.

Kelly happily allowed herself to be pulled along behind Bastian. At least it was something different; something besides those dreaded blocks.

Some kids with autism could never shake their obsessions with certain objects, which made it all the harder for them when they couldn't have them for one reason or another. It made Kelly's heart soar that Bastian had begun taking an interest in other things.

"See?" Bastian said, pointing at a painting resting next to his bed. His eyes were shining with delight at this latest treasure.

Greta was right. The painting was ugly. It was very obscure and crudely done. It was a mess of muted colors and various shapes, yellowed slightly with age. Although Kelly could tell that it was supposed to be a city, it looked like something a kindergartener would paint. Why Bastian would like it was anyone's guess.

"Ooh, pretty," Kelly lied, trying very hard to sound sincere.

"Yup, it's a city. Bet you can't guess which one," Bastian chirped.

"Hmmm, let me see," Kelly pretended to be thinking. She had no idea really. It didn't look like any city she'd ever been to.

"It's New York City," Bastian told her excitedly before she even had a chance at guessing, then prattled on, "New York City has eight and a half million people. Half a million Chinese people, a million Greek people and over a million Jews," he crowed wrinkling his nose with apparent distaste.

"Huh. New York City you say? What is it with you and New York City lately?" Kelly laughed and ruffled Bastian's hair playfully, trying hard to ignore his new fascination with populations, but pleased just the same with the improvement in his pronunciations.

"I'm going to go there soon. I have the map now, so I know how to get there," he told her matter-of-factly.

Kelly assumed that he had meant the map that she had been bringing in her bag for Bastian to use.

"That would be fun to go to New York City Bastian, but I think you will need a much better map than the one I bring for you to look at," Kelly told him, playing along with his story.

"Not that map, silly," Bastian giggled, "this map." He

reached down and tried to pick up the painting, but could only push it towards Kelly.

"Silly goose. That's a painting, not a map." Kelly chuckled, wondering if he still didn't have a good grasp of the meaning of the word. He had developed his language skills very quickly. Faster than she had ever witnessed before.

"But it *is* a map. You just can't see it. Mommy couldn't see it either. How come I can, and you can't?" he asked Kelly earnestly.

Playing along with what she assumed was a game, "Maybe you have super power special eyes."

"I do have special eyes," Bastian told Kelly, "That's how I could see that I'm going to New York. I just have to find my friends, maybe at school, and get something first. Then I can go to New York City."

Kelly chuckled at his tale. He seemed to be developing a healthy imagination. So many children with autism were very literal, never allowing for role-play or anything that was not exactly as it was.

At the rate he was going, he wouldn't need her for much longer. The thought suddenly made her sad, though she knew that was the goal all along.

"Well, I hope you do get to visit New York City someday, Bastian."

Back at the table, Kelly couldn't tell that Bastian had begun taking the medication at all. That he wasn't showing any side-effects seemed odd to her. He appeared normal. Quite animated, in fact. She was able to complete her lesson plan with him and happily agreed to let him study her map after as a reward. He was able to correctly identify all of the continents and several major cities, reciting the populations of each by race and origin.

The kids that she'd worked with before who took that particular brand of medication always showed a remarkable difference in the amount of energy they had. They almost always became fussy and more tired. While it lessened the violence to some extent, (poor kids didn't have the energy to fight), it also made them less able to focus and prone to falling asleep while she worked with them. Bastian, on the other hand, was full of energy and eager to learn. Kelly waited until Greta was out of earshot before asking Bastian about it.

"Bastian, your mom told me that you went to see the doctor the other day and he gave you some medicine to try. Does it make you feel any different?"

"It did make me feel different, so I'm not going to take it," he told her.

"What do you mean you're not going to take it? Doesn't your mom give it to you in the morning with breakfast?"

"She does give it to me, but I don't swallow it. I spit it out in the potty when she isn't looking."

His honesty surprised her, and the fact that he was smart enough to think of doing that, but it put her in an uncomfortable spot. She herself didn't agree with the medication, but knew it was very wrong to encourage Bastian to lie to his mother.

"Bastian, the doctor and your mom think that you should take the medication. It's not nice to lie to them about taking it."

"I don't lie," Bastian corrected her. "I just don't tell her I spit it out."

He had a point. Technically, it wasn't lying to omit certain information. It really was amazing how fast Bastian was advancing. In the past half hour, he had shown her remarkable reasoning skills, but something about it just didn't seem normal.

"In any case, Bastian, I think you should probably tell your mom that you don't want to take the medication. The doctors and your mom need to know."

"I don't want to tell mommy. She'll make me take it. I scare her."

It was sad that Bastian had picked up on what Kelly had been suspecting for a while. Greta was becoming wary of Bastian, but for him to think that wasn't right.

"Your mom loves you very much, Bastian, and you have to trust her. She and your doctors know what is best for you. If you're not going to tell her that you're not taking the medication, then I'll have to."

"Please don't tell her, Kelly!" Bastian began to cry. "I can't take that medication," he sobbed.

Kelly hadn't meant to make him cry but she couldn't, in good conscience, allow him to deceive his mother.

She reached out to hug him, but he pushed her away and jumped down from his seat, racing into his bedroom.

Kelly followed and found him flopped belly down, sobbing hysterically into his pillow.

She walked quietly over to him and gently began to rub his back. He sat up and looked at Kelly with tears streaming down his little face.

"I can't take that medication, Kelly. I can't take it because when the doctor gave it to me, I couldn't hear my soul."

CHAPTER TEN

Munich, Germany

Magdalena rubbed her belly gently as she rocked back and forth in the chair Adolph had salvaged from the Jews' house. She'd made sure to wash it thoroughly before she brought it into the small cottage they shared.

Her mother would have called it nesting, but really, the thought of her skin touching where one of them once sat made her stomach churn. She was insistent that they had an odor. Sour, like milk gone to waste.

Lately, at night, the repugnant smell of the Jews invaded her dreams, waking her and making her run to the water closet. She'd spent hours washing everything he brought home from their burning homes, but even with her nose stinging with bleach, she could still smell them. Even her own Adolph smelled of the Jews every time he came home.

She hated being pregnant. It was an accident, really. She thought about ridding herself of it somehow, but Dolphie had been so excited when she told him, and so proud. She almost felt guilty. She hadn't had the heart to tell him that it wouldn't be right. It couldn't be.

She'd never been one for nostalgia, but given her circumstances that night, and with Adolph out for an evening meeting, she found it difficult to keep her mind from reminiscing. The war would be over soon. She knew it, even if he didn't.

She had been thinking back to Adolph's first days in the Bavarian Army. How impatient he'd been. She'd done all she could to keep herself from howling with laughter when, after his first day at his post, Adolph paced around the room fuming in his baggy green undergarments as she ironed his uniform.

"But you told me that I was to be an official. I'm nothing more than a message boy!" he cried indignantly.

"Dolphie, I keep telling you that you need to have patience. A *Gefreiter* is nothing to be ashamed about," she'd sighed.

"It just seems so pointless. If I am to be of this great power you speak about, then why should I stoop to this level? Everyone will laugh at me. No one will take me seriously. If I'd stayed and fought for the Habsburg Empire..."

Magdalena's temper flared and the iron she held almost scorched his pants. "We've had this conversation. I would not have you fighting alongside of those disgusting pigs. If they want to produce an army of mutts..." she'd fumed, "imagine mixing Austrians and Jews! I honestly can't believe you're still going on about that even after I showed you what was to happen. Why must I hold your hand every step of the way? When are you going start trusting me?" She glared at him, but the sight of him standing there so skinny, looking like a frightened child in nothing but his shorts, softened her again. She knew he hated it when she got mad at him, and she really had no intention of irritating him when she needed him focused.

"Look, Dolphie. This job you are to do is of great importance, though I know you can't see it now. The papers you are to deliver have all of the information you need. You will be privy to private conversations and have the opportunity to meet with the very people who will be the ones to raise you up."

"Well, you didn't need to poison me to keep me out of the Habsburgs," he stated with a note of irritation.

On the day he'd been required to take the physical examination to be considered for the Austrian army, he'd fallen severely ill. He knew it was her. For his own good indeed! He'd almost died!

"It was all for the greater good my dear," she had told him.

In that first war, it was almost as if she needed to take him by the hand and lead him every step of the way. He hadn't understood the rules. Magdalena couldn't just make an entire army respect him with her power. It helped, but it was something he had to earn, carefully and methodically. He needed to prove himself. She'd been with him through her dream eyes during every battle, every wound. Nurturing him every step of the way.

Those days were long gone. He no longer needed the coaxing. He killed willingly now, and with such savagery. It was the savagery that Magdalena mulled over, as she sat waiting for him that night.

He'd taken over her duties in the Order in his free time, made up in part by some of the Aura people who had been touched, like Magdalena, and communists that felt the way Adolph did. There was really no way to win such a war without a lot of help from the aura. They all knew it would be very difficult if the Americans got involved.

The nations fighting were very powerful and fraught with corruption and greed. It was comical that everyone involved thought it had to do with acquiring land.

Yes, Germany had taken Poland, then Czechoslovakia. Magdalena ordered the collection of amber from the regions taken. Her visions had been showing her the crystalized gold resin for some time. They would need bunches of it, though she couldn't see clearly the reason.

They'd gathered up the Jews in each place they defeated. She supposed that if they kept thinking it was all about the land, it would more easily hide the real reason. It was all she could do just to keep Adolph safe from so many people that wanted him dead. Some people called their Order a cult and mocked him for practicing such witchery, being the man of power he'd grown to be.

He recruited eleven good officers and began teaching them, as Magdalena had taught him, the power of mind persuasion...deception.

The Jews had been identified and so many were captured. She ordered that the ones in captivity be sterilized so that if they did manage to escape, they couldn't reproduce. However, it proved to be too time consuming and expensive the conventional way, so she hired a group of doctors to try different ways. Castration was the cheapest and most effective.

It was easy to get them to comply with anything she wanted when the aura was used. They almost went willingly to their own deaths. Such stupid people. Anyone so stupid deserved to die.

It hadn't bothered her so much before the pregnancy that the children were being exterminated along with their vile parents. She'd witnessed many killings, and she was as unfazed as she would have been squashing a spider. But with the pregnancy came her ever-changing emotions.

She'd found herself in dangerous territory.

Leaving a meeting of the Order a few weeks before, a group of members, along with Magdalena and Adolph, came upon a small boy begging for food on the street.

The star he was supposed to wear to identify him as a Jew had come unpinned and was dangling from his coat. He couldn't have been more than four or five. He was so small and skinny. She remembered looking into his eyes. That had been a mistake. Something about his eyes staring at her, so needful, so helpless, and yet still with a child's sparkle made her soften. She remembered looking at his tiny outstretched hand and wanting to take it in hers and protect him. She'd tried to shoo him away quickly before the others could do him any harm, but it was too late.

Adolph snatched him violently up off the ground by his impossibly thin arms. He cried out as one of them snapped, probably brittle from lack of milk. Glistening with bright red blood, a small bone poked through his taut skin.

Adolph's chief officer grabbed the child's legs and they began making a game of tugging him back forth as they laughed and admonished him for wearing his star incorrectly.

A woman, probably the child's mother, ran towards them from her apparent hiding spot, screaming and crying for them to please stop. Magdalena could see that she was with child, though the only part of her body that held any weight at all was her belly. Adolph let go of one of the child's arms just long enough to grab the gun from his belt and shoot her in the gut. As she fell, her arms were still reaching out for the boy, her face, pinched with pain, was still pleading.

The poor little boy tried in vain to wiggle free, crying and reaching out for the dead woman, but it only caused more strain on his limbs and he pulled a leg out of its socket. Wailing pitifully from pain and loss, the child looked to Magdalena desperately for help, perhaps sensing her unease.

Magdalena tried to get Adolph to stop.

"It's enough, Dolphie" she murmured, trying to sound nonchalant. She was not sure what bothered her more...the violence or the feelings it was invoking. "Put him down and let him be. He'll find his way to the chamber." They didn't hear her, or if they did, her plea was ignored.

Another officer joined in, snatching the tattered star from his coat. The straight pin was still attached and so he re-pinned it, only this time through both of the child's own lips instead of his coat, sealing his puckered, drooling mouth partially shut. The officer shouted as he did so to the dead woman in the street. "See what you've done, you stupid Jew? We might have spared him if you hadn't broken the law." Then to anyone else who might be hiding within earshot, "And to the rest of you...anyone caught wearing their star in such a manner can expect the same or worse."

Magdalena saw that the child was nearing the end of what his little body could take. She turned her face away as his muffled cries became weak. He'd grown pale and listless. His body was sagging and his extremities had all come out of their joints, but the men kept it up, pulling hard in each direction until they literally pulled his arms and legs off from his body. His blood splashed to the ground and his head thumped dully onto the dirty street.

Magdalena barely made it to the bush where she violently lost the contents of her dinner. She sat there a moment, sobbing while her own baby kicked inside of her. She thought briefly of the tiny life inside of that woman and wondered if it could be spared.

Even thinking about what those Jews did to her so long ago didn't make her feel better about what she had just witnessed. That child was so far removed from those men it seemed unnecessary.

Adolph, sated as he always was after a killing, went to her and rubbed her back gently as she heaved. "What's wrong my dear?" he asked of her. "Are you not proud? Did you not teach me well?"

She didn't know what compelled her to go out again that night after Adolph had fallen asleep. She ran back to where the woman with child had been shot with the intent of trying to cut the baby from her; to possibly save it.

When she got there, she saw that even though the woman must have endured horrible suffering in recent years, even in death she was not safe. The scavengers had picked clean what was left of her. She was naked, devoid of even her dress. Everything of use had been taken by the savages. Magdalena was disgusted, but not surprised. Vile, filthy Jews!

She pulled a knife from her pocket and quickly, but carefully, slit the woman from rib cage to pelvis. She cut the sack surrounding the fetus and gently tugged the baby out, slashing the cord to set it free from the dead.

Though she tried so hard to roust the child to life, it wouldn't be spared. Magdalena noticed that the bullet had grazed the side of its skull and a portion of brain poked through a splintered hole among its fine, matted, and blood soaked hair.

She wept as she took one of its tiny fingers into her own hand. Even though it wasn't to term, it was perfectly formed, its tiny lips drawn up into a pout.

Magdalena immediately thought of her aura. She'd never used it for trying to save a life, only to take it, but oddly she felt the strongest urge to summon it to save the baby. She told herself that it was merely for scientific purposes, to see if it could be done, but she couldn't call upon the others to help. They wouldn't understand. There wasn't anything she could do. Surely an act like that would require more than what she could produce without more tea, and she needed to save her dwindling supply.

She felt like a fool as she walked home that night, rubbing her belly for comfort as she did.

Yes, she had taught him well. Though he'd never hurt her, he wouldn't dare, a child was something different. They were so small and vulnerable, like the little boy with the mis-worn star.

She loved Adolph very much, but she'd have to do what was needed to protect their child. She didn't know what sex it was yet, but something about their child was important.

A sudden cramp in the lower half of her belly brought her out of her stupor. Her pains, intermittent before, were becoming steady. It was clear that her labor was in full swing. She was both excited and fearful. This was to be her first and only child. It was bittersweet, for she knew that she'd only have the child for such a short time. They wouldn't survive the war. No one would let them. She was sure of that.

Magdalena was hoping that her maternal instincts would not keep her from handing him over to the care of others, if the need arose. No matter what happened, she would need to safeguard the future at all costs. Even at the cost of her own life. She didn't trust herself anymore after the way she'd reacted to the death of the Jew boy and baby.

She was relieved to see Adolph walk through the door. "It is time, Dolphie. Time for you to meet your baby."

Hours later, utterly spent and still in shock, Magdalena lay curled up in a pool of her own sweat and urine, shaking with blood loss and residual pain.

Even the sight of her Dolphie holding their little boy did little to ease the trauma of what she went through.

She had no one to tell her what giving birth would be like. She didn't have any close female relatives, and she certainly wasn't one for female companionship.

She only had the vague memories of her mother, but she seemed to remember that her mother had an easier time. Of course, she had already had children before Magdalena helped her with the last. Maybe that was it. Maybe it was just supposed to be harder the first time. Thank God this was to be her last. One child.

When the pains first started, they'd been bad but not unbearable. A little more than the cramping she experienced once a month. Painful but tolerable. She'd expected some measure of discomfort, but nothing could've prepared her for what she went through to produce their son.

Dolphie wasn't much help, but it was a comfort to know he was there for her. She wasn't so sure if he would want to be, but she was glad he opted to stay with her instead of going for celebratory drinks with his officers.

Whether out of loyalty or fear, it didn't matter much to her. He'd held her hand and offered a cool cloth during the worst of it, but that was about all he could do.

While the mid-wife was very efficient and did what she could, it was a difficult birth from the beginning. Severe cramping had begun within an hour or so of the first pains, and then there were hours and hours of increasingly horrifying pain, causing her to vomit and soil the sheets.

The baby's head was very big and Magdalena had a hard time passing it through. She needed to use every ounce of strength she had to keep him from slipping back up into the womb, so the mid-wife wouldn't give her anything that would make her drowsy, though Dolphie threatened the poor woman brutally.

Finally, she felt a sharp pain and sticky wetness that could only be blood. It seemed at one point as though she were going to be ripped completely apart when she finally heard the cries that could only mean the baby had come.

Sweet relief was only for a moment before the mid-wife began the process of stitching Magdalena back up to stop some of the blood flow.

She wanted to kick her away, but Dolphie placed the baby into her arms, and for a moment she was lost in its beautiful little face. A boy. Dolphie was so proud. She wept with relief, despair, and happiness all at the same time. Never once had she felt such conflicting emotions.

He was absolutely perfect. Of that she was sure. He had tufts of blonde hair, curled slightly from the wet, sticky blood, and when he opened his eyes to look at her, they were blue, just like she'd hoped for.

His little button of a mouth puckered and he began to cry. Dolphie took him immediately and began to rock him. He amazed her somehow with his gentleness, when lately all she'd seen from him was violence. She was at once comforted and relieved.

She was very thirsty, but seemed to lack even the strength to ask for a cup of water.

Luckily, the mid-wife appeared at her side with water and some powders that she produced from inside of a folded paper. She told Magdalena that it would ease her pain and help her to sleep.

Grateful, she took what was offered to her and closed her eyes as she waited for some relief. The one thing she thought of before she drifted off was that she would have to do everything she could not to get too attached to this baby.

She wished that it could be different. That they were just two regular people living two regular lives, but it was just not the way it was. They had a mission to carry out, and unfortunately, the casualties would be on both sides.

No matter how much her womanly emotions wanted to love that child, she would nurture him and protect him until it was time, then she would have to let him go. No matter how hard it seemed at the time, she knew that it would be better for everyone if she remained as indifferent as she could, so she could hand him off when the time came and never have a moment's remorse. That would be very dangerous.

Months passed, and despite what she kept telling herself, it was nearly impossible not to fall in love with their beautiful little boy. She couldn't help herself. He charmed her right from the start.

He was such a quiet baby. Not even prone to midnight fussing which allowed her and Dolphie plenty of sleep. The mid-wife had told her to rest as often as she could because a baby could keep them up all hours. Not her Josef. He slept through the night and woke up with smiles for everyone.

She kept waiting to see the signs, knowing that they could come, but at the same time so wrapped up in motherly bliss that it didn't seem to matter. She would take him as he was. She couldn't imagine loving him any less if he *were* to be mentally retarded.

It really was very different for her to spend her days entertaining a baby. In some ways, it made her feel ordinary; just like any other homemaker or mother. Though having a baby warmed her heart beyond anything she'd ever experienced before, she also couldn't help but remember, painfully, her own baby sister from so long ago, and how she would tickle her and make her giggle.

Magdalena's mother often left her to care for that baby while she did her outside chores. Magdalena loved her so. Sometimes at night, she could still hear her screams.

It was tiring for her, though, and a bit boring to stay home day after day while Dolphie fulfilled his duties. She felt at times as though she were getting cabin fever, but there wasn't anyone to watch her little boy, so she had to wait until he could hold the bottle on his own.

One night after Dolphie came home from a meeting, she sensed that something wasn't quite right. He seemed to be losing a bit of his edge, and from what he'd told her, there was some fighting amongst his men.

She thought it might be worth the risk to leave Josef and get out for a bit. Maybe go to one of the meetings of the Order. She did need to get away just for a little while, gain some of her strength back. She was getting soft and she didn't like it.

The next day Magdalena propped up a bottle for little

Josef and gathered her coat. She checked in on him once before leaving to see that he was sleeping soundly. Her conscience pulled at her a bit as she opened the door to leave, and she felt all at once guilty about leaving him alone. She'd almost decided to stay, but then silently ridiculed herself for being so ridiculous. If she was going to get back to her old self, then it was time to get her strength back and start acting like the woman she used to be.

With that, she shut the door and headed out into the chilly night air. Dolphie would be surprised, but hopefully pleased to see she had returned from her motherly stupor. Even he, lately, hadn't understood her emotions. It was high time that she got on with the planning. Dolphie didn't know it yet, but they were about to lose a battle, the beginning of the end.

She was shocked to see the wretched decline of their normally picturesque city. Garbage was strewn everywhere, and windows were broken out in many of the buildings. There was no one left to maintain order.

Most of the young men were fighting battles in Czech, or had been dispatched to fight in other areas. Most everyone left behind were the old, the women, and the very young. It was almost as if she'd been asleep for the last few months.

Of course Dolphie told her bits and pieces about what was going on, but she knew that he held a lot from her, just as she did from him.

Magdalena arrived for the meeting just in time to find the men in a heated discussion. They hadn't even noticed her arrival.

"I'm telling you, we have to plan for the worst. Hope for the best but prepare for the worst." One of Adolph's officers was appealing to a crowd that was clearly not being

Kristy Gherlone

receptive.

The murmuring throughout the crowd told Magdalena that somewhere along the way Adolph had lost control.

Another of Adolph's officers stood up and addressed the group.

"I just think if there is a chance we could escape when the time comes, we should at least try. Leave the Jews and flee. What would be left for them anyway, except a broken country without any food or shelter? Isn't it better that we should leave than die in the company of such heathen?"

She never should have left him alone with this. You don't ask people to follow you...you command them to.

She shut the door loudly and everyone turned to see her.

Adolph came rushing to her side, his pleasure at seeing her was obvious but so was his embarrassment. He should have been embarrassed! She'd taught him better than that. With talk of the United States joining in the war, everyone should be nervous and on point. Not thinking about running away like a bunch of cowards.

Adolph took her hand and led her to her usual spot at the head of the table. He seemed relieved that she could now take over.

All eyes were on her, waiting for her to speak.

"My visions have told me that we need at least ten more chambers to achieve our goals. Once the Americans invade this country we may not have another chance to finish our task, at least until they leave. I want the prisoners who are still strong enough working to build the other camps and to maintain the rail lines. The ones who are at least a little able should be harvesting what is left of the fertile grounds to feed the workers. This is not the time to balk. There's much to be done."

In truth, they still had some time, but she needed to motivate them as much as possible. That they weren't going to survive the war was something she couldn't share with them.

In fact, once the United States stepped in, they would, most likely, all be rounded up and shot. Their own countrymen would give them up to save themselves. Even the aura wouldn't be enough to save them. But she needed their continued trust. She needed to give them hope. She couldn't take the chance that any one of them would flee, or risk being shot outside of where she could find them. She needed the bodies intact and accessible. Until it was imminent, she wanted them working as hard as they could on the extermination.

The building of Auschwitz helped, but they would need many more camps. While it gave her a great deal of pleasure to know that the trains were packed daily with them, hauling them off to the places that still had room, and that there were hundreds of them dying every day, there needed to be more. She knew that there were many in hiding, and that some had fled to other countries. It made her sick. She wished that her aura was strong enough to reach them all.

The officers grew quiet. Everyone was reluctant to disagree with Magdalena, but it was *their* lives that she was talking about. The officer that spoke before stood up and again appealed to the crowd, and to Magdalena.

"If what you say is true, then what's the point in continuing until after they leave? Why should we risk capture or even death if they are truly coming? I think it may be better for us to go into hiding now, flee the country before the Americans arrive. What if your visions are wrong?"

Magdalena's temper flared. She didn't like to be questioned.

"Adolph, I asked you to choose your officers wisely. You obviously didn't follow my advice." She stepped forward, took a knife from her boot and stabbed the man in the throat. Gasping loudly, he fell. He tried to speak out, but could only manage a gurgling, bloody froth. No one offered him any sympathy or help.

Adolph's cheeks flamed with shame. He hated feeling so stupid.

It was clear that Magdalena was back in control.

"Franz Doicht, come forward and take this man's position." Magdalena knew for some time that Franz had been waiting patiently for a positon of higher rank. At least he wouldn't be a whining fool.

He didn't need further coaxing. He stepped over the fallen man and took his seat to the right of Adolph. He couldn't hide his pleasure, despite the violent death occurring at his feet. That was exactly what Magdalena needed to see. It wasn't a war for the weak spirited.

Winning or losing didn't matter much to Magdalena. She cared nothing of land acquisitions nor treaties. She just needed to keep them all going long enough to exterminate the rest of those wretched Jews. They were well on their way to eradicating the disgusting pigs that plagued their country. By the time the Americans got there it would be too late to save very many of them, and that was the important part.

Those who managed to escape to the United States would have to be killed eventually. Both she and Adolph had heard rumors that quite a few had left pre-war and were making their way to a city in the United States. New York City. A good place for them as far as she was concerned. She'd heard the stories of their crime-ravaged streets, poverty and diseases spreading through the over-crowded buildings. Well, at least if they stayed put, they would know exactly where to find them when the time came, if their own stupidity didn't wipe them out first.

Satisfied that the meeting was back under control, Magdalena linked hands with Adolph, and the others followed suit, as they had on many occasions, signifying that they were about to be brought into her vision. Though it was a false vision, she knew they wanted to see for themselves.

The next few years passed quickly, but successfully. Magdalena was able to divide her days between motherhood and leading the Order.

While she was pleased to know that every single day more and more of the Jews were being loaded on to trains and brought to the ever increasing work camps, it had become clear that little Josef would not entirely escape the fate she'd worried about from the beginning.

He was a beautiful boy, thankfully. At least he didn't have the mask of retardation that often marred the faces of children like him. His malady lay deeper within, where it couldn't be seen at first sight.

She began to see the signs after his second birthday. He wouldn't speak. He wouldn't look anyone in the eyes, and though she longed to hold him tight, he stiffened at every touch. He wailed pitifully if his clothes were too tight or if his socks weren't straight. He would hold his hands to his ears and scream if noise levels became too loud for him. There didn't seem to be any logic to his tantrums.

When it started, Adolph had no patience for Josef. He was convinced that the child was stupid, and frustrated himself by trying to force the poor boy to do tasks that he simply couldn't do. He was ashamed of him. A man who valued intelligence so highly could not possibly have reared such a stupid boy. If he ever suspected anything, he never said. Though Magdalena knew he'd have to be told eventually.

Adolph struck him only once before Magdalena put a stop to it. She was convinced that loving patience would pull him out of it.

She would strap him in to a special seat that attached to their table and read to him, and draw pictures, or do puzzles. It was in that manner that she began to see that Josef was not the idiot boy his father feared him to be. He was, in fact, brilliant.

It started with the puzzles. The child couldn't clothe himself but he could put together puzzles that many intelligent adults couldn't figure out. His father suddenly became more intrigued, bringing home increasingly more difficult puzzles to do. Adolph would bring his officers by and he'd watch proudly as Josef placed the last piece in a matter of minutes, captivating his audience.

Then began the math equations. Josef would write them everywhere...on the walls, on the rocks outside. Anywhere there was a blank spot; Josef would fill it in with an equation to solve. He had folders of paper filled with math problems.

Adolph told Magdalena about the doctor he'd hired to

perform some experimentation and studies on human subjects. Some of them were willing subjects who were paid a small stipend for their participation, and some were extracted from the work camps. It began as a way to help German military personnel in combat situations.

The experiments involved explosives. How long did an individual have once it was triggered and how far would he have to run to escape the blast?

Those who were injured in the testing were also used. If one man lost an arm and died from blood loss, but another lost his arm and lived, could they attach the dead man's arm on the living?

It was all very useful, fascinating work.

From there, under the direction of Edward Vat, the new surgeon and psychotherapist that Adolph had also hired, there were other experiments as well.

Magdalena saw a lot of genius in his work. His children's studies were of particular interest to her.

Dr. Vat found a way to manipulate a child's brain manually by removing the skull cap and stimulating different areas. Using an electric probe, he would touch it to the various exposed parts, thus awakening areas that otherwise appeared silent.

In one particular case, a perfectly ordinary Jewish child of about seven had the left portion of his brain probed in just such a way. Though he had no history of any musical talent, when the electric impulses were administered, he was able to play the piano as well as any seasoned concert pianist.

Magdalena and Adolph were invited to attend a concert featuring his remarkable abilities. The theater was packed with uniformed officials and well-dressed wives; everyone delighted that Adolph had also given them the night off to enjoy such an unusual event.

Magdalena found it interesting that though the top portion of the child's head was missing and his brains were exposed to the open air, the little Jew child played as if there were nothing amiss.

Unfortunately, Dr. Vat's assistant became a bit overzealous with the electric impulses, which caused a nasty fire, thus ending the concert.

They'd invited Dr. Vat over for dinner on many occasions. Magdalena found him to be highly intelligent and admired his ethics. Not once had he ever performed any of his experiments on the Germans.

He'd taken up a fascination with Josef. He found it very interesting that there seemed to be parts of Josef's brain that were stimulated without the use of probes.

He wanted to take Josef in to the hospital for testing, but Magdalena balked. The thought of Josef being in pain for even a moment was very displeasing to her.

However, a vision came to her one night. She saw Dr. Vat extracting some blood from Josef's chubby arm and then from the small of his back.

He injected the blood intravenously into the neck of a woman, who lay silently on a table next to them.

Before her dream eyes the woman's belly began to grow with child. Her vision jumped forward and she could see the same woman holding her newborn child. Magdalena peeked into the folds of the blanket to find a blue-eyed child blinking back up at her. He looked like her Josef!

The vision jumped again. Magdalena was on a street. There were many women holding the hands of children like her Josef.

There was a clock on a church tower. Magdalena could see that the hands were spinning too fast. Every time the bell rang another mother and child would come out of hiding until the street was overcrowded with them. Their numbers grew with the passing of time!

An army of light haired children let go of their mother's hands and walked together in unison towards something Magdalena couldn't see. They were chanting a prayer in her language. Her aura language! In their wake, they left the lifeless bodies of the Jews.

Magdalena shared her vision with Adolph. It was decided that Dr. Vat could do his testing. Both she and Adolph could see the benefit of building such an intelligent army. It was ingenious, really.

Magdalena left him at the hospital with a strict warning that he would not be harmed. She would visit him often.

CHAPTER ELEVEN

Present Day

K elly pulled up to the school a few minutes late. The traffic was usually heavy during the week, but that day had been especially bad with the start of a new school year. The University campus that held the nursery school was a mob of new freshmen running around nervously, their arms loaded with books, trying to find their classes while the juniors and seniors lounged around on the lawns poking fun.

It wasn't good planning to have the start of the nursery school year coincide with the start of the college year, but that's usually how it went. It would be almost impossible to find a decent parking spot, she thought, as she circled the lot for the third time. If she'd stayed on campus that year instead of opting for an in-town apartment, it wouldn't have been an issue.

Finally finding one of the only remaining spots, she hurried over to the main entrance to see that the little yellow bus was already parked at the curb at the front of the school, waiting for Kelly to collect Bastian and escort him into his classroom.

Bastian's team suggested that he should start taking the bus from the very beginning so it would become routine and not as stressful when he started kindergarten the next fall, and Greta had agreed wholeheartedly. She could have easily brought him every day since she worked so close by, but she readily agreed to the bus taking him. Kelly couldn't help noticing that Greta was becoming more and more wary of Bastian. From what she'd told Kelly, she'd been spending more of her time at the lab, leaving Bastian with sitters. So it was decided that Kelly would meet him at the bus and bring him into the school.

"Hey there Sugar Plum," Kelly called to him from the open doors in the front of the school bus. "Ready to start school?" she beamed at him.

"Yes, I have my backpack," Bastian answered, smiling as he held up the new Spiderman backpack his mom had bought him.

Kelly was relieved that he didn't seem to be the least bit nervous or agitated by the change in routine.

"Did your mom pack you a good lunch?" Kelly asked, as she took his hand and helped him down the stairs.

"Yup! She packed me a sandwich and some carrot sticks. I'm going to share my carrot sticks with my new friends, but not any of the bad kids, because they can't have any, but you can have some if you want cause you're a good kid."

"Well thank you, Bastian. That's very nice of you. Let's hope there aren't any bad kids here, though, and that they're all nice." Kelly chuckled, rumpling his hair. He could really amuse her with his honesty.

Kelly and Bastian had met with Bastian's teacher, Miss Carol, before school began. She'd been invited to a team meeting so that a teaching plan could be worked out for him.

She was fairly young, not unattractive, but perhaps a little proper. That was Kelly's initial impression. She definitely seemed up to the challenge of taking on two children with autism as opposed to the one that was normally enrolled.

While there would be the one other child at the school with autism, each was entitled to an individualized plan, or IEP, based on their own specific needs, Carol had told her. No two children were alike, so while they would be attending the same class, they might be doing very different things.

Bastian had made so much progress since he was first diagnosed, the decision was made that Kelly would attend only a portion of his day. She was supposed to help him with the social piece of his plan, but he would also have some time on his own to see how he managed with the typical children at the school.

"Well if it isn't Bastian and Kelly! Welcome," Carol exclaimed happily as they entered.

The cheery classroom brought back memories of Kelly's own childhood. The minty smell of stick glue and wax crayons, along with the construction paper leaves taped to the windows signifying the start of fall, made her feel instantly nostalgic. Letters of the alphabet hung around the top of the room as did some pictures of zoo animals, just as she remembered her old nursery school as having. Bastian pointed things out excitedly as the room buzzed with the excitement of the other students, but he immediately stopped when he spotted a wall map. He let go of Kelly's hand and scurried over, immediately reaching up to run his fingers over the inked lines, as if they were something that could be felt.

Kelly pulled Bastian back to show him the felt board that was in the center of the room. Fastened to the middle was a cutout tree devoid of leaves, but holding red apples instead. Each apple contained a child's name written in perfect penmanship. She pointed out his, but, uninterested, he wiggled out of her grasp again and went back to the map.

Most of the other students, already there and at play, looked up only briefly to see their new classmate before continuing with what they were doing.

"Here's your nametag, Bastian," Miss Carol offered, approaching him at the map. She bent down to give him the laminated star bearing his name written in gold glitter.

She winked up at Kelly, "I know none of the children can read. It's more for the teachers. We have a lot of names to learn. It..." but she didn't get a chance to finish her sentence, because just as she began to pin the tag on Bastian's shirt, he jumped back away from her, horrified.

"Oh no, Bastian. I'm not going to hurt you. I'm just going to put it on your shirt, just like the other kids," she promised pointing towards the other children, who were all wearing theirs.

"No, No, No!" Bastian hollered loudly. He stamped his feet, making the other students stop what they were doing and stare in surprise.

He leapt back towards Carol, snatched the laminated nametag, and attempted to tear it up, though he couldn't do much more than twist it. Frustrated, he ran to the front of the room, and tossed it into the trashcan that was next to Miss Carol's desk.

Before Kelly had the chance to stop him, he bolted towards a little blonde-haired girl in braids and ripped the star from her dress, tearing a hole in the delicate fabric. She began to cry, but Bastian went on to the next student, a husky red-haired boy, and attempted to snatch his nametag. Kelly got to him first and quickly pulled him off to the side. He thrashed about angrily, trying to get back to the kids, who were mostly either crying or looking on in surprised silence by then.

"Bastian, stop!" Kelly demanded, trying to get him back under control. She got onto her knees, at eye level to Bastian, and gently directed his face towards hers. The technique would normally redirect him, but he struggled fiercely to free himself.

"Stop," she ordered. She held onto him tightly, and pulled his face towards hers again. "Look at me. I need you to stop." Bastian looked into Kelly's eyes briefly, but still squirming, quickly looked away.

Held too tightly to move, Bastian had no choice. His eyes made their way back to Kelly's. Finally, she felt him begin to relax, just a bit.

"I have to get the stars, Kelly," he whispered, earnestly. "They don't go on those kids." He pointed towards the sobbing children that Carol tried to soothe.

"Bastian, what do you mean? They're only wearing them so that Miss Carol and the other teachers can learn their names."

"No. They don't get stars," he protested seriously, as if that would explain everything. He looked at Kelly with such blue-eyed innocence; she couldn't imagine what was going on in his head.

"They go on these kind of kids," he grabbed hold of her hand and pulled her towards a very small, dark-haired child, who was sitting on the floor holding a book.

Bastian's face held a look of disgust as he pointed towards the little boy, whose nametag indicated that he was Jacob.

"He has to keep his star," he stated, matter-of-factly.

Jacob's lip started to quiver at Bastian's accusatory

finger. He jumped up, scurried towards Miss Carol, and hid behind her back.

"Okay, Bastian. That's enough," Miss Carol scolded gently. "Class, let's all take our nametags off for now. You can bring them up to me, and when Bastian's feeling a little bit better about it, you can have them back." One by one, they shuffled up to her desk, relieved to be rid of them, as they had caused such an issue.

"Miss Rose, can you hold down the fort for a moment while I speak with Kelly?" Miss Carol asked of the classroom helper.

Kelly reluctantly left Bastian and followed Carol into the hallway, knowing that she was in trouble for not having a better handle on him. Rightfully so, she thought. She was, after all, paid to keep a close eye on him and prevent those types of outbursts and behaviors.

He was just so unpredictable sometimes. He seemed fine, getting off the bus. She never would have expected his mood to turn so quickly.

"Well, it's clear to me that the team was right in sending in an aide to work with Bastian," Carol began. "I must admit that when I met him, I found him to be well mannered and especially smart for his age. I actually doubted that he had autism at all. After today, however, I think I'm going to recommend that an aide be placed with Bastian full time while he is here. I just can't take the risk with the other students if he's prone to this type of behavior. As it is, I am going to have to explain to twenty different parents this afternoon why their children are upset, and one has a ripped dress."

Kelly was disappointed. He really had been doing so well. These setbacks made her wonder just how well she was getting through to him. She'd told Greta that Bastian hadn't been taking his medication, and with that information, she was betting that Greta made him. As much as Kelly disagreed with it, if he were taking it, it should have helped prevent such an outburst.

While it was true that he was still displaying some very odd behavior at home, she felt that the progress he had made was beyond the initial expectations.

She hadn't seen any true aggression in a while, and the times that he did seem out of control, Kelly was always able to put a stop to it by forcing him to look at her face and by speaking calmly to him.

"I'm truly sorry, Carol." Kelly felt the need to apologize even though she knew there was little she could have done to prevent a behavior that was so unpredictable.

"I know, Kelly. It's not your fault," Carol, to her relief, reassured gently. "I've worked with a few autistic children in my day, and I know how hard it can be. But I was under the impression from the meeting we had that Bastian wasn't a violent child." She looked at Kelly quizzically.

"Bastian had some trouble early on, from what his mom and the intake nurse at the hospital told me, before I started working with him, but I've never, personally, seen anything like this. As a matter of fact, his aggressions have only been minor incidents until today. Just a bit of biting and hitting when I push him too hard. His mom did just start him on a new medication, which should be helping with stuff like this. However, he hasn't had the chance to play with other children very much, so it would've been hard to predict how well he'd really do."

"Well, let's monitor him closely and see how the rest of his day goes. If we need to readjust his IEP, then we should probably do it sooner rather than later. I'd like to talk with Greta and see what her thoughts on this are. If he hasn't been aggressive in a while, and is now becoming so because of a new medication, perhaps the dosing should be changed."

Kelly agreed. If Bastian were to make a habit out of scaring the other children and acting out, it wouldn't be a very fun experience for any of them.

At that, Kelly peeked into the classroom to find Bastian sitting with another student, quietly playing blocks on the rug. She decided to watch him for a few minutes. Carol joined her, and they both were relieved to see that they were taking turns lining up the blocks and giggling at each other. It looked like Bastian had found a friend.

"What do you suppose his issue was with the name tags?" Carol asked suddenly.

"Who knows? That kid sometimes, I swear. I do know that he loves playing with his blocks. Maybe it's the shapes. You know, circles, triangles, squares…Autistic children are very absolute. He may have rejected the stars based solely on the fact that they were a shape he doesn't use often, or can identify with."

"That seems logical, I suppose," Miss Carol agreed, but then appeared to think of something else. "But why do you suppose he was okay with Jacob wearing his?"

"I couldn't tell you. Your guess is as good as mine. He has weird ideas sometimes, and he can be quirky like all autistic children can be at times, but for the most part, he's a pretty good kid and I love working with him." Kelly concluded, smiling broadly, as she watched Bastian chattering animatedly with the other boy.

"I can see how much you like him. That day that I went to Greta's house for the meeting, I could tell. The connection you have with him is obvious. It's a shame that you couldn't be here with him all day, if that's what's decided."

"I know," Kelly responded a little regretfully. "Between my senior thesis, looking after my professor's mother, and working with Bastian as much as I do, I'll be lucky to find any time to sleep."

Carol patted Kelly's arm sympathetically. "I hear you. I work here all day and then I have a part time job on the weekends bartending at the Highland's Tavern on Elm."

The proper teacher was a bartender? Kelly was secretly glad. Maybe Carol wasn't as stuffy as she thought.

"I know that place! I've been there a few times. It's rowdy, but fun." Kelly was having a hard time picturing teacher Carol working in such a place. The thought made her chuckle a bit to herself.

"Well, I figured that I'm not going to meet any guys here at school. All of the male teachers are either taken or too old. Are you dating anyone?" Carol asked, but then reddened. "I'm sorry, that's none of my business. I'm just curious by nature, I guess. But if you don't mind my saying, you are way too young and attractive to be single."

It was Kelly's turn to blush. It had been a while since someone other than Helga or her mother had paid her a compliment, and they didn't count.

"Aww, thanks. You made my day. Don't even worry about it. I'm rather nosy, myself. But no, I honestly haven't had the time for dating."

"You should come by the Tavern sometime again soon. Friday nights are usually the best nights for getting a little eye candy, if you know what I mean," Carol winked at her.

Kelly was getting ready to tell her that she'd probably take her up on that, but she was stopped short by a piercing scream from within the classroom.

"Oh God! What now?" she asked as she darted into the classroom, frantically trying to locate Bastian.

Unfortunately, she didn't have to look too far. Bastian and the boy he had been playing with were both standing over little Jacob, who was flat on his back on the carpet, screaming, and writhing in pain.

Miss Rose reached the boys just a fraction of a second before Kelly, and scooped Jacob up off the floor.

Kelly took Bastian aside. "What happened?"

"He wouldn't wear his star, Kelly," he told her.

"But Bastian, what did you do to Jacob? Why is he crying?" Kelly's heart sank as she looked over towards Jacob to see a small splotch of red, quickly spreading, on the white polo shirt he'd been wearing.

"I didn't do it. It was Kurt," he accused; pointing to the boy he'd been playing with on the carpet.

"What did Kurt do, Bastian?" Kelly asked fearfully.

"We just wanted Jacob to wear his star, but he wouldn't do it, so Kurt had to make him wear it. I just held his arms because he kept wiggling around."

"But why is he bleeding?"

"Cause Kurt wanted to make sure Jacob couldn't take his star back off, so he put it right there." Bastian started to pull Kelly towards Jacob to show her, but Jacob was having none of it, and began shrieking again, burying his tear streaked face into Miss Rose's shirt.

Miss Rose lifted Jacob's shirt gently to assess the damage, and Kelly was horrified to see that the nametag had been pinned to Jacob's bare chest. Trickles of blood oozed out of the tiny holes surrounding the safety pin.

Some of the kids who had been looking on with both

curiosity and concern for Jacob began screaming and running from him.

Carol quickly swooped in and gathered up Jacob to bring him to the nurse's station.

Kelly was at a loss for what to do. The entire classroom was now a symphony of crying, startled children.

She did her best to soothe some of the children, while Miss Rose tried to gain control over the classroom again. Even though it wasn't her place to do so, Kelly got some of the children engaged in various activities, while keeping a careful eye on Bastian and Kurt, who by that time had resumed their quiet play on the carpet.

The school principal came in after a time and asked Kelly if she would bring Bastian and Kurt down to his office. Their parents had been called and would be arriving soon.

Fabulous. Kelly knew that Greta was going to be very upset. The very thing she had been worried about all along had come true on Bastian's very first day.

She felt like a complete failure. She never should've left him alone. Not even for a minute, but it was too late for regret. She would know better next time, if Greta or the school allowed him to continue.

Bastian began to cry. Kelly stopped in the middle of the hall to soothe him.

"I didn't mean to hurt Jacob," he sobbed.

Kelly's heart pulled a little as he latched onto her, hugging her around her neck, hiccupping deep sobs into her hair. She knew that he'd never truly mean to hurt anyone. He was such a sweet boy. He'd just never had the opportunity to interact with other children. He didn't know how, the poor kid, she thought.

"I know, I know," Kelly soothed. "Jacob will be okay." But

Kelly wondered just how okay he would really be. Surely, something as traumatic as this would stay with that little boy for a long time. Kelly doubted that he would ever feel completely safe at school again.

CHAPTER TWELVE

Greta stared out the window into the darkness, not paying any attention to the TV she had turned on out of habit. What was happening to her son? What was happening to her?

She'd been half expecting a call from the school all that morning, and was not surprised when it came. She was surprised, however to hear what actually happened. And horrified.

While she had nightmares about Bastian since that horrible time at the hospital with Dr. Goldenberg, everyone kept assuring her that he was improving. Everyone told her that he was definitely ready for school.

She knew what he was capable of, but Bastian's team of therapists kept telling her that he was better. They'd given her a false sense of security when they told her that Kelly would be going along as his aide, just in case he should regress.

While it appeared to be true that Bastian hadn't actually been the one to pin the nametag to that poor little boy, the thought of Bastian holding him down so another kid could made her sick to her stomach.

And where the hell was Kelly during all of that? Out chatting it up with Bastian's teacher! What in the hell were they paying her for if she wasn't going to do the job?

Kristy Gherlone

As soon as she thought it, she knew it was not a fair assessment. Even though she had struggled with her feelings towards Kelly, she knew that if anyone was suited for working with Bastian, it was her. Kelly adored Bastian, which was more than she could say of her own feelings lately.

Ashamed, she thought of how grateful she was when the school told her that the bus would be picking Bastian up each day and bringing him home. She couldn't bear to hear what would come out of his mouth next. She couldn't bear the way he looked at her.

While he'd made great strides since he was first diagnosed, with his progress came a whole new set of worries. He could talk, but the way he did frightened her. He was now making regular eye contact, but when he looked at her, all she could see was anger and contempt. And if it wasn't that, it was dismissal.

He seemed to jump from speaking a single word to making full sentences overnight. First, his interest was geography. Then he'd moved on to populations, then to casually asking questions about the work she did at the lab. It was unnerving.

She didn't doubt for a minute Kelly's theory on autistic prodigies, but instead of being proud of him, she was downright freaked out. She didn't want to feel that way towards her own child, but lately he'd really been making her uncomfortable, and the thought of being alone with him more than she already was scared her.

She was seriously giving the Weisenhoff School some thought. If he *were* to go there, it would cover the entire week. She would have Wednesdays to herself, and Saturday she could get a sitter while she worked.

It was annoying that Kelly never seemed to mind his weird behavior. She'd been watching the two of them when Kelly came to work. He would say something so totally off the charts, and Kelly would either laugh or dismiss it as though it were nothing out of the ordinary. It was almost as if Kelly were better suited to be Bastian's mother than she was.

Kelly had more patience and energy. She was never fazed by his oddities. She almost seemed to encourage his peculiar interests. She'd been really stuck on her theory that Bastian was a savant, and spent a lot of time trying to draw out what Greta wished would just go away.

Kelly showered him with kisses and hugs and he let her, but when she tried it, he pulled away.

Greta loved him from birth, of course. She supposed that all mothers had an innate tendency to love and protect their children. She loved him still. She wanted so badly for him to feel just a fraction of what she felt for him; to be able to show her some affection or love of any kind, but all she got from him lately were demands, as though she were his servant instead of his mother. It was making her grow to resent him.

She wondered if it had something do to with her own upbringing. Perhaps she was making some of the same mistakes her parents had without realizing it. She tried to be loving and understanding, yet firm, but family legacies could be hard to shake.

Maybe it wouldn't have been so hard for her if Bastian had been just a normal kid. Why couldn't he just have been normal? It was so embarrassing sometimes. At some point she was going to meet the other parents whose children attended Bastian's school. She knew by then they probably would have all heard about what happened. They were probably already talking.

She'd been so determined in the beginning to make sure he had a happy, fun upbringing, to have what she lacked as a child. Now it was all she could do to tuck him in at night. She didn't even want to be alone with her own son.

For his part, most of the time he barely even paid attention to her. He probably wouldn't have even cared if she told him to go to bed and didn't say another word to him. Except lately, when she'd gone into his room to give him what she felt more and more was an obligatory hug, he'd ask her a lot of questions about her work and what she did at the lab. It was almost as if he were interrogating her. A child of his age taking an interest in something like scientific formulas was just plain weird.

There was also that stupid painting! She wished she'd never let him bring it home. He took it to bed with him, studying the pattern as though it might contain all of the secrets to the universe. When she was four, she was still eating Play-Doh! Where Bastian came up with some of his ideas she couldn't even imagine.

Maybe the medication hadn't been such a good idea after all. She had to admit that when the idea was introduced to her, she had been lured in by the possibility that he would sleep a lot more. In truth, it seemed to be doing the opposite.

A small sound startled her from her thoughts. She whipped around to find Bastian standing in the doorway to the living room. She suddenly became aware of the news channel that was on and the images of violence from the fighting that had broken out in Serbia and quickly snapped it off.

"Bastian, what are you still doing up? I tucked you in

hours ago."

"What was that on the TV you were watching?" Bastian asked with an undeniable look of curiosity on his face.

She limited what he watched on TV, but it was inevitable that, eventually, he'd accidentally see something he was too young to understand. She hoped that he hadn't been standing there for too long watching all of that. She hadn't been paying attention, but typically CNN seemed to televise the worst images. She could just imagine what he'd seen. She didn't want him to be frightened, or get any ideas.

"It was just some people fighting way over on the other side of the world. Nothing we need to worry about," Greta replied as casually as she could. She searched his face, looking for signs of fear, but instead saw something else.

"I used to fight like that, I remember about it sometimes." The beginnings of a smile played on his mouth.

There it was again. He was so odd!

"Bastian, why would you say that? You're a little boy. I've been with you just about every minute since you were born. You've never fought like that. Those kinds of fights happen between big people."

She should have just let it go, she knew, but she was fed up with everyone going along with every weird thing he said just to appease him.

Ignoring her outburst, Bastian asked, "Can you turn it back on, please? I want to see."

"No, I think you should just go back to bed. That kind of fighting isn't something you should see. It's very sad to see so many people get hurt," Greta got up to try to usher him back to bed before he could creep her out with anything else. He started to go along, walking beside her in small steps, but stopped short. He looked up at her, straight into her eyes.

"The weak will always perish, just as they should." She saw his eyes become very dark, and it was as though, for a moment, she was looking at someone else. For just a fleeting second she thought she saw something reflecting in his eyes. She looked again but it was gone.

It was enough. She'd had enough! She couldn't even imagine where his thoughts came from. He seemed to have something in his brain that had already been there. Something from before he came to exist that he was drawing on. It scared her. She shivered with the sudden thought.

She wouldn't allow herself to engage him anymore that night.

"Bastian, go back to bed now," she stated as firmly as she could, trying to maintain some type of control, but the quaver in her voice betrayed her. She was intimidated, and from the look on his face, he knew it. It pleased him.

"I will go back to bed. But I don't want *you* to bring me," Bastian told her defiantly. He headed back towards his room alone.

That was more than fine with her. She was going to her own room and she was going to lock the door!

The next morning, Greta arose to find Bastian asleep on the couch, the TV tuned in to the same station that she'd had on the night before.

Bastian awoke just as she turned it off.

"Mom, can we go to New York in April?" he asked her sleepily, rubbing at his eyes.

"Bastian, did you watch that TV all night after I told you to go to bed?" She refused to answer the ridiculous question, angry at his defiance.

"Yes I did. And can we?"

Greta expelled her breath and tried to calm inwardly. She didn't have any intention of getting herself upset. She had to go to work.

"No, we can't. You have school and I have work. What is it with you and New York? Why do you want to go there so badly?" She was curious, but also wary of the answer.

"The man on the TV said they're opening a new museum, and I really need to be there. When it opens, it will be my time to go."

"Bastian, I honestly don't have time for this today. I can't imagine why you think you have to be at a museum in New York and I don't care. There is no way we can go. Go and get dressed. Rachael will be here soon to look after you while mommy goes to work," she told him firmly, her patience dwindling by the minute.

Bastian glared up at her and he began breathing rapidly through his nostrils. His face became aflame with anger. She'd seen that look before, and didn't like it. So much anger for such a small boy.

"Well, I have to go. If you're not going to take me then I really have no use for you, do I?" He jumped up and kicked her as he headed towards his room.

It was too much. She stifled her frightened, bewildered sobs with her hand, which was still shaking as she headed towards the shower. The sooner she got ready for work, the sooner she could leave and someone else could deal with him!

CHAPTER THIRTEEN

K elly was happy to be heading over to Professor Stein's. She hadn't been able to go for a couple of days because of the reports she had due, and of course her other work responsibilities.

The first part of the school year was always the hardest. The professors laid down their expectations and doled out hefty amounts of homework, trying to determine who really wanted to be there and who was only there to fill a requirement. They usually had it figured out by Christmas, and after the transfers, things would start to relax. Until then, Kelly would have zero free time.

She'd been missing Helga and also needed to make a lot more progress on her thesis. They'd been doing well, working on it every chance they had. They'd already put in several weeks of studies, and Kelly was completely fascinated by the *Tungri* language, but it was going slower than she'd hoped.

Helga was an apprehensive teacher. She cautioned Kelly that it was a language that wasn't supposed to be carried over, and that by teaching Kelly it was breaking an old pact that the Aura people had made. She didn't know what could happen.

Kelly didn't put a whole lot of stock into all of that talk, even after what she'd witnessed Helga do at the Steins' dinner. It sounded like plain, old-fashioned superstition, like never letting a black cat cross in front of your car. It didn't really mean anything.

Kelly was fully aware that she wouldn't be learning *Tungri* at all if it hadn't been for Helga's encounter with Bastian. She still insisted that it *was Tungr*i that Bastian spoke that day.

"My Kelly," Helga greeted her with a warm hug and kiss on the cheek as she walked through the front door.

"Mm, smells good in here. You've been baking again." Kelly closed her eyes, and drank in the heavenly aroma of fresh bread wafting from the kitchen as she returned the kiss to Helga's soft cheek.

"What can I say? Is what I do." Helga chuckled proudly, returning to the kitchen once again to set the timer.

She called out to Kelly, "Has that child said anything else recently?" She always got right to the point, first thing.

When Kelly didn't answer right away, she made her way out to the table, which had become their work area and stared, waiting for a response eagerly, but nervously.

It had become her new ritual. Every time Kelly went to work on her thesis, Helga would ask Kelly this same question, but she tried to avoid answering. Talking about him only seemed to upset her.

"Not that I know of. Well, not to me anyway, but then we're really trying to encourage Bastian to use English and not babble." As soon as she said it, she wished she hadn't. She knew Helga really believed that Bastian was speaking her language, and no amount of arguing would dissuade her of that. She braced herself for what was surely to come.

"Is not babbling! I'm tell to you! You have to believe me! How are you to figure out why he's here? Figure out what

Twelve Urns

he wants?" Helga's voice rose with agitation.

Kelly found it difficult to explain to Helga the work they were supposed to be doing with Bastian. Helga saw Bastian, not as a little boy in need of services, but as an enemy. A danger.

"I know you don't understand," Kelly explained softly. "Even if what you think of Bastian were true, the fact of the matter is that I do have a certain set of rules that I have to follow as his aide. I can't just go against what the team has decided. I would lose my job."

"Is okay, Kelly. I sorry. Is just that I love you like daughter and want you to be watchful. Dis is why I teach to you my language. So you vill know. This vill prove to you what I already know."

Both deciding the matter settled for the moment, at least, they began their work, which for once, Kelly conceded, was work. It was a lot tougher than any other language she had studied.

Tungri, while in part was what the German language itself was derived from, it wasn't much like German at all. It may have had some similarities, but none of the words were even close to any other language she'd ever heard.

Spanish was the easy one to learn. It just made sense. You could take a word in Spanish and it would resemble closely the same word in a bunch of different languages.

Sitting there with Helga going over the basics was a struggle.

After working for two hours without a break, Kelly could see the fatigue growing on Helga's face, and had to admit that she felt almost as tired as Helga looked.

"I think we've done enough for tonight," Kelly told her, yawning loudly. "I'm so tired I could fall asleep sitting up."

❖ 197 ❖

"Is okay, my Kelly, I tired too. I get a blanket from the closet. You sleep here tonight. Then I can make for you my special sweet bread in the morning

Kelly wanted to protest, but she was just too tired. She closed her eyes and rested her head in her hands. It felt like only a second, but when Helga nudged her awake and handed her a cup, she realized she must have been out for at least as long as it took to brew a pot of tea.

"You drink dis tea and you vill feel much rested after not driving home so far." Helga patted Kelly's hair lovingly and went to gather a pillow.

Normally, Kelly would have driven home no matter how tired she was. She didn't like to sleep anywhere but her own bed. Home, at her parents' house was one thing, but even as a child, she hated sleepovers. However, the thought of Helga looking after her, just this once, seemed so comforting. The cushiony couch together with the snapping fire glowing in the fireplace were too inviting to resist. She took a few sips of her tea and felt like she barely had the will to get up from the table.

"Okay, you win. I'm too tired to argue." Kelly stifled another yawn. She hoisted herself out of the kitchen chair and plodded towards the couch. All of the hard work was taking its toll, she thought, settling under the warm blanket Helga had laid out for her.

"That makes me much happy my Kelly. I worry about you driving around so late at night. You vill sleep soundly," Helga told her confidently, as she handed Kelly the pillow and tucked her in tightly, just like her mother used to do.

Kelly could feel Helga's lips brush her forehead tenderly. She had to force her voice to murmur a goodnight before falling into a deep sleep.

Almost immediately, she began to dream, but it didn't seem like a dream at all. It was too real. It was like watching a movie and also being part of it.

Kelly looked around the unfamiliar room through half foggy sleep eyes. She could sense that it was a place not of the present. The floor was bare dirt instead of wood, or linoleum, or tile. An oil lamp burned dully in the corner next to a paned window. There didn't seem to be anything around that required the use of electricity.

She tried focusing on the voices she could hear murmuring. "You will give me that seed. You will give it to me because if you don't, bad things will happen."

Only then did she see past the dream haze to find that there were two women in the room with her. They were seated at a pine wood table that was badly scarred with age and use.

There was something very familiar about the woman sitting on the left. The voice. She knew that voice! Kelly had to squint through the fog to make out the face. Of course! Helga! A younger Helga! How strange to see her like that.

Logic told her that she must be dreaming, but she could smell something baking and could see the smoke rising from the fire in the woodstove next to her. She reached out to touch it and immediately felt the sting of its burn. Withdrawing her hand quickly she saw that it was already beginning to bubble.

Where was she? She knew it had to be a dream, but it all seemed so real.

"I keep telling you! I keep telling all of you! I will not give it up. You know very well that it's the last one. I may need it for something else someday. It's better that I hold onto it until it is absolutely necessary."

Kelly could see the pleading look Helga was giving to the unknown lady. She could feel her fear. She didn't like to see Helga that way, though she knew it wasn't the Helga she knew today. She could see that this Helga was much stronger with youth, but Kelly could detect a tremble in Helga's hand as she tried to brush off the other lady.

Kelly went closer so she could offer some kind of comfort to Helga, but she moved apparently unseen by the women. They continued their bickering as if they were alone.

She reached out to touch Helga's shoulder but her hand moved through her as if she were a ghost. It was so odd. She was there. She knew she was there, but if they knew, they were ignoring her.

"I will tell you this for the last time. Give me that seed." The woman was more forceful that time. She stood and brought her face in closer to Helga.

Kelly heard a shuffling of shoes behind her and quickly turned to see a small boy peering in through the window from outside.

His face was somehow familiar but she could not place where she'd seen him before. He saw her, though. She knew it. He brought a small hand up and offered her a wave of hello. He looked right at her.

Something about this was so familiar, like déjà vu, but as she wracked her brain trying to remember, the women's bickering became louder, jolting her attention away from the window.

"I told the others that you wouldn't part with it. I told them that you would be the stupid fool that you've always been. You shouldn't have gotten two seeds anyway. You already planted one tree. It's not fair!" the woman raged with indignation.

Helga sat with tear-streaked eyes, shaking her head back and forth and wringing her hands. "I can't. I just can't! You know it was for my..." She cast her eyes downward and her tears spilled onto her lap.

"You need to show me where you hid it, and give it to me willingly. Give it to me now! Magdalena's baby is to be born very soon, and no matter what we have said to you, you either do not believe or you are choosing to side with her. While we may not be able to force you to give it up, rest assured, there will be consequences. If we are all to suffer, you will suffer right along with us. That baby must die. Die before he is born."

Kelly saw Helga try to stand, to escape the other woman's wrath, but was promptly halted with a forceful hand.

The woman waved a finger over Helga's face and at once, it was if she were choking.

"I will take from you the power to speak. Maybe then, you will come to your senses. You are making a big mistake in letting her child be born. A strong, new tree and all of the teas it would produce could prevent it from happening and from the destruction that will surely come from its birth. We warned you that he should not come to be. That child is to be born for one purpose! It will come to no good! You are failing to heed the warning for whatever reason has gotten into your fool brain. You are not fit to speak our language. You are not fit to be of the Aura people!"

Kelly tried to stop the woman from harming Helga any more. She reached out to push her away but got a handful of air instead.

It was so frustrating! She was there! She knew it. She

could still feel the burn on her finger, she could smell the earthy smell coming up from the floor. Why couldn't they see her?

Kelly screamed, testing her voice in that strange place, but it was as if she, herself, had lost the ability to speak. All she could manage were a few halting sounds. She tried to force her voice out, but the more she tried, the harder it became.

The woman with Helga shook her head in anger and frustration. She started for the door, but turned, and storming back, waved a finger in her face.

"*They are coming.*"

Kelly began to feel a grinding fatigue wash over her. She had to try hard, with every ounce of strength she had, to stay awake.

She felt the need to sit, to sleep. It was urgent. She was so tired. She looked around for a place to rest but found none. She flopped to the floor, kicking up a hill of greasy dirt as she landed. Her eyes were closing but she could still hear the woman talking to Helga.

"You know as well as I do that there aren't many of us left. You are the only one left that can stop this. You are the only one left with a seed. I can do nothing now but punish you for going against what the rest of us have decided. I know by our own law that I must offer you some kind of clause that will release you from your punishment at some point in time, so I offer you this. You may not speak again until you hear the language of our people."

With that, the woman began to cackle hysterically. "The foolish will die," she called out to Helga. "The foolish will die." Kelly could still hear her demented laugh fading as she walked away.

Kelly tried so hard to make herself get up. She wanted to check on Helga, but it was like there was something heavy on her chest, and her eyelids felt as if they had been glued shut. She fought hard, but it was no use. She was just too sleepy. She heard Helga calling her. Maybe she did know that she was there, but that woman just took Helga's voice. She couldn't be calling her.

All at once, she was back at the professor's house. The familiar scents of Helga's cooking still lingered in the room, as did the warmth of the fire.

Her heart raced erratically with the effort of trying to wake herself, and with the strangeness of what she'd just witnessed.

It was a moment before it began to beat normally again, and for her to fully open her eyes. Her head was pounding.

"So now you know."

Kelly jumped at the sound of Helga's voice and turned to see that she was sitting right next to her, rocking patiently away in her chair.

"How long have you been sitting there? And now I know what?" Kelly asked completely bewildered, still trying to get a grasp on reality.

"Is funny you don't yet know it." Helga smiled a small, shy smile, suppressing a laugh, Kelly could tell.

"Kelly, *miep liesebere, hoble ausit min worshete*." (Listen to my words).

"What are you talking about? Listen to what words?" Kelly asked, thoroughly confused.

What in the hell was going on? Had she been dreaming or not? Was she still dreaming? Her head was so foggy. What words was she talking about? It took several minutes before it dawned on her.

"Oh my God! I'm speaking *Tungri*! And I understand what you're saying!"

"Yes, my Kelly. You vill be able to know it better now. No more lessons. We haven't the time. I give to you some of my thoughts. Some of my memories. With that comes my language. Is in your head now." She sat smiling a proud, motherly smile.

How could it even be possible? It was just too much. Up to the point of meeting Helga, she'd been pretty sure that she had a firm understanding of how the world worked. Helga was introducing her to things that were very unfamiliar to her and frightening. Helga's world was a strange one that just shouldn't exist.

"I know is a lot for you again, Kelly. Is a lot of nonsense you do not know of or understand. You were not of these things. I was. My life began with dis knowledge. I would not to pass it to you Kelly, but I am sure that your Bastian is what I tell to you and I am very frightened." Her smile gone now, Helga became very serious.

"That baby to be born in my memories, the baby the lady spoke of...he...he was not to be right. He was born of two people that were not supposed to breed. It was forbidden and punishable by nature," she cleared her throat and continued reluctantly. "That baby, he growed to be something even his parents could not expect. While he was not right, he had knowledge of things he could not have learned anywhere. He was wise beyond his years but he was just a baby in so many other ways. He could not look you in the eye but he could tell you so many things it would be impossible to write them all down. Most of all he was beautiful. The most beautiful child anyone ever seen. He was loved and protected by first his mother, and then the doctors who spent much time being with him. They testing him. They doting on him. They spent many of their hours ignoring the other patients, to work with him, helping him to be smarter."

"His parents left him to the care of those doctors. Was not until much later that I found the reason for dis. He was to be a weapon in a war that had nothing to do with you. A war that could not be won in that time, but with help of that child, the promise of being won at later time. That time is now, my Kelly. They are coming; she was right in saying dis."

Kelly was lost. It didn't really make any sense. A baby born more than half a century ago could not possibly have anything to do with the present, with her, or with Bastian. Could it?

CHAPTER FOURTEEN

G reta arrived at work exactly on time, which was a rare occurrence lately.

Bastian had begun fighting with her most mornings about getting dressed, brushing his teeth, and about a thousand other things. The Christmas season had also begun, and the requests from the school kept pouring in for snacks, plates, napkins, and gifts for the exchanges, which meant she had more to round up in the morning.

The day before it had been her turn to send in the snack, and she'd been late in spreading the peanut butter on the celery sticks, which meant Bastian missed the bus again, and she'd had to drive him.

To her surprise, it worked out better than she thought, even if she did have to endure Bastian's weird questions on the way. It was nice to hear from Bastian's teacher, first hand, that Jacob suffered no lasting damage, though he did change schools. It was also nice to hear about Bastian's progress, and to meet his little friend, Kurt, that he talked about so much.

He really was cute. It was hard picturing such a sweet boy doing something as horrible as pinning that nametag on another child's skin. She had demonized him in her mind, but seeing him for the first time set her more at ease. It made her feel a bit better, in a way, knowing there were other kids like Bastian.

Kurt asked a lot of questions, mostly about her work, and begged her to allow Bastian to go to the Weisenhoff School like he did. She promised she'd think about it.

After the episode with the television, she'd made the decision to start doing things a little differently with Bastian. She wasn't going to allow him to push her around anymore. She needed to take back some of the control that he clearly thought he had. She had been thinking more and more about the school. It could help to keep him in line.

Which is why, that morning, she made it to work on time. She hadn't put up with any of his whining, hurried him despite his protests, and ignored his complaints of not feeling well. Driving him occasionally was one thing, but she definitely didn't have time to do it every day.

Thankfully, Bastian's bus had been early and she was able to get him off to school with minimal effort, so it was a surprise when Bastian's school called. She'd just started the testing phase of her newest idea for a formula.

"Ms. Hall, I have Bastian here in my office. He's complaining that he has a tummy ache, and he looks a little pale. I took his temperature, and it's one hundred and two. Unfortunately, it looks like he might be coming down with the flu that's going around."

Damn it! Greta thought. Not again! Not today! She knew she was going to get into a lot of trouble with Jack if she kept taking time off. In addition, the thought of being alone all day with Bastian wasn't a pleasant thought.

She really was needed at work. The government overseers were pushing hard for her to finish the project. They wouldn't be pleased to hear that she would need to be out again.

Well, there wasn't anything she could do but pick him up and bring him home, she thought miserably. She hurriedly dumped the chemicals she had been working with down the drain and grabbed her coat off the hook.

"Umm, Greta? Where are you going?" Jack stopped her just as she reached the door.

"Bastian is sick. I'm really sorry, but I have to go and pick him up," she told him.

"But we have that meeting today with the team from Alpha One."

"Oh no! I forgot all about that!" Greta cried, checking her watch. Nine o'clock. They were supposed to be there in half an hour.

The Alpha One team had set up the time to come and talk with Greta and Jack about additional funding for the work they'd been commissioned to do.

They were already annoyed about the time it was taking to get the formula right, and were getting worried about the cost.

While Greta didn't exactly agree with helping the government find a way to make bombing materials even more deadly, it was her job, and that meeting could mean the difference between getting more money to continue the testing, or job loss and the risk of having to close down the lab completely.

She also didn't relish the idea of another visit from Major Barnes. He was the man in charge of Alpha One team, and he always gave Greta the creeps. Not only was he a harsh critic, he could be downright rude. There was definitely something about him that wasn't right.

Great. What in the hell was she supposed to do? She couldn't leave him at the nurse's station.

The only logical, (but not very ideal), solution she could think of was to run and get him and have him sit quietly in the lab until the meeting was over. Jack wouldn't be happy about it, but a lot happier with that than with her missing the meeting altogether. It would probably give Major Barnes something else to criticize her about too, but what could she do?

"Give me fifteen minutes and I promise I'll be back in time." She raced out the door despite the startled and annoyed expression from Jack.

"Now you listen to me. You're not going to give mommy a hard time," Greta scolded, as she practically dragged Bastian down the hallway to the lab. "You're going to sit still and be very quiet until I finish my meeting, and if you're a very good boy, then I'll stop and get you some ice cream on the way home." Greta knew with her new resolution to stop letting Bastian rule the roost she shouldn't be bartering with him, but it was too important. She needed him on his best behavior.

His feverish, glassy eyes told her that he should be sluggish, but he wasn't a typical child, so, naturally, he fought her every step of the way.

When she wrestled the door to the lab open, however, Bastian straightened up and walked in, instantly fascinated with all of the equipment. Greta had all she could do to keep him from knocking over the delicate glass vials in his excitement.

She hadn't been wrong about Jack. He was not happy at all about the tiny visitor, and doled out some strict rules for

Bastian of his own, telling him to sit in the chair that he provided and not to move. Bastian stuck his tongue out at the harried man, but Greta decided to ignore it.

"It's only until the meeting is over and then he'll be out of here," she whispered with assurance.

Twenty minutes into the very stressful meeting, Greta found, to her embarrassment, that she was in trouble for spending so much money on Nitro methane, a chemical that they'd already tried.

In the midst of her scolding, Bastian kept getting out of his seat and getting into things, but to her amazement, Major Barnes didn't say a word to her about it. In fact, he seemed delighted with Bastian, barely taking his eyes off him. She should've felt relief, but for some reason it was unsettling.

She also had the beginnings of a monstrous headache.

She knew the Alpha One team members were merely advocates for government's money, and all they really wanted to know was what had been tried, what failed, and the reasons why. She was finding it impossible to explain without making it look like they weren't wasting the taxpayers' money.

What the government wanted was for them to find a way to make their particular bomb better. Cleaner. They wanted more testing done to see if it could be made to be more sensitive to detonation, so it could be used without boosters, in addition to being able to sustain a little water infiltration without its ruination.

Greta was just about to go into some of the failures when all of a sudden her stomach roiled and a wave of nausea hit her. She bolted from her seat and raced to the bathroom just in time.

Kristy Gherlone

Several minutes later, she was alternating between throwing up and having severe diarrhea. Damn flu!

"Greta? Are you okay?" Jack opened the door the ladies' room just a crack and called in to Greta.

"I think so. I just need another minute. I'm so sorry. This hit me so fast. Is Bastian okay?" she choked, suddenly panicked as she remembered that Bastian was in a room full of strangers and dangerous chemicals.

Greta was surprised to hear Jack chuckle. "I don't think you need to worry about him. He's been entertaining our guests the whole time you've been in here. When you're both a little better, I think I may need to talk to you about giving that kid a job!" He laughed as he shut the door, leaving Greta baffled as she washed her face and took a quick sip of water.

"You don't have to use diesel. My friend Kurt from school said that diesel is expensive. Molasses would work the same way plus it won't evaporate." Greta quietly entered the room and was astonished to see that Bastian appeared to be holding the meeting. He held a piece of paper in his hand that contained a bunch of different equations in his childlike writing.

The Alpha One team seemed to be thoroughly enjoying themselves. They were taking turns asking him questions, getting a kick out of the quick, intelligent answers he fired back.

"This is one hell of a kid!" Major Barnes quipped to Greta, finally noticing her return. "Where did he learn all of this stuff?" he asked with laughing disbelief, "Did you know that he can tell you the exact population of any city?"

Greta didn't think it was so funny. Not funny at all. Where he got any of the stuff he came up with was

❖ 212 ❖

downright scary to her, and definitely not a laughing matter.

The fact that her child was weird had at least been contained to his team and school, but now it was spilling over into her work. She never should have brought him here. She was embarrassed beyond words.

"Bastian has a pretty active imagination," she lied.

She needed to get him out of there before he made things worse, she thought.

"I'm sorry but we really must go. Bastian is only here today because the nurse thinks he may have the flu. Unfortunately, it looks as though I've caught it too. We'll have to finish this meeting at another time."

"You know, my wife is on the board at the Weisenhoff School," Major Barnes offered, ignoring her plight for the moment, "I'd love it if you would bring Bastian by to meet her. He has autism right?"

"Yes, but how did you know?" Greta asked, genuinely surprised.

"Call it a hunch. Anyway, it's a part time school for children who are gifted. Many of those children have autism. It gives the students the opportunity to work with scientists and doctors in any field of interest, really, and sometimes the kids are able to come up with theories on their own that most people haven't thought of before. They're able to test them out and play around with things they wouldn't normally have access to. The staff really works with them to help them develop the skills they're born with, but lack the tools to define. Bastian mentioned his friend Kurt, from his school. I believe he's in our program," he finished, looking at Greta hopefully. She'd never seen him so animated.

"I don't know," Greta responded hesitantly, "I really appreciate the offer, but I'll have to give it some thought. We really should go before one of us gets sick again."

In truth, she had already made the call to the school, and Bastian had a meeting set up for Wednesday. She didn't have any idea that Major Barnes' wife worked there, and could only hope that he would have minimal involvement in her work.

The team and Jack had no choice but to let them go. It was obvious that Greta was not well enough to continue.

"Just out of curiosity, how much about geography does Bastian already know?" Major Barnes asked Greta as she opened the door to leave. It unsettled her to see that he was no longer smiling, but merely looking at Bastian with curious wonder.

"Greta, I need to go back to that lady's house," Bastian told his mother as he sat at the table, piecing together another intricate puzzle, coughing slightly still after a couple of weeks, though his flu was nearly gone.

Greta was annoyed with the way Bastian had taken to addressing her lately. At first she ignored it, but then decided if the goal really was to take back control, it wouldn't help to let him do whatever he pleased.

"Bastian, I'm not going to tell you again. Don't call me Greta. I'm your mother and you need to start calling me mommy again, or mother, or ma, or whatever, but you're not to call me by my first name. It hurts my feelings. And what lady are you talking about?"

"But you aren't really my mother," he told her casually,

placing the last piece in the thousand-piece puzzle, not even looking up from his work. "The lady that was selling the nice things in her yard."

"Bastian, what are you talking about? Of course I'm your mother. I'm not going to play these games with you today. If you don't stop it, you're going to spend the entire day in your room," she told him angrily. She didn't have any intention of spending another day in the house with him and his weirdness. It was bad enough that she'd been cooped up with him for too many days already with that dreaded flu.

"Well, you aren't. I don't belong to you. My mother had me a long time ago. Long before you were born. And can we?" he asked, jumping down from his chair.

Fearing that he was going to say something else disturbing, she decided to use one of Kelly's tactics and redirect him before it got out of hand again. Getting down at the same level with him, she took his face in her hands and tried drawing his attention to her eyes.

"Bastian, you need to stop. I don't want you talking about stuff like this anymore. Do you understand me?"

"And I don't want *you* touching me!"

Hoping to change the subject, Greta decided to ask him about his new school. She'd heard from his teachers that he was doing great and learning a lot, but she really hadn't had the time to ask Bastian about it.

"It's fine," he told her, as he wiggled out of her grasp and took a step back, wiping his face where she had touched him, as though it disgusted him.

Though she tried very hard not to take what he said and did to her personally, his behavior was really getting to her.

"The volunteer, Ms. H says that I remind her of her little

boy. He had aw… awfulism too," he told her, completely
messing up the word autism. He'd been doing so well with
the pronunciations of things, it tickled Greta just a little
when he messed up. It made him appear more normal. He
always had trouble with the word autism, but that was the
best yet!

Greta couldn't help but smile, though she managed to
suppress a laugh, as she didn't want to make fun. 'Awfulism'
was a fairly accurate description, she thought.

Before she could correct him he added snidely, "She's
nicer than you." Greta's heart sank once again.

"Bastian, just stop it. You're not being very nice," Greta
told him.

"I mean it. I don't want you touching me," Bastian told
Greta, jerking himself away even farther.

Hurt tears formed in her eyes and she looked away so
that he wouldn't see them. She'd given birth to Bastian, fed
him, nurtured him, read to him, and he couldn't even bear
to look at her, let alone have her touch him.

He never acted that way with Kelly. He always allowed
her to touch him when necessary, and he openly gave her
affection. Lately, with all of the time she'd been spending
with him at home and at his school, he was getting even
more attached to her.

Kelly was supposed to be helping her get back the son
she knew and loved, but it appeared that the opposite was
happening.

Still stinging from the rejection, it crossed her mind that
she should just give him to Kelly. However, she was
immediately sorry and ashamed for the thought. What kind
of a parent was she to think something like that?

After talking with Kelly and the team about his behavior

as of late, they decided to try a storyboard. It was supposed to help Bastian make the social connections that children with autism seemed to be lacking.

Kelly would make up a pretend scenario, such as seeing someone Bastian might know at the grocery store, and then use cut out characters on a felt board to act out a story to help him with appropriate greetings. He did okay with verbalizing what he should be saying, although his words sounded forced, and almost robotic. In real life situations however, he didn't remember to apply what he learned, or he simply didn't want to.

Paula told her that it would take time and that, eventually, he would make the connections, but Greta wasn't so sure. Bastian was getting worse. She couldn't deny that anymore.

The team had been planning to do a silent observation of Bastian at play in his nursery school. They were hoping to identify and correct any issues they saw in his communications with peers, and tailor the storyboard to fit his real life experiences. However, it wouldn't do anything about the problems she'd been having at home, so the next time Kelly came, she was definitely going to ask her what to do about that.

"Did you know that two percent of the population in California is Jewish?" Bastian asked suddenly, wrenching Greta out of her thoughts.

Perhaps sending him over to that lady's house wasn't such a bad idea.

A day away from him might give her some time to come up with a new plan. It was obvious that the medication wasn't working. She was going to have to call Dr. Jackson again and see if he could fit her in.

Kristy Gherlone

While it was true that Bastian had autism, it seemed like he might have something else as well. Something in his brain wasn't right.

Pulling a piece of folded paper out of her wallet, Greta grabbed the phone, and after deciphering the shakily written number, called Cora.

"Bastian, go and get dressed."

CHAPTER FIFTEEN

"**I**'m so glad you called. Been thinking about your little guy since you was here for the sale. Didn't think you would, but awful glad you did," Cora gushed, smiling widely as Bastian rushed up the driveway and straight into her arms. It delighted the older lady immensely, but hurt and angered Greta once again. Cora was nearly a stranger, and Bastian didn't seem to have any trouble doling out his affection to her.

"Are you sure you don't mind watching him for a while? I really hate to put you out." Greta asked the question, but only out of politeness. She could see that Cora was more than happy to have him.

"Nonsense. Been hoping to see him again. Been kinda lonely around here, this being my first winter without my Rich, and all my quilting chums gone south for the winter. No siree. I wouldn't dream of going to Florida. My Rich and I used to love the snow. Course..." She didn't have a chance to finish her sentence because Bastian took her hand and started pulling her towards the door, making Cora chuckle.

"Bastian," Greta called to him, "you behave yourself." She gave him a stern glance.

"Oh, don't you worry none about this little guy. He and I are gonna have a grand time, aren't we?" She rumpled Bastian's hair playfully.

"He has some activities in his backpack in case he gets bored," Greta reached down to give Bastian a quick kiss goodbye, but she needn't have bothered, because he instantly pulled away. Greta gave him a sigh and shot Cora an embarrassed look.

"I don't know what's gotten into him lately. He acts like kissing his own mother would be a crime."

"Oh don't go worrying about that. My boys went through that phase. Acting like they hated me, until of course one of 'em needed something or was sick. He'll get over it. They always do," Cora told Greta with a reassuring nod. Bastian impatiently tugged on her, and she happily allowed herself to be pulled inside.

Greta hesitated a few minutes before backing her car out of Cora's driveway. Something just wasn't right with that kid and it had nothing to do with phases. He simply wasn't normal, not even for a kid with autism. It just seemed to her like his behavior was particularly odd. Perhaps she should have mentioned something to Cora about Bastian before just dropping him off like that. After watching him for a couple of hours, she probably wouldn't welcome him back ever again!

Thank God Dr. Jackson was able to fit her into his schedule, she thought as she began to pull away reluctantly. Her train of thought turned to focus on the appointment. If the doctor could give Bastian something that would help even a little, she wouldn't have to worry so much.

One thing was for sure; she simply couldn't deal with Bastian the way he was. Dr. Jackson was going to have to do something, even if it meant keeping Bastian in the hospital for a while until they got him straightened around.

As Greta drove on towards the appointment, she was

worried more for Cora than for Bastian and that, in itself, was troubling.

"Do you have any more of those pretty pictures?" Bastian asked happily, as he slurped up the rest of the cocoa Cora had given him to drink at the kitchen table.

She snickered at his chocolate mustache and went to get a wet cloth to wipe it away.

"What pictures, Bastian?" Cora asked as she dabbed at his face, which made him crinkle his nose.

"Like the one you had at your sale. You know. The one you gave to me." Bastian gave Cora an exasperated expression; as if she should have known all along what he was talking about.

"Well, I wouldn't have called it pretty," Cora scoffed, "but I'm awful glad you're enjoying it. As a matter of fact, I do have one more. A much smaller one. My Rich brought two paintings back from the war. The one I gave to you, and another that I liked pretty well, so I hung it up in my downstairs room."

"Can I see it?" Bastian asked, but didn't wait for her to answer. He jumped down and raced out of the kitchen.

"Of course you can, but wouldn't you rather go outside and play?" she called after him as she tried to catch up. "We could build a snowman. When my kids were little we always made a snowman with the first sticky snow. Oh gosh, we used to have a good time, just me and the boys rolling up big snowballs. One year... oh, be careful on those, Bastian," Cora cautioned as he started to run down the stairs to the basement ahead of her. "Those steps are slippery and ain't very big. I don't want you to fall. Anyway, one year..." she went on, snapping on the light as she descended after him.

"You talk a lot," Bastian observed as he kept moving down the stairs.

"Suppose I do." Cora laughed, following him down, "I'm glad you're here to talk to. Otherwise I'd be talking to myself and you know what that means?"

"Yup. My mother told me that only crazy people talk to themselves. That's why she always gets mad at me when I talk to my blocks at home. She thinks I'm crazy, but I'm not crazy. She just doesn't understand my language and it makes her mad."

Cora stopped on the steep, narrow stairs, "Course you're not crazy. You're a very smart, sweet little boy," she reassured, rumpling his hair.

Bastian ducked as if to avoid further contact, and jumped off the last step, immediately racing around the nicely finished basement until he found what he was looking for. He stood on his tiptoes, looking up at the small painting and studied it carefully.

"Yup, that's it. I have to bring it with me," Bastian told Cora matter-of-factly. He went in search of something to help him reach the painting, and finding a chair, struggled to drag it over to the wall. He climbed up, and stretching as high as he could, attempted to take it down.

"Now hold on there, Bastian," Cora scolded gently, reaching over him to put the painting back in place. "I'm afraid I'm not ready to part with this one."

"But I need to have it," Bastian told her forcefully. "Anyways, it's not yours," he snapped, giving her a look of contempt as he reached up to take it once again.

"What do you mean it ain't mine? Course it's mine. My

Rich bought it for me! I'm sorry if it makes you mad, Bastian, but you can't have it," Cora told him firmly. She set the painting in place once again and then, taking him by the hand, helped him down from the chair and tried to lead him back upstairs.

Bastian wiggled out of her grasp and stood stubbornly where he was, drawing his lips into a pout.

"How about you and I go back upstairs and I'll fix us a nice snack to watch in front of the TV?" Cora offered as recompense. "I bet I can find some cartoons on this time of day."

Bastian stood firmly rooted right where he stood, furrowing his brow into a terrible scowl, but then suddenly brightened.

"Okay," he seemingly relented. He took her hand and allowed Cora to escort him back up the stairs.

CHAPTER SIXTEEN

K elly just needed a little distance. Some time on her own to process what had happened to her. At least that's what she told Helga as she ran out of Professor Stein's house that morning after the dream. She could see the hurt and concern on Helga's face as she left, but what did she expect?

To think that she had woken up from that dream speaking an entirely different language! It was a little more than she could wrap her mind around. Strange words and definitions had been floating around in her head since she woke up.

Then there was the little matter of what she had witnessed while she was supposed to have been sleeping.

She knew then that she had been present, either sleeping or awake, to the event that Professor Stein had spoken about. The same event that he'd witnessed as a little boy when he spied through the window. It *was* him that she'd seen at the window. She didn't know how it was possible, but it was true. She'd been there.

When Professor Stein and Helga had invited her over for dinner the evening that Helga performed her magic act at the table, Kelly had all but convinced herself that it was just that. A magic act. She hadn't known why it was so important for Helga to want Kelly to believe that it was all real, but whatever the reasons were, it didn't matter. Kelly was from this day and age, and things like that just didn't happen in normal life. How could anyone expect her to just accept what was going on and actually be part of it?

The dream was more than just that, and she knew it. There really wasn't any way to dismiss what had happened to her. She couldn't explain it away or come up with any other explanation than she had actually been in that tiny farmhouse and she had, indeed, been witness to a real life curse.

The Band-Aid covering her burn was a frightening reminder that if it had been just a dream, she couldn't have been injured. If all of this was really happening, then could it be possible that somehow Bastian was tied in?

She would also need to see Bastian with this new-found knowledge of hers. Soon. If there was a grain of truth to any of this, then she was going to start asking him some questions. It may not be the right thing to do, and it could even get her fired, but the dream had fully convinced her that there was definitely something going on.

She arrived at home to her phone ringing. It was probably Helga checking on her. She was going to let the answering machine pick it up. She loved Helga dearly, but she meant what she told her about needing time to sort things out for herself.

She was surprised to hear not Helga's voice, but Jason Hardwick's! Her long time school crush.

Thinking quickly, she decided it couldn't hurt to answer. She had liked him way too long just to brush him off, though there couldn't have been a worse time for him to call, with her mind still reeling from recent events.

"Jason, hi, I'm here. Just walked in actually." She was

grateful that he wasn't there to see that she was blushing again, or her disheveled state of confusion.

"Kelly! Good! I was hoping to catch you. I'm here in Boston for the night. My boss sent me out here to meet with one of the writers at the Boston Globe. He's doing a piece on a building of my design, but as it turns out, he was called away unexpectedly and didn't have the time to see me. I was kind of hoping that you'd be free for dinner tonight?"

Kelly's heart skipped. He was actually asking her out! After all of those years of hoping that he would, he finally was. She just wished the timing had been better. With everything going on in her head, and everything she still needed to think about, dating seemed like a ridiculous idea. So unimportant compared to everything else that was happening.

However, he was familiar. He was from home. He felt safe and far removed from all of the drama going on. Something that could keep her connected to this world, and right then she desperately needed that.

The distraction could be good for her. There would be plenty of time for sorting everything out later. She needed this. Normalcy.

"Umm, yeah. I think I can free up my night. That would be really nice." And it would, she thought.

"Sweet! Should I pick you up, or do you want to meet somewhere? Any good restaurant suggestions?"

"How about I pick you up, and if you're up for it, I know a really good Italian restaurant in the North End."

"Sounds great. And Kelly? I'm really glad you're free. I haven't been able to stop thinking about you since I saw you back home."

She couldn't suppress the giddy delight she felt at

hearing those words, despite the feeling of dread that still lingered in her belly. It was a nice reprieve. How long had it been since she'd actually felt truly excited?

After hanging up, she made a determined decision to try to forget all of her worries for the day. Maybe even splurge on some new clothes and get her hair cut. Everything else could wait. She never asked to be brought into any of this, so everything would wait until she was ready, she thought with a great deal of resentment.

Despite her best efforts though, Helga kept entering Kelly's thoughts throughout the day. The look of desperation, sadness, and guilt on her face as Kelly left in a huff, made her feel a bit sick.

Helga needed her and desperately wanted her understanding. No matter how far removed Kelly was from all of the events she spoke of, she seemed to be asking for help. What kind of a friend would she be to ignore her pleas?

It was nice to have someone to care for and who cared for her that lived so close by. She loved being in Helga's kitchen with her, sharing tea and conversation. Helga gave her the feeling of family when hers was so far away. However, it appeared as though Helga was trying to drag her into something that was just too unbelievable and strange to comprehend. How could she just ask Kelly to put aside all rational thinking and just accept everything that was happening?

While she couldn't deny that she had been given a language in her sleep, and Helga did seem to possess something she could only describe as magic, it was just so far removed from her everyday life and everything she'd come to believe about the world.

It was going to take some time and perhaps a lot more

convincing before Kelly could say with any honesty that she believed any of it.

❖

Kelly's date with Jason ended up being better than she could have hoped.

The evening's conversation flowed more easily than she thought it would. Though Jason was curious about Kelly's life and asked her lots of questions, she kept the conversation focused on her schoolwork and her thesis. She chose not to discuss how she'd recently been able to add another language to her list of fluency, though he was fascinated that she could speak so many. She could never hope to think that he would have the tiniest bit of understanding about what she'd been going through. She didn't understand it herself. If she had brought any of it up, he probably would have thought she was insane.

His part of the conversation centered mostly on his work. It was clear from his description that he was not only good at his job, but he really seemed to love what he did.

As they sat in the low light of the restaurant and peered out at the city around them through the giant looking glass windows, Jason was able to point to a few of the towering buildings above as buildings he had a hand in designing. All that time of living there and walking right past those same buildings and she had no idea. It was endearing when, as he explained his latest accomplishment, his face lit up like a child.

It was interesting that they also shared some common ground, as he seemed to enjoy working with an architect on his team that had autism. From what Jason had told her, he was quirky and distant, but his intelligence and architectural creativity went unrivaled.

He always insisted on keeping his designs secret until opening day of the building, but usually astounded everyone with his revolutionary designs, which is why he was allowed to be so evasive.

As Jason talked on, despite the great time Kelly was having, a tiny seed of unease worked into her brain. She tried to push it out, but it persisted. She couldn't identify where it came from or what it was about, but it was there just the same.

When she dropped him off at his hotel, he leaned in to kiss her, but stopped with that. He wanted to take it slow so that he wouldn't mess anything up. It turned out that he'd had a crush on her all through high school too, but was too shy to ask her out. It was funny that she never saw him as being shy, though she could not remember him ever dating anyone else, either.

The next day she was pleasantly surprised to answer her doorbell and find the floral deliveryman there with a large bouquet of roses and a note telling her that he wanted to see her again as soon as possible. She couldn't even suppress her smile.

When her phone rang, she jumped up and immediately answered, thinking it might be Jason, but regretted it as soon as she heard Helga's voice. She was not ready to return to the Twilight Zone just yet.

"My Kelly?" Helga quavered, sounding so small.

"Yes, Helga. Good morning," Kelly sighed, with a hint of resignation. She knew that Helga was worried about her, and wouldn't leave her alone until she was sure she was okay. It was comforting in a sense, but she wasn't ready to discuss what happened yet.

"Kelly, I worry for you. I upset you. I'm sorry for that, but I hope you know that there was no other way." Kelly could hear the concern in Helga's voice. "I want you to come tomorrow. I want you to come so you can help me with planting."

"I'm sorry, Helga, but I'm going to see Bastian tomorrow. We have a team meeting of sorts scheduled. I can't miss it, and anyway, how can we plant anything? The ground is still frozen."

"This kind of planting can be done any time of year. Please tell me that you'll come. If not tomorrow, then soon," Helga pleaded.

"I'll try to come the day after, but I'm not making any promises." She needed time, but she also didn't want to hurt Helga's feelings, or make her worry more than she already was.

"Okay, my Kelly. Please be careful tomorrow." Before Kelly could say goodbye, she heard the audible click indicating that Helga had hung up on her end.

She came to a sudden realization. The entire conversation she'd just had with Helga was in *Tungri*! She wondered why Helga was suddenly so much easier to understand. In her native tongue, she was able to speak with clarity and without the usual, sometimes hard to decipher accent. Thanks to Helga, Kelly could understand it perfectly.

Kelly hoped it wasn't going to be an automatic thing; to start speaking *Tungri* without realizing it. God! She hoped that she hadn't reverted to that language at dinner with Jason. He hadn't given her any funny looks, so she supposed she was safe.

When Kelly's phone rang again, she hesitated to answer, but was glad she did.

"Kelly? It's Jason. I just wanted to give you a quick call. My plane is getting ready to take off, but I didn't want to leave without telling you what a great time I had."

"I had a great time too. It was really good to see you," Kelly grinned with delight.

"I know it might be a little too soon to ask, but my boss is throwing a big party for the grand opening of our museum, and I'm wondering if you'd like to come to New York? I'd love it if you'd be my date."

While she was overjoyed with the invitation, with everything going on, there would be no way she could get away. Her heart sank.

"I really wish I could, but I just can't get away right now," Kelly told him regretfully.

"No, I understand. I know you're probably really busy," he murmured, sounding dejected.

"Believe me, I'd love to. You have no idea. I'm going to be honest with you, Jason. I really like you. I have liked you for as long as I can remember, and I would rather come to New York to see you again more than you can imagine, but I've gotten in a little over my head. Working, school, and this damn thesis are going to be the death of me! In a couple of months I'll be done, and then you can take me anywhere you want," she offered with a small laugh, hoping that Jason wasn't taking her 'no' as a clear rejection.

"You've got it," he said, brightening. "Okay, gotta turn my phone off. Can I at least call you once in a while?" He asked quickly.

"I'd be very disappointed if you didn't."

CHAPTER SEVENTEEN

"Well, I think the important thing is that Bastian is making some progress. I'm fairly certain we're on the right track, and it's my recommendation that we continue with just his therapies, and see what kind of progress can be made, in let's say a month. If Bastian hasn't shown any new improvements by that time, then I think we could try a different medication, but for now, I want you to stop his current medication altogether," Dr. Jackson told Greta efficiently, as she sat in his office, getting frustrated.

"But haven't you been listening? He's not improving, he's getting worse. The things he says to me! The way he acts! I don't see any of that as progress," Greta argued. Frustrated tears formed in her eyes.

After describing to Dr. Jackson the way Bastian had been behaving, she'd been hoping he would recommend hospitalization, or at the very least prescribe an arsenal of behavior meds, but it was clear that he wasn't going to do any of that. He didn't seem in the least concerned.

It was almost as if he'd had a complete change of heart since the last time she spoke with him. He seemed different. He seemed cold and uninterested.

He offered no sympathy nor any suggestions for how to deal with Bastian's increasingly disturbing behavior. Not to mention his suggestion to stop his medication. From what she'd read, they were supposed to be tapered to avoid withdrawal.

"Also, I would severely limit television and perhaps start increasing the time he attends the Weisenhoff School. It seems to be good for him. I received a call from them just a few days ago. They informed me he was doing quite well with his studies, though that wasn't really the reason for their call," he proclaimed, looking up at Greta for her reaction.

Greta was suddenly alarmed. The school never mentioned to her that they called Bastian's doctor.

"Oh?" she queried, trying hard to keep her voice even. "What was the reason for the call?"

"They had some concerns about you actually, Greta," he stated carefully.

"Me? Whatever for?" she raised her voice with genuine shock. She couldn't imagine where the conversation was headed, but she didn't like it one bit. They had no business contacting her son's doctor without her permission, even if he was on the contact list. How dare they!

"Well, from what they reported, you don't seem to be on board with his program. They also told me that you don't seem to be very interested in the progress he's been making, and that they barely see you at all. They complained that more times than not, they have to relay any pertinent information to the various babysitters that either drop Bastian off or pick him up."

"That is a bunch of bull! I'm very interested in his progress. I guess I just don't understand what their mission is supposed to be. I get that Bastian needs time to explore his interests, but what's the point of knowing a bunch of places on a map if he can't share the knowledge appropriately. I'd rather he had more training on how to fit in with his peers," she shouted, getting madder by the minute. "As far as the babysitters, I do have a job, you know. A very demanding job, as you do. I can't be with Bastian every minute. Surely you must understand that. I've seen the pictures of your own kids on your desk. I don't suppose you've considered staying at home to raise your kids instead of working?"

The whole thing was ridiculous. She always worried about people seeing her as unfit, and it appeared as though her worries would not go unfounded.

"This isn't about me. It's about you, and it's about Bastian. Everyone is just concerned that you aren't doing the best you can with him. That perhaps you might even be trying to hinder his progress. Look, from what the school has told me, Bastian is a brilliant, funny, warm, and caring little boy. Not at all what you've described to me. They said that he is inquisitive, and has taken a keen interest in geography, showing remarkable skill. From what Bastian has been telling his teacher, you forbid him to even talk about it at home."

"That's not fair," she faltered, because even as she said it, she knew that there was some truth to it. Though it shouldn't be a crime to want Bastian to be normal, and encouraging his incessant recitations of geographical locations and populations wouldn't help him with that.

He was weird, and she was tired of people staring at him as he went on in the grocery stores, doctor's offices, or anywhere he went. He just wouldn't shut up about it.

Lately, he'd begun reciting the various New York City streets, along with the instance of people by race in each neighborhood. It was embarrassing.

As determined as she was in the beginning not to care what others thought, it was different now that she was a parent, and it bothered her a great deal to have people looking at Bastian as though he were a freak.

The doctor closed Bastian's file, indicating that the topic was closed. He took out a pamphlet that he had pulled from a drawer next to where he sat.

"I'm sorry, but there really aren't any quick fixes for autism. I know it's difficult, and it must be frustrating at times, but you need to be doing everything you can to encourage Bastian to be the person he is, not what you want him to be. While I don't recommend quitting your job, you really should consider hiring someone on a more permanent basis to look after him, or have him spend more time at the Weisenhoff, which I feel would be the best thing for him. There is a parenting class for parents of children with autism starting up next week. I think it would be beneficial for you to go," he offered, handing her the pamphlet as he got up from his desk. "There's really nothing more that can be done right now."

"A parenting class isn't going to help me!" Greta cried. "I'm not the problem here, it's Bastian. I'm telling you that I don't feel safe in my own home. Something is seriously wrong, and if you're telling me that you're not going to do anything about it, then I guess I'll have no choice but to find myself another doctor," she delivered the ultimatum with determination.

"I'm sorry, Greta, but I honestly can't recommend hospitalization at this time, or medication, or anything else you're asking me for. To be honest with you, I'm a little sick of parents like you coming in here and demanding that I fix your children. Stop being a whining little bitch. You people make me sick. If you all had your way, you'd take your genius children and turn them into blathering idiots just like the rest of you. If you can't handle Bastian, then perhaps you should give him up. There are plenty of people who can't have children that would be glad to take him," he stated coldly, and with malice.

Greta was horrified. A whining bitch? Never in her life had anyone talked to her like that! And to hear something like that from a professional; her son's doctor? She fumed with sudden anger.

No matter what kind of a parent she was, she knew she didn't deserve that. Something was very wrong with Dr. Jackson. Maybe he was having a nervous breakdown, but whatever it was, she didn't have to stay there and take it. She'd put her trust in the hospital and Dr. Jackson, and she couldn't help but feel betrayed.

Too shocked to do anything else, she quickly grabbed her things, headed for the door, and slammed it as she left. She wasn't going to give him the satisfaction of seeing her cry.

She nearly ran into Jane, as she rushed down the hall, trying hard to hold herself together.

"Greta! What's wrong? Is something the matter with Bastian?" she asked, genuinely concerned, recognizing Greta right away. At least Jane hadn't completely lost it, Greta thought bitterly.

"No. Well, yes. Actually something seems to be wrong with Dr. Jackson." Greta broke into scared, confused sobs as she relayed the entire story to the sympathetic nurse.

Jane gave Greta a look of apology. "Oh no. Not you too?" Motioning for Greta to follow her into an empty patient room, she whispered, "You're not the only one to notice. The hospital has been getting calls all week. Dr. Jackson is not quite himself right now. He made calls to the parents of every single patient of his demanding that they take them off their medication right away. No explanation. When some of the parents protested, he apparently told them that they were bad parents and he wouldn't treat them any more if they couldn't follow his directions. I probably shouldn't be telling you this, but I put in my notice today. He's been downright abusive to work for lately. I honestly can't stay here another minute," Jane told Greta, getting teary-eyed herself.

"I'm so sorry Jane," Greta told her, giving her a sympathetic hug, though she was still shaken herself. "If it makes you feel any better at all, you will be missed. You've been a great nurse."

"Do you want me to take you to administration so that you can file a complaint? I'm not supposed to encourage it, but I'm leaving anyway. There isn't anything more they can do to me," Jane asked Greta as they walked together back into the hallway, both feeling a bit better after the talk.

"No. No, thanks Jane. I just want to go home. I'll definitely make my complaint, but for now, I think I've had more than I can handle."

"I understand. Please take care of yourself and don't take anything that Dr. Jackson said to heart, okay?"

Greta knew one thing for sure as she drove away from the hospital for the last time; she was definitely taking Bastian out of that school.

She stewed silently as she drove towards Cora's house. Where did he get off saying the things he did? She wasn't perfect, but she really was doing the best she could under the circumstances. Blathering idiots? She couldn't get the stream of insults out of her head.

She wasn't wrong about Bastian and she knew it. Just like she knew something was wrong with Bastian in the beginning. She knew now too.

Dialing Cora's number and not getting any answer, Greta assumed that they were probably outside playing in the snow. Good, she thought. She decided all at once to let him stay there a bit longer, then she'd be able to go home, calm down, and have her lunch in peace, but as she pulled into her driveway, Greta could tell immediately that something wasn't right.

She *thought* she'd closed and locked the front door when she'd left that morning, but she could plainly see that it was slightly ajar.

How weird, she thought. It wasn't like her to forget to lock her door, but with all of the distractions lately, it didn't really surprise her too much.

It did surprise her, though, to hear the TV as she neared the door. She knew for sure that she'd shut that off before leaving.

"Hello?" Greta gave a tentative holler as she entered, but didn't really expect an answer. It was unlikely that anyone would be in her house, except a robber, and a robber wouldn't be watching TV. She must be losing it, she thought with a defeated chuckle as she went to turn it off, but stopped short when she saw Bastian sitting on the couch.

"Bastian? What in the world are you doing here? Where's Cora?" She was stunned and completely confused to find Bastian calmly eating ice cream in front of the television.

"I got bored when Cora fell asleep, so I walked home," Bastian told her, not even looking away from the program he was watching.

"Bastian, that was very, very bad. Do you know how dangerous that could have been? You're way too young to be walking around without an adult. Do you have any idea of what could've happened?" Greta demanded, reaching to grab the remote control off the coffee table so she could turn the television off.

"Well nothing did happen and I was watching that," Bastian snarled as he reached up to rip the remote control back out of her hand.

"I've had just about enough of your smart mouth and your rotten behavior. Go to your room!" Greta grabbed hold of the remote once again, but Bastian held firmly, clenching his teeth with the effort.

They played tug of war with it for a few seconds, but Greta won, which sent Bastian sprawling backwards, infuriating him.

He stuck his tongue out, screwed up his face and spit in Greta's direction, though it merely landed on the carpet, missing her altogether. It didn't matter. She lost it, and advancing on him, smacked him squarely across the face.

Shocked, Bastian's hand flew up to rub his reddening cheek and he shrank away from her.

Oh my God, she thought, horrified. What had she done? She was instantly sick to her stomach.

She closed her eyes in shame. She tried, unsuccessfully, to stop the stinging tears that threatened. Warily she opened them, fearful of the damage, but the look on Bastian's face told her that the blow had only stunned him. It was clear that it hadn't really fazed him in the least. On the contrary, he stood regarding her with a look of profound smug pleasure.

Completely exasperated with herself and Bastian, and at a loss for what else to do, Greta scooped him up, stowing him under her arm like a football, carried him as he kicked and thrashed, and deposited him in his room, closing the door tight.

She was losing it. She couldn't believe that she'd hit her child. Something even her own parents had never done. Never mind that he probably deserved it, walking home all by himself and sassing her that way, she was the adult and should have a lot more control of her emotions.

She was so ashamed. Hot tears began again, and this time she couldn't hold them back. Not wanting Bastian to hear her, she ran to her room.

It took some time for Greta to get control of herself, and feeling only slightly better after a good cry, she knew she couldn't put off calling Cora any longer. The poor woman was probably frantic, though it was partly her fault, Greta thought. She shouldn't have fallen asleep while she was supposed to be watching her son.

Greta peeked her head out of her room, checking to make sure that Bastian was nowhere in sight and dashed for the phone. She dialed Cora's number, and though she let it ring through several times, didn't get any answer. It both bothered and angered her that Cora probably didn't even realize that Bastian was missing and was probably still asleep. She vowed never to leave Bastian there again.

Greta went to check on Bastian. She could hear him in his room, probably lining up those stupid blocks. He only babbled that way now when he was playing with them. Grateful that he'd at least stayed there, Greta tip-toed away so she could begin making dinner in peace.

She took the hamburger out of freezer and threw it into

the microwave. Spying Bastian's backpack by the counter, Greta saw something odd, partially sticking up through the top zipper. Curious, she decided to unpack it while she waited for the meat to thaw. She was surprised to find a small, ugly painting.

Chapter Eighteen

❖

"Kelly, Gretchen, Paula? This is a surprise. I wasn't expecting you until this afternoon. Was there a change in the schedule?" Miss Carol asked, confused as she met Kelly and the team in the school hallway on her way back from the teacher's lounge.

"No. Today is observation day, remember?" Paula scoffed with annoyance.

"Oh, that's right! Today is the day you're supposed to observe Bastian silently to see how he's doing socially."

"Yes. I'm surprised you don't remember. You might want to start setting appointment reminders on your phone, like I do. Anyway, I don't get much of a chance to talk with you Carol. How is he doing? Socially, that is? Is he getting along with the other children?" Paula kept a brisk pace as they walked on towards the classroom. Carol had to practically jog to catch up just so that she could answer.

"No different than usual, I guess. He still only plays with Kurt when you're not here, Kelly, pretty much ignoring everyone else. But in truth, I'd rather see it that way than what we experienced on Bastian's first day," Carol snorted.

"Yes, I heard about that. It was very unfortunate. Still, I was hoping that he would make more friends. I know that Kelly has been trying hard to get him to begin play sessions with others," Paula stated.

"He seems to do okay while I'm here, but obviously I can't control what happens after I leave," Kelly pointed out.

"No one said you could." Paula stopped as they reached the class, and gave Kelly a look of warning.

"So, will you be checking in when you're done, or heading out?" Carol asked.

"Leaving. Today is just for observing. Please don't tell Bastian that Kelly is here. I don't want him to be distracted," Paula instructed Carol.

Kelly suspected that being a distraction had nothing to do with Paula's decision not to tell Bastian she was there, but she wasn't going to argue. In fact, she was glad he wouldn't be able to see her. If there was any grain of truth in what Helga had been telling her, she knew that she'd have to watch Bastian when he didn't think anyone was watching.

"Okay, well, happy spying," Carol told Kelly, shaking her head with a laugh as she entered the classroom, closing the door quietly behind her.

Kelly, Paula, and the other members of the team went to the observation window and looked around until they spotted Bastian. He and Kurt were playing with the blocks behind the bookshelves, away from the others.

They watched as Bastian lined up a row of the black blocks. Kurt moved in and placed a row of red blocks behind his. Kelly could see their lips moving and remembered that they hadn't turned the volume up on the speaker. She wished they were just a little bit closer so she could hear more clearly.

Suddenly, Kurt got up and kicked Bastian's row of blocks, knocking them all out of formation. Kelly braced herself for what certainly would be Bastian's protesting scream, but instead, he began to shriek with delight, and got up to do the same with Kurt's blocks, which in turn made Kurt laugh.

Paula made some notations in her file, and shook her head in disappointment.

Bastian and Kurt got down once again and began to line the blocks up differently. This time, Kurt took the black blocks and Bastian rounded up a group of yellow.

Kurt placed the black blocks into a long line, being extra careful to arrange them evenly apart.

Kelly watched as Bastian put the yellow into a circle. Each block touching the next, as though they were in unison.

What happened next was startling. Bastian selected a yellow block, being careful not to knock over the others, and heaved it at one of the black blocks, which knocked it over and out of line. He would then place the yellow block back into formation and choose another. He repeated this process until all of the black blocks were down.

They watched as Kurt took the black blocks and placed them under a gray blanket that was lying next to them on the carpet.

It was chilling that each time a black block went down; they'd both look at each other and smile. Kelly got shivers. A bad feeling rose in the pit of her stomach. She reached down to turn the volume up higher.

"If we had a fire we could burn them," Kurt giggled, looking towards the blanket.

"There will be a fire. They will all burn," Bastian told him reassuringly, patting the blanket roughly.

The realization hit Kelly all at once. Bastian was speaking *Tungri!* Bastian and Kurt, she thought in terrified amazement. How could it even be possible? How could she have missed it right from the beginning?

These kids weren't lining up their blocks to be linear...they were lining up their armies! My God, what Helga had said was true!

"You see there, Bastian is still showing signs of aggression, which could be why the other children don't want to play with him," Paula pointed out to Gretchen.

She was just as blind as Kelly had been. They had no idea of what was going on! To all the rest of them, the children were playing and babbling.

Kelly couldn't hear Bastian and Kurt over the team as they discussed Paula's observation. She tried turning the volume up more, but it was at the highest level.

"You know, it might be a good idea for Kelly to spend an extra hour with him each day at school. I'm sure the time would be approved, if you agree, that is, Kelly," Paula asked, but Kelly wasn't paying attention. She needed to know what else they were saying!

"Paula! Could you please shut up? I can't hear!' Kelly begged desperately, shocking Paula into silence.

"They are here. I have seen one, one of the men from the time before," she heard Bastian say before Paula dragged Kelly away from the window.

"That was very rude, Kelly. What's your problem?" Paula demanded angrily.

Kelly looked towards the boys once again. Kurt was stomping on the blanket as Bastian beamed with pleasure. "I have to go. I'm sorry!" she yelled as she ran down the hall leaving Paula and the others gaping after her.

She could only hope there was a way to stop it, to stop them before it was too late.

CHAPTER NINETEEN

Germany 1945

A ny guilt Magdalena felt in leaving Josef at the hospital in the care of Dr. Vat for so long had left her. The Americans were on their way, having just crossed the Rhine River, and it was only a matter of time before they would all be killed. At least *he* was safe...for now, and for now was all they really needed.

The work that Dr. Vat had been doing with him was nearly done. However, if they decided to drop a bomb on them as they'd been planning to do with Japan, then all would be lost. Knowing that the Jews would be killed right along with the Germans gave her no comfort. Too many of them had escaped to the United States.

Josef was the key to a complete eradication. She was convinced of that, as was her Dolphie. With the proper tutelage, Josef had designed some ingenious weaponry. Using her visions from long ago for placement, engineers had already been sent to the U.S. to plant the devices Josef had designed. While they didn't have the technology yet to be used, they one day would. The amber would keep them safe until it was time. Now they just needed a future army to be there to see that the job got done, and Dr. Vat had seen to that.

He theorized that if he were to inject some blood and spinal fluids extracted from Josef directly into the brain stems of his female test subjects, then his condition might be able to be duplicated, and he wasn't wrong. In doing so, he was able to alter the genes of his subjects so that once they became impregnated, at least one of their offspring would be very much like Josef, and the ones who weren't would carry the gene to be passed on.

Dr. Vat, himself, impregnated quite a few subjects over the last few years, and with pleasing results.

Over time, the condition would spread, branching out and growing in numbers with each passing year. More and more children like Josef would be born. A good number of them would be of superior intelligence, blonde haired, blue-eyed, beautiful children.

He was quick to caution that not all of them would necessarily possess the same kind of intelligence that Josef had. For some of the children, a lot would depend on their environment and upbringing. However, given their condition, most would be given every opportunity to flourish. They would be taught, and their genius would be undeniable. They would go on unsuspected while their skills were drawn out of them and expanded upon. Some would be scientists, some would be architects, and some would be mathematicians. Whatever the case was, they were sure to be of use in the next war.

Magdalena was the one to suggest the addition of a blood and tissue specimen from both she and Adolph. She wanted them all to carry little pieces of them inside, in their memories and in their genes. Magdalena wanted them to know what they were fighting for. She wanted them to be able to see for themselves.

The latter thought made Magdalena smile, for it ensured that they would know what needed to be done. They wouldn't be able to control the urge. Adolph and his officers would be there to guide them. Soon their ashes would be placed in the urns so their bodies could be returned to the living in the next century. They wouldn't look the same, but their souls would be restored.

Magdalena hastened her steps in the chilly April air. Her dream eyes were showing her that Adolph was getting ready to flee, to hide. He had become paranoid and delusional. His depression of late made him very hard to reason with, and she couldn't bring him into her visions to show him what was to be. He wouldn't be able to handle it in the state he was in.

She'd had to take his mandrake root from him so he wouldn't see her thoughts. He was sure he'd lost it. Maybe that it had been stolen. He'd been frantic looking for it. He was sure that without it everything would fall to pieces. He never understood the limits of the aura. They'd done the best they could. The war was already lost, but he refused to believe it.

Their time together was very nearly over. His time in this life was finished, but she needed his death to be controlled. He'd been receiving threats every day for months. If she didn't act quickly, then someone was going to get to him first, and then perhaps she wouldn't be able to find the body. She would not do the job herself. She couldn't. Even to her, it wouldn't be right. She'd killed his officers that morning. Eleven officers. It was easier than she thought it would be. They were so trusting that she didn't even need to use her aura. She'd called a meeting of the Order. They only balked slightly at the change in venue. The quiet farmhouse in the country ensured that she wouldn't be interrupted.

As for Adolph, there was really only one way to do what needed to be done. She'd have to show him the truth about who he really was. It would be enough to send him over the edge. To know that he had Jew blood in his veins would be more than he could bear.

Magdalena found her Dolphie as she had left him that morning…unshaven, disheveled, and still looking for his mandrake root. The house was nearly turned upside down in his efforts.

"You can stop looking now, Dolphie. I know where it is," she told him quietly as she entered their house for the last time. Her heart pulled as she saw his face light up. His childlike face. His sweet, sweet face, even in his maddened condition. He would always be her Dolphie. Her lover. Her only brother.

His eyes went to her blood soaked coat.

"Erhard had it. Your very closest friend and best officer," she lied. "I had to be forceful with him until he would tell me where it was hidden. You are to go to the old farm house. The one we lived in when we first came to Germany. You will find him there. I will get your root and bring it to you."

CHAPTER TWENTY

Present

"**M**y Kelly! I knew you were to come. My dream eyes told to me." Helga met Kelly happily at the door with a kiss, ushering her in out of the cold.

Helga could see that Kelly was visibly upset. "My poor Kelly, you come with me." She led her to the couch next to the fire and gave her a sympathetic pat.

"I take it you saw Bastian today?" Helga asked, raising her eyebrows in question, though she already knew the answer. At Kelly's hesitant nod, Helga hurried into the kitchen to get her some tea and cakes, as if food could cure everything.

"I knew when you realized truth, would be hard," Helga hollered over the whistling of the teapot.

"Hard?" Kelly cried, "Hard isn't the word I would use. Try disturbing, unbelievable, frightening. Those are the words that I would use. Let me ask you something...if you've known about this your whole life, why didn't you ever mention it to your son? And why didn't you just give that woman the damn seed in the first place? If you'd given it to her, wouldn't it have prevented this whole thing?" Kelly clamored. It wasn't fair that she'd been brought into this. The whole thing was madness.

She had so many questions and so many things running

through her head, she didn't really know what to ask first. She wanted answers. She wanted someone to explain to her how any of this could possibly be real.

Helga came back into the living room carrying a tray with steaming china cups and a plate heaped high with little cakes and cookies and placed it on the coffee table in front of where Kelly sat.

"Kelly, try to understand," she began in her language, but Kelly interrupted.

"English, please. I've had enough *Tungri* for today," Kelly pleaded, still reeling from what she'd witnessed.

Helga looked at her sympathetically and sat down beside her.

"When my cousin come to me so long ago and asked me for that seed, I just lost baby. My husband and I try so long after Gerhard was born. Finally, I pregnant but lost it. Same happened again a few months later. When she comes to me I just been pregnant for fourth time. We were more hopeful that time, because by fifth month it still inside, but I woke up one night with pains and she comes. Oh! She was so small but so beautiful. I hold to that sweet baby girl and I pray and I pray, but she die. My aura could not save her. I cried for many days. My heart hurt me to think about that *kleines (little)* baby. I could not bear to see anyone go through same loss as me, even if she not good person." Not able to hold in her emotions, Helga began to cry. Deep sobs wracked her tiny frame and she turned away, embarrassed by such a display of emotion.

Kelly could see that it was very difficult for Helga to talk about, even after so many years had passed. She got up and grabbed the tissues from the end table where Helga kept them and handed one to her, rubbing her gently on the back until she quieted.

Sniffling, Helga collected herself and began again. "No one really knew for sure that her baby would be that way and be used in that way. It was vision, but I didn't want to believe it. The others could not make me believe it. I was so bad with the grief. I could not help the others kill her baby. She was my relation. All of our relation. She had bad life. She was touched by bad aura. Not her fault. Something bad happen to her when she was young, but after we not allowed to see her anymore. Then we hear that she die with parents in fire, but I see her many years later. I recognize her eyes. She had most beautiful eyes! I know by seeing them that she not died. She pretend that she don't see me, that she did not know me, but still, I remembered how kind she was to me when I was little girl before the bad thing happened. No matter what she became, she did not deserve to have her baby taken from her," she rationalized. "No one is deserved to that," she said with conviction, shaking her head.

"When her baby comes out, and we hear the stories of his illness and what he could do, it was too late to do anything about it. It would be what it would be. No one could get close to it anyway. She guarded that baby. I was glad because I didn't want to hurt that child. I had hope it would be okay, that the others were wrong."

"When war ended and every one of those people die, there was no reason to bring up subject again. We hear that his doctors did something with his blood. He put it into other people, but we not know reasons until much later when doctor's journals were found and published. His work was all just theory anyways, we thought. Many years passed, and when nothing happen, and most of my people die, I try to forget."

While Kelly found the story to be very compelling and her heart grieved for Helga's loss, it still didn't add up. "So what does this have to do with what's going on now? What does any of this have to do with Bastian and his ability to speak *Tungri*?" It still didn't make sense.

"I hear tell through the years of children born more and more with illness like her baby have, I believe your Bastian is one of those," she said softly, turning her face away from Kelly in shame, before whispering, "After her baby was born, there was nothing to be done. There was nothing anyone could do. It was what it was. I knew was all my fault, but what could I do? I live my life and forget. I do good job forgetting until I meet your little one."

"Helga," Kelly began softly, "I'm so sorry for all that you had to go through back then. I really am, but do you honestly believe that Bastian; that all children with autism, are somehow related to your cousin? That his autism was caused by something that doctor did so long ago?" she asked incredulously.

"Is okay, my Kelly. Was long time ago. I foolish to cry about it now. Yes, I don't just believe it. I know it. Bastian is the way he is because I was a sentimental fool, even back then. The most important thing is that you know now what he is. What they all are. His is of bad blood. He is dangerous. Is my fault, but I cannot change the past. I am old woman now. What am I to do?"

"What I don't understand is, why now? Why is all of this happening now? What changed?" Kelly asked.

"Not just now, my Kelly. Is happened all around us for years, but everyone was blind to it. You remember the little one who flew the plane to the school?"

Kelly nodded vigorously. She had just talked about that with Paula not that long ago.

"Was Jewish school, was it not?"

Kelly couldn't deny that it had been. All of those children dead along with everyone on the plane. She'd known it was a Jewish school, but never thought of it as a target. Why would she have? To her it was just a senseless accident. It could've crashed anywhere.

"How about the one who make bomb and blew up Jewish Community Center?"

Finally, it was all starting to make sense, if there was any sense to it. It began to dawn on her that all or most of the tragedies involving autistic children were centered on the Jewish community in some way. Every single incident she could think of involved Jewish people in one way or another. Why hadn't she put it together before? How blind could she have been?

Suddenly she thought of Bastian's behavior at school with little Jacob on the first day. He was adamant that he was the only one who should wear the nametag. The laminated star. Weren't all of the Jewish people in World War II forced to wear stars as markers of their race? Could Bastian really have something in his blood that made him predetermined to hate Jewish people? To want to do them harm?

"While I agree that you do have a point, there have been plenty of people with autism that have done good things too," Kelly couldn't help but add. She didn't want any of this to be true, and was really grasping at anything she could.

"I know what you talk about Kelly, but you think of this; that boy, the boy who made medicines out of plants? He was hero, no? What happened after he make medicines?

Think back to what was in news after."

Kelly wracked her brain but couldn't remember anything specific.

"The Ashkenazi disease in Jewish community is what happened. No one could explain why so many children come down with it at such young age. Usually it not comes out until old age, but all those kids, maybe hundreds, were diagnosed in just couple years. All bad cases. Many of them die. It was that boy. It was those medicines. I tell to you. He mix them in with vaccine. Each year it getting worse, like it coming to boiling point. More and more of those kids do terrible things."

Kelly suddenly remembered hearing something about that, but again, she never would have tied that to any targeting against Jewish people.

"Why didn't you ever alert the authorities or at least tell Professor Stein so that he could do something, if this was your suspicion?"

Helga scoffed, "Ever since I lose my voice, people treat me differently, like I stupid. They talk to me louder, like I cannot hear. They talk slower like I cannot understand what they say to me. They would never hear me say those things about their precious little ones. They do not want to know of those things. They would not listen. They would think I crazy old woman. Even now, with my voice comes back to me, they would not listen. No one listen to old lady."

She was probably right, Kelly thought. Look how long it had taken Helga to convince her, and even then, she didn't want to fully believe it.

"When I was at Bastian's school earlier today, I overheard him talking to another boy with autism. I heard him speaking *Tungri*, just like you said. Bastian told Kurt not to worry, that 'they' had finally made it from the time before. He'd seen one and they would all burn soon. Do you think they could be planning to do something like those other kids did? And who do you think 'they' were?

Helga suddenly paled, "He said time before? Are you sure?"

"I'm sure. My *Tungri* is perfect, thanks to you." Kelly rolled her eyes dramatically in mock annoyance.

"My God, she did it," Helga exclaimed in disbelief. "She did it."

"Did what? Who are you talking about?" Kelly asked nervously.

"Magdalena. My cousin. There is still much you do not know Kelly," Helga told her. She got up and went to the mantle of the fireplace where a row of nicely framed pictures had been carefully arranged in an attractive display.

Kelly had seen the pictures many times before, but never really looked at them. Helga pulled down an old black and white one framed in cracked porcelain and handed it to Kelly.

The picture showed a crowd of people, most of them wearing black overcoats and haircuts that dated the picture to be sometime in the thirties or forties.

At first glance, because of the excited expressions on many of the faces, it appeared as though it was a picture of a parade, perhaps, or some kind of special event.

Kelly smiled politely and tried to hand it back to Helga, confused. What did a parade have to do with anything?

Helga shook her head. "Look. Look closely."

Kelly studied the photo once again. Only then, did Kelly actually see what the picture was all about. In the distant and hard to see background, high on a platform, was the likeness of a man that could only be Adolph Hitler, and next to him a beautiful woman. Kelly was stunned!

"My cousin was wife of a very important man. Most hated man of all time," she stated, looking cautiously at Kelly.

"Oh, you aren't going to tell me that your cousin was married to Adolph Hitler? Are you serious?" Kelly nearly shrieked.

"Dis is what I tell to you. Is true. What no one knows is that he was husband yes, but also her brother." Kelly started to interrupt again, but Helga motioned for her to wait.

"All we know is after bad thing happen when Magdalena was girl, he was born. We not know all of the details; only what us little children overhear our parents talk about late at night. They sent him away to be raised by others. Does not matter now. Is in past. But what is important is that when they growed and he became man he was, they did not finish what they set out to do." She looked at Kelly questioningly.

"Exterminate the Jews," Kelly declared darkly, remembering all she had read about that awful time during World War II.

"Yes, my Kelly. They wanted to kill them all. She vow to get them all, and even though her teeth were blackened from drinking the teas, some escape and then war stop."

"Teas?" Kelly asked, "Like afternoon tea, tea?" What does tea have to do with anything?"

"When you are of aura people, you get a seed to plant. It grows into a mandrake tree. The roots, branches, and bark get ground into tea, which feeds your aura and keeps it strong. The more tea you drink, the stronger the aura becomes. Brings extra luck when you need it most. When war was almost over, her tree would have been nothing but dry roots. She made much tea in her life to help with killing those people."

Kelly had a sudden thought. "It was that tea, that mandrake tea you gave me when I slept here wasn't it?" Kelly asked indignantly, glaring at Helga. She knew there had to have been a reason for the crazy dream!

"Yes, my Kelly. I sorry I deceived to you, but was necessary," she reasoned, casting her eyes away quickly.

Kelly decided to let it go, but she made a mental note not to drink any more tea unless she made it herself!

"Anyway, so you think that they created little autistic kids to finish what they started?" Kelly asked in disbelief.

"It wasn't the original intention, but yes. Adolph had vision of blue eyed, blonde hair perfect race. Intelligent, beautiful people. When their Josef comes out, he like dis. It was not planned, but it was a happy consequence for them. They want to make more, but they could never make a whole army together. They need help."

"And that's where the doctors came into play," Kelly stated blandly. "But that doesn't explain who the other people are from the 'time before'.

"I getting to that Kelly. My people believe that when you die, your soul is not die. If burn body, and place in urn, it goes on to live in another time. Next century. If buried in ground, it stay inside of person and cannot get out. Magdalena knows to put her husband and his men into the urns. She send them here to help little ones. To lead them. To make sure they finish job."

"So it's like being reborn? Like I was Adolph Hitler in a

past life?" Kelly asked jokingly, though she didn't find anything funny about any of it.

"Not exactly. Is not work quite like that. If come back from urn, you only get a little while. You go into the living and take over for a time. Not too long, but is chance to live again," Helga told her casually, as if it was nothing at all.

It was crazy. Completely nuts, Kelly thought, and something else was not adding up. She did some quick math in her head.

"How old were you when Professor Stein, well Gerhard to you, was born?" Kelly asked slowly.

Helga stopped pacing and went to sit down next to Kelly. "I was twenty-seven," she stated, staring down at her hands that she worked nervously in her lap.

Kelly blinked rapidly a couple of times, trying to grasp the meaning behind the answer. "But, if you were twenty-seven plus when Magdalena's baby was born and the war ended in nineteen forty five when he was the age of seven, then that would make you…"

"I'm one hundred and four, but is no matter, Kelly," Helga told her, getting up again to pace. "Yes, I'm old. All of my people live long times. Is how we know our love ones come back from urns. We see our loved ones again. They not look the same but they are the same inside," Helga told Kelly, pointing to her head and heart simultaneously, "something happens and they just come. Something triggers. A memory goes in and takes over. They recognize us and seek us out. We see them again and they not lost to us. But she not send those men back to see love ones. She send them back to finish what she could not all those years ago."

It was too much to think about. Helga being one hundred

and four. Children with autism being born killers. Helga was related to Adolph Hitler. Maybe Kelly would have time later to sort it all out in her head, if that was even possible. The real question though, was if those men, Adolph included, were sent into the year two thousand and sixteen to carry out what they tried to do so many years ago and failed, what could she do about it? Could any of it be stopped?

One thing Helga said was certainly true. No one would believe her, and they definitely weren't going to believe Kelly. Why would they?

Helga, as if she were reading her thoughts, answered Kelly's unspoken questions.

"There may be something that can be done. I'm going to have talk with my son. I'm going to have to convince him to take me to Austria. Yes, I must go to Austria soon as possible," she told Kelly decisively, "and you and I...we must plant seed. My second tree. The tree meant for my baby that died. We go plant it now. Will bring much luck. My old aura very weak."

"Austria? Why Austria?" Kelly asked, surprised.

"I'm going to have to go and right the wrong I did all of those years ago by not giving them my seed," she told Kelly, but seeing Kelly's confusion added, "Magdalena's tree would be there. Maybe at her childhood home. She had to have planted tree to do the things she did, to help Adolph do the things he do. Like I say to you, it would be all but dead now. All used up for all of the help she had in doing what she did. She must have drank the teas until it was nothing more than a pile of roots beneath the earth. I go and find it. I kill last of its roots. Then maybe it stop. As long as there is the tiniest of piece, she still has the luck. We go, Kelly, we go right now and plant my tree. I save seed all these years. I need tree to give to you luck. We need strong luck, my Kelly," she proposed earnestly.

Not wanting to leave Helga alone, Kelly stayed that evening to help prepare dinner, though she couldn't imagine eating after everything she had just heard.

She helped, reluctantly, to make the necessary plane reservations, and was able to get Helga and Professor Stein on a flight the following day. Helga was adamant that it would have to be done as soon as possible, and though she tried to get her to wait until she had first spoken with her son, she insisted. They didn't have time to waste.

Helga appeared tired and shaken after divulging so many of the secrets to Kelly that she had hung onto all those years.

It must have been a heavy burden to carry all that time, Kelly thought. To think your whole life that you were partly to blame for the deaths of so many Jews without any way to tell anyone.

As crazy as it all sounded, Kelly was fully convinced and was ready to help in any way she could, though she couldn't imagine how.

They planted the seed. Kelly was amazed to see it sprouting before her eyes, though the ground was still half frozen from the winter that hadn't yet released its hold. The tender fronds peeked out from the crusty earth and unfurled as though they couldn't wait to feel the sun after so many years of being hidden away.

With a little help from Kelly, Helga knelt down and gently clipped a tiny piece of root that had already begun snaking its way through the icy ground and handed it up to Kelly.

"To keep you safe, my Kelly. To protect from harm. We stay together now in my dream eyes. We will always be together."

Kelly held back her tears. The gesture from Helga made her feel overwhelmed with love for her aging friend. She didn't know why, but her heart began to ache as though she had suffered a great loss.

Neither of them was very hungry, and Kelly felt exhausted and a little down, so she told Helga that since Professor Stein would be coming in soon, she was going to go home and leave them to their talk. She bent down to give Helga a kiss goodnight. Helga surprised her by capturing her around the waist and hugging Kelly tightly.

"I love you like daughter, my Kelly. You are good girl." She let go and reached up to give Kelly a kiss on the cheek. Kelly noticed a hint of tears in her eyes, which made her uneasy.

"Is there anything else I should be doing while you're away or anything else I need to know about?"

"Just be watchful. Very watchful. If they here, if they come from urns, then there is something going to happened. Something big. Keep eyes open to news."

"Okay, get some rest. Good night Helga. I'll see you in a few days. We'll figure this out. Please be safe in Vienna," Kelly told her, suppressing a big yawn, and with some reluctance, turned to leave.

"Goodbye my Kelly," Helga told Kelly sadly as she shut the door.

CHAPTER TWENTY-ONE

❖

G reta was still groggy after a hard sleep in which she had many strange dreams. She couldn't remember them all, but she'd woken up feeling nervous.

Grateful it was a furlough day for her from work and that Bastian had school, she stepped outside into the early morning light and grabbed the paper off the front step.

She would let Bastian sleep a little longer that morning and enjoy a cup of coffee and some quiet time before rousting him, she thought, settling into her seat at the table.

Scanning the National section, Greta was happy to read that they had finally completed the Holocaust Museum they'd been talking about in New York. It was about time they gave those people a decent memorial, she thought.

Though she would love to see it, opening day would be a mad house, as they expected thousands of visitors. New York would be tough to get in and out of with all of that traffic. It would probably be like that for months until the newness wore off. Perhaps she'd visit next summer, she decided.

Not finding much else of interest, Greta went straight for the local news.

Checking the headlines for stories of interest, one caught Greta's immediate attention.

BRIGHTON WOMAN FOUND DEAD IN HOUSE DUE TO APPARENT FALL

Seventy-seven year old lifelong resident of Brighton Hills, Cora Simms, was found dead in her home by local authorities after sons alerted police that they had not heard from their mother in days. Both children, Dane and Markus Simms, reside outside of the state.

They informed local officials that their mother phoned them every day since they had moved out of the home, which they once shared with Cora and her husband, Rich Simms, who died last year, but that it had been three days without the ritual morning phone call.

They each made several calls to the home that went unanswered, and could not reach anyone they knew to check up on Simms.

Police performed a wellness check and noted that Simms' car was in the garage, and the front door was ajar.

After entering Simms' home and completing a thorough search, they discovered a body at the base of the stairs leading to the Simms basement. the body has been positively identified as Cora Simms.

In a disturbing turn of events, the medical examiner told news 9 that Simms suffered a broken leg and hip, and it did not appear as though Simms died immediately after the fall.

The examiner stated that it was difficult to tell exactly how long Simms survived before succumbing to her injuries, but that there was evidence that Simms did at least try to get herself to the phone to summon help.

At this time, officials are saying that there is nothing suspicious about the death, and it has been ruled accidental, but could not comment on the reason the front door was open.

Greta put her hand to her mouth and stifled a gasp, "Oh my God, how awful. That poor woman." She thought about the day that she'd dropped Bastian off. She'd been so happy to see him.

How awful it must have been for her to lay there broken and in pain with no one to help her. She wondered if that was the reason Cora hadn't answered the phone when she called. It made her sick to her stomach to think of her laying there as Greta was trying to call, and that she and Bastian were probably the last people to see her alive.

Putting the paper aside, she took her coffee cup and tossed the last drops of cold liquid into the sink.

She'd planned to spend the day cleaning out some of Bastian's unused toys, but it looked as though she'd be making a trip to the police station instead. At least she could clear up the mystery of why the door had been left open, knowing that Bastian was the most likely cause.

"Bastian," Greta whispered, quietly opening the door to his bedroom, not wanting to wake him too abruptly and risk putting him in a foul mood. "It's time to get up."

She shouldn't have worried about making him grumpy. Bastian jumped out of bed with unusual enthusiasm, pulled the blankets up and over his pillow and pushed past her, heading towards the kitchen. She found him, a few moments later, already dragging his chair over to the cupboards to reach his favorite cereal.

"I'll get that for you today, Bastian," Greta offered, reaching over his head to get the Lucky Charms he insisted upon having morning after morning.

"I'm sorry to have to tell you, but I have some very sad

news," Greta told him with reservation, as she poured the cereal into a bowl and added milk.

She thought it would be a good opportunity to bring up the subject of death, though it certainly wasn't a pleasant topic. He was a little young, but she was going to have to tell him eventually, anyway.

She was around five when she first remembered learning about death. Her mother told her that everything and everyone died.

They had been on a walk and saw a dead squirrel in the middle of the road, that day. Greta wanted to pick it up and bring it home and make it better, but her mom explained that it wouldn't get better because it had died. Greta asked what 'died' meant, and her mom explained that it had gone to the sky to be with someone named God, and wouldn't run around anymore and play. It didn't make sense to her, at the time, because she could see the squirrel, so to her, it hadn't *gone* anywhere. She hoped that Bastian would have an easier time with *her* explanation.

Bastian had already brought his chair back to the table, and was tearing through the newspaper she'd left there.

As usual, he was ignoring her and had thrown all of the pages to the floor except for the National Weather map, which was always on the last page. Greta watched as he ran his fingers over the lines, tracing the states carefully. She wondered for a moment just how much he'd really understand.

"Mrs. Simms died yesterday," she told him sadly, sitting down in the chair across from him at the table.

When he didn't say anything, she asked, "Do you know what that means?" She was hoping that he wouldn't be too upset with the explanation and want to stay home from school.

"In any war, there are always casualties on both sides," Bastian stated blandly, looking up from the map only briefly, before pushing it aside to focus on the cereal bowl. He quickly singled out the marshmallows and slurped them from his spoon messily, dribbling milk down his chin.

Greta should have guessed that his reaction would be completely out of the ballpark. Bastian was weird. Plain and simple. It seemed that no matter what was presented to him, his reaction would shock and disturb her.

"We're not playing war today, Bastian," Greta replied dryly, "I was being serious. Cora fell down her stairs, broke her leg and died." It came out a little harsher than she had originally intended, but he didn't seem to care at all.

"Okay," he chirped. "I have to go get my pictures. I have to bring them to school today." Without any show of emotion for the woman he'd been so adamant to spend time with just a few days before, he pushed the bowl away, jumped down from his chair, and headed to his room.

Greta decided to let it drop. She could see there would be no point in pushing the issue. Either he didn't get the seriousness of the situation, or he simply didn't care. She would only frustrate herself by continuing with the subject.

Sighing, Greta went to his room to make sure he picked appropriate attire for school, and found him trying to cram both of the paintings that Cora had given him into his backpack.

"Bastian, you're not bringing those paintings to school. They're too big for you to carry, and they won't let you get on the bus with them."

"Then I won't take the bus. You will drive me. I need to bring them because I have to use them today."

"I honestly don't have the energy for this today, Bastian. You're not taking them, and I'm definitely not driving you. I have something I have to do this morning. Put them down and get dressed, you're going to be late," Greta told him firmly.

"I am bringing them," he sassed back, still trying to fit the largest one into the pack. "You go and get dressed. I'm going be late, like you said," he bossed smartly.

Greta silently counted to ten in her head. She could feel the stress working into her shoulders, tightening them and making her head ache. Bastian had a way of making her feel like she wanted to strangle him, and she'd made a pact with herself never to touch him in anger again.

"Enough, Bastian." She grabbed a clean shirt and pair of pants from his orderly dresser and threw them at him. "Put these on and let's get going. Now," she told him forcefully.

"No," he told her, holding his ground.

She hated to do it, but really didn't have a choice. Greta picked up the clothes she'd thrown at him and wrestled him out of his pajamas.

He struggled, trying to kick her, but she held him fast, forced each little arm into a sleeve, and did the same with his bottoms, being careful not to hurt him in the process.

When she finished, she picked him up and carried him out to the living room under her arm, and once again used force to put on his coat and shoes, as Bastian dug at her arms and kicked at her. He began loudly reciting the surrounding towns and city streets.

Still holding him tightly, Greta snatched his lunch off the counter and carried him to the bus, which was already patiently waiting, and deposited him at the door.

Satisfied that he was safely on the bus and feeling a bit

smug that she hadn't given in, Greta went to get ready.

Greta sat timidly in the crowded, noisy visitor's area of the Brighton Police Department, waiting for a detective that had the time to speak with her.

It was clear that they'd been busy the night before, and were still working on the residual cases they hadn't been able to get to yet.

A disheveled man sat next to her reeking of stale alcohol and cigarettes. He randomly blurted things out to no one in particular, slurring his words and dribbling spit as he spoke.

"Bitch don't know nothing! Tell me she's gonna throw my ass in jail. I'll throw her big fat ass in jail." He swayed to the side and wiped clumsily at a bit of spit that had landed on his cheek as he spoke.

Greta tried to inch away from him, but found the company on the other side to be just as bad. A large breasted woman in a skimpy mini skirt, low cut shirt, and smudged red lipstick was entertaining a man across the room by inching her skirt up.

He smirked, and waggled his eyebrows, egging her on.

The woman elbowed Greta accidentally, but instead of apologizing, gave Greta a look of contempt before continuing with her show.

"Ms. Hall?" A voice yelled over the noise.

Greta's head snapped up. Thank God! She was grateful to see that someone had finally come to get her. She was starting to worry for her safety, sitting out there will all those creeps.

"I'm sorry that it's so crazy out there today. It's been nuts around here lately. I don't know what's going on, but geez Louise we've been busy," the officer complained as Greta followed him. He led her down a long, narrow hallway, lined with framed pictures and awards, and into a tiny, overly warm office.

He motioned for Greta to sit. There were two guest chairs, and she chose the one that didn't look quite as beaten up and dirty as the other. The old wooden furnishings had probably made their way around the station, and had definitely seen better days.

"What brings you in today?" He took off his glasses and rubbed tiredly at his eyes.

"Well, I feel kind of foolish now for even coming in with this. I can see that you're all very busy. I probably should've just called," Greta began nervously. "It's just that I read in the paper this morning that Cora Simms passed away, and that when the officers arrived, they found her front door open."

"Yes, that's a fact. Did you know Cora, ma'am?" he asked.

"Not very well. It's a long story. My son, Bastian and I went to a yard sale of hers not too long ago. She became rather fond of him, Bastian, that is, and asked that I bring him back to see her sometime. You see, she'd given him this painting..."

"Painting? Did you say painting?" the officer interrupted. He straightened up with sudden interest, and put his glasses back on. He took out a pen and a pad of yellow lined paper and looked at Greta inquisitively.

"Well, yes. You see, at the yard sale, Bastian fell in love with a painting that she had for sale. When I wouldn't buy it for him, she insisted on giving it to him."

"Can you describe this painting, ma'am?" he asked, as he

poised the pen over the paper. Greta wondered what the painting would have to do with anything.

"Umm, well, it was a big painting. It had a large wooden frame. Actually, it was very ugly," Greta chuckled nervously, "Even Cora said so herself. But that's not really why I'm…"

The officer interrupted again, "How large would you say the painting was, if you had to guess? Eight by ten? Maybe eleven by thirteen?" he suggested, clearly becoming much more interested with Greta's visit.

"Oh, I don't know, but much bigger than that. It was at least three feet by, oh I'd say two and a half," Greta guessed, and used her hands to show the size the way she remembered it. "But what does the painting have to do with anything?" then laughed with a sudden thought. "Was it stolen?" she asked incredulously.

"No, no, nothing like that." He chuckled lightheartedly. "One of her sons, Markus, I believe, called in yesterday. He flew home to settle his mother's affairs and close up the house. Told me that a painting was missing from the basement. Said his mom loved that painting. It was supposed to be his when his folks passed away. Thought maybe it'd been stolen, and wanted to call and report it, especially since he'd been told about the front door. I thought for a minute that you were going to clear up that mystery, but from how you described the one she gave to your son, it couldn't be the same one," he stated, disappointed, putting the pen back down onto the desk.

"Well, actually," Greta began again slowly, "Bastian asked a few days ago if he could go over and visit Cora. I had some errands to run so I called and asked if she wanted to watch him for a while. She was more than happy to do it, the sweet woman, and so I dropped him off with her for a while. When I finished doing what I had to do, I tried to call, to tell her that I would be by to get him, but she didn't answer. I decided to go home first and let them visit a bit longer, but when I got there, I found Bastian."

The officer looked confused, "So what you're telling me, is that Cora brought Bastian back to your house and was waiting there for you when you got home?" he asked, obviously beginning to lose interest.

"No, Cora wasn't there. Just Bastian. He said that she'd fallen asleep and that he'd gotten bored and walked home by himself. Of course I was horrified, you see, Bastian is only four and he has autism," she stated, and thinking once again about all of the things that could have happened to him, shivered a little.

"So, I guess I'm confused as to why you're here? Are you here to report that Cora was clearly unfit to babysit your son? The woman is dead, so there's really nothing I can do," the officer told her with an air of annoyance.

Greta felt her cheeks redden. "No, not at all. While I was a bit upset that Cora fell asleep on the job, if that's what you'd call it, I was only here to tell you that *if* the front door had been left open, then it was probably Bastian who left it that way. I believe he may have been the last visitor she had," she stated defensively, wishing, all of a sudden, that she hadn't come. "My son has a hard time remembering to close doors, and as a matter of fact, when I got home that day, I thought I had an intruder because my front door was open," she explained further.

"Oh!" The officer exclaimed, finally finding the point to Greta's visit. "I see. Well, that clears that up. You know? You're probably right. Well, good. Okay. I'm glad you came

in. At least I can finish up that section of my report anyway."
The officer stood, stretched his back and rotated his head
side to side, which made a loud cracking noise. He held out
his hand to shake Greta's.

He looked at her expectantly when she didn't get up.
"Was there something else?"

"Well, you mentioned that other painting and I might be
able to clear that up as well. The day that Bastian walked
home from Cora's house, I emptied out the backpack he
brought with him, and I did find a small painting inside. It
was about ten by thirteen. When I questioned him about it,
later on, he told me that Cora gave it to him."

The officer sat back down, "Ah, well. I guess that does
clear that up. How attached would you say Bastian is to
that painting?" He smiled, hesitantly.

"He'll get over it," Greta scoffed. "I'll go get it and bring
it down so you can give it to Cora's son. He should have it.
Anyway, it would most certainly mean more to him than it
would to Bastian."

"I'm sure Markus will appreciate it very much. Thank
you. He was pretty upset about it. Thanks again for taking
the time to come in. Looks like I'll be able to close this case
for good." He stood as Greta did, and reached out once again
to shake her hand.

Driving home, Greta was grateful that Bastian was at
school. She didn't want to have to deal with how mad he'd
be if she had to forcibly take the painting away from him.
This way she could just do it and explain what happened
later.

Kristy Gherlone

He'd be mad for sure, she thought, pulling into the driveway, but too bad. Another life lesson for him.

Damn front door! She thought angrily, slamming the car door, instantly mad at Bastian. She could see right off that it had been left open again, but then remembered that she'd been the last one to leave.

There was no way he could've walked home from school, she thought, relieved. Then she wondered briefly if she should be.

Taking a cautious first step into the house, she was glad to find nothing out of place. Everything was exactly the way she'd left it, except she couldn't remember leaving the cereal cupboard in the kitchen wide open. She went to close it and saw that Bastian's Lucky Charms were gone. Had she used up the box that morning? Well, there certainly wasn't a neighborhood cereal thief that she'd heard of, she laughed to herself. She'd have to put them on the shopping list and call a locksmith.

On the way to Bastian's room to gather up the painting, she saw that her answering machine's light was blinking. Pushing the button to listen in case it was the school, she was surprised to hear that it was her boss.

"Greta, sorry to bother you on your day off, but could you please give me a call when you get the chance? There's been a break-in at the lab. Some of the materials that you've been working with are missing. I don't think I need to tell you how dangerous that could be. Just give me a call okay?"

Oh my God, Greta thought. She always knew that this was a possibility someday with all of the terrorist activity.

The experiments that she'd been doing were classified, so no one could possibly know how they worked, and if they did, she was fairly certain they wouldn't want to take the risk. She felt herself relax a bit, knowing that no one in the United States had access to the Nitrolite needed to make the bomb work.

Used in combination with the other materials, the reaction it produced could be devastating and would kill thousands of people, but without it, the others chemicals were fairly harmless.

She only received a small quantity of Nitrolite, which she'd mostly used up in the testing phases. She still had a tiny bit, but it was locked in a vaulted safe.

The chemicals were all stored apart and unlabeled, thus eliminating the possibility that they could be identified, or that anyone would guess that they were to be used in conjunction with each other.

Of course, the Alpha One team retained a small quantity to be doled out as budgeting allowed. The amounts together would be enough to do a great deal of damage, but there was really no way anyone outside of the Department of Defense could know that.

No one had the code to her locked safe but her, and even if someone did manage to break in, the little bit she did have would only be able to produce a whiff of smoke.

Besides, the only place to get more of the material was in Russia, and they were damn near impossible to barter with, plus they had no idea what it was being used for, or what it reacted with.

It was probably just some dumb kids hoping to get high by mixing the contents of whatever they'd found. The internet was a lovely tool for making people believe that anyone could become a home pharmacist.

Satisfied with her thought process and the painting now forgotten, she grabbed her keys off the counter where she had thrown them only moments before. No doubt Jack would be at the lab with the Federal Agents who would definitely be combing the place. She'd have to give them a complete inventory.

Racing out of the house, she didn't hear the phone ring once again.

❖

"Greta! Thank God you're here!" Jack met Greta as she walked into the lab.

As she expected, the place was alive with police officers and Federal Agents.

"I came as soon as I heard your message. So what did they take?" she asked, immediately heading over to her station to take stock.

The lab was a mess of broken glass and strewn about papers. Greta walked carefully over the littered floor, trying not to cut her feet.

She could see that the locked refrigeration units had been broken into. The unwanted contents were knocked over, and some were still leaking fluid onto the tiled floor.

"They took pretty much everything of any value. Everything you were working on," Jack informed her, following her as she inspected the damage. "Including what you had in the safe," he told her solemnly, and stopped, placing a light hand on her shoulder.

"What did they do? Rip it out of the wall?" Greta asked surprised.

"No, someone apparently opened it using the combination."

"That's impossible," Greta insisted, not believing it. "No

one had the combination but me, and I keep the code locked up in my safe at home."

"Greta, stop for right now. We have to talk," he told her, giving her a look that suddenly made her uncomfortable.

She'd never seen him like that before. The usually stoic man was a mess. There had to be more going on than she knew.

Following him reluctantly in to his office, she closed the door behind her.

Motioning her to sit, he began, "The Federal Agents are going to be speaking with you soon, and I want this to come from me first. I owe you that much at least," he said with reservation.

"Okay," Greta muttered nervously, "What's going on?"

"The chemical that you've been working with, the Nitrolite, didn't come from Russia, and isn't exactly what you thought it was."

"What?" Greta stood up abruptly and angrily, getting ready to give him a piece of her mind.

"Sit down!" he yelled, pointing to the chair again. "Before you launch into a speech about ethics and safety protocols, I want you to know that it wasn't my idea. I had no choice."

"What do you mean you had no choice?" Greta was furious, and rightfully so. It was of the utmost importance that a scientist knew each and every component of the material they were working with to avoid dangerous fumes, fires, and burns. He knew better than that. He put her at risk, and he had no business playing with her safety like that!

"If it's not what I thought, then what the hell is it? Exactly what the hell have I been working with here these last couple of months?" She watched as Jack seemed to struggle with what he was about to say. It must be pretty bad, she thought. He looked like he was about to be sick.

"Look, the Alpha One Team brought me in on this a while back. They presented me with an ultimatum, and unfortunately, it wasn't a very good one. You either worked on this project or they were shutting us down. The problem was that I couldn't tell anyone, including you, what the project was. I couldn't tell you what it was made up of, or what its intended use was for. It was classified. They cautioned me that if I told anyone, anyone at all about it, they would pull the funding and we would both be out of a job. I don't know about you, but I'm not in a position to lose my job."

Greta glared at him, feeling like her head would explode in anger.

"They assured me that you wouldn't be in any danger," he offered.

"I understand that you wouldn't want to lose your job, but to tell you the truth, I'd rather be alive and without a job than dead. They had no way of knowing what I would try or how it would react. They gave you assurances that they didn't have any business giving. Jesus, Jack, I have a child. What in the hell did you expose me to?"

"Nitrolite is a two-part explosive with some pretty serious residual side effects to the victims that manage to survive the blast. You were chosen to work on this because you're good at your job. You have a knack for identifying the contaminants that could potentially cause a bomb to fail. You are very good at making a neat bomb, at isolating the usable components, and identifying potential barriers, leaving it clean, if you will. You should be proud that your work has been recognized by the government and that they came to us with this," he offered hopefully, but Greta wasn't buying it.

Proud? She was still way too angry, "I don't understand why they would tell you, but feel it necessary to keep me out of the loop. They value my work, but they can't trust me with the information I needed to do my job? It doesn't make any sense, and you still haven't told me what the hell we are dealing with here. I want to know if in a couple of months I'm going to come down with cancer or some other illness." She watched as he squirmed, struggling uncomfortably in his chair. Beads of sweat trickled down his forehead. He pulled a tissue out of a box and dabbed at them.

"The fact of the matter is, Greta, they simply wanted to keep you out of the loop because you're a woman." Jack chucked the tissue into the trash and held up his hands to silence her before she could begin, "Yes, you're a very gifted scientist, but you're a woman and you're a mother. Two very good reasons why they didn't feel they could tell you everything. Before you start accusing me of being sexist, the hard facts are that women, especially mothers, are more prone to falter on matters like this when it comes right down to it. They didn't think you would work on it if you knew what it was. It's that simple."

"For Christ's sake, Jack, tell me what it is, so that I can formulate my own opinions. It can't do any harm for me to know now. It's gone!" Greta's voice rose, as her patience dwindled even further.

"Well, you know the frustration that you've been having at not being able to rid the Nitrolite of that unknown compound that you kept finding on your test results?" he asked.

"Yes, it's been driving me crazy and you know that. If you tell me that you've known all this time what it is, I'm going to quit right now!" Greta threatened. It had been driving her nuts for months, because no matter what she used, no matter what she tried, it kept popping back up. She could get rid of it briefly only to do another test and there it was, multiplied. It had been extremely frustrating.

"You couldn't get rid of it because it was meant to be there. It wasn't meant to be stripped. They know how good you are at your job, and that you would find it and try to destroy it, so it was designed to stay. You were just supposed to get rid of everything else, leaving the clean bomb and that component."

"Come on, Jack! Tell me what it is before I lose my mind!" Greta demanded.

"The bomb you've been working on is perhaps the most ingenious bomb of all time, and probably the most disturbing bit of weaponry ever built. Made to be compact so it won't be large enough to kill off the compound within, it gets placed in a special unit that's been embedded into concrete and surrounded by amber, which absorbs some of the shock and makes it undetectable by dogs and scans. The bomb explodes upwards, instead of outward, which keeps the blast radius small, let's say a radius of less than a square mile. It's designed to kill by explosion, just like all bombs, but during detonation, it also releases your unknown compound into the air. It adheres to the victims that didn't die in the initial blast." He paused, but cautiously continued.

"The compound, which they have nick-named 'Spade' pretty much does just that. It renders all of the surviving victims unable to reproduce. Worse, they unwittingly carry it home with them. It imbeds into their skin and is later secreted through bodily fluid. They're meant to pass it on to their relatives, like rats carrying poison back into their nests. A whole population of people completely sterile. No way to carry on their genes."

"Oh my God, Jack. That is probably the most horrible and unethical thing I have ever heard," Greta declared in shock, trying to think of what reasons there could possibly be to want to do something like that.

"There's more," he stated blandly.

Greta didn't know if she wanted to hear more. The government had come up with some pretty awful means of torture in the name of war, but this was, by far, the worst she'd heard of yet. They were right about one thing, if she'd been asked to do this willingly, the answer would've been no. Not just because she was a woman, but also because it was wrong on so many levels.

He continued despite the look of horror on Greta's face. "'Spade' can be manufactured to sterilize certain gene sets. For instance, if it ever came down to where we were in imminent danger of World War III, and our biggest foe was, let's say, the Muslims, they could tailor the compound to target people who are only Muslim. That way if our soldiers were caught in the cross fire, it wouldn't hurt them. They'd be able to go on and reproduce, but..."

"Not the Muslims," Greta finished for him, starting to get the idea. The whole thing was disgusting.

"You see, you know as well as I do that with the production of nuclear bombs, if it ever came down to another war, a lot of people would die. Perhaps everyone would die, I don't know. But with this bomb, we would be able to effectively stop the offending nation at its roots. The entire mindset of those people would eventually be wiped out. If they can't have children, then they can't teach hate and violence. No matter what has been tried in the past, people always hide, always persevere. This way, even with one bomb, maybe a few carefully placed, they get everyone, eventually."

"You sound like you're condoning this! You can't tell me that you agree with this, Jack. It's not right! You're not closed minded enough to think that every single person within a race thinks exactly the same. That every one of them would do the same things, have the same ideals. We are scientists, not God! We have no right deciding who lives and who dies!" Greta cried.

"Don't give me that, Greta. We play God every day. If we didn't, then every single person who got cancer would die," he defended loudly, but then softened.

"If this whole ridiculous idea didn't come from the Russians, who did it come from? Do I need to worry about my heritage now? Am I at risk because I'm German?" Greta scoffed, still outraged.

"No! No. You're not at risk. I would never have agreed to this if you were in any danger," he told her with apologetic conviction.

"If not me, then who? The Muslims? Was this supposed to be some kind of punishment for 9/11?"

"No. It came from the Germans. Your heritage," he answered, with misplaced satisfaction.

The realization hit her all at once. "When are they going to leave those poor people alone? Haven't they suffered enough?" Greta asked incredulously, remembering all that she had ever heard about World War II. The Jews again. The Germans just couldn't leave it alone.

"Is that what it's set to now? Is it carrying Jewish genes?" Jack gave her a small nod, "Well, then, I'm glad that I failed at this job. I'm glad that I couldn't find the right vehicle to drive that bomb. I never could get the formula right, and without a good mix, I'm happy to say that it won't work. Whoever has stolen it has wasted their time," she promised with self-satisfaction. She wouldn't have been able to live with herself knowing that she had helped to create such a vicious weapon.

"There's more," Jack said again, with resounding apprehension.

"Oh my God, what now?" Greta asked, on edge once more.

"It turns out that the Alpha One Team was going to shut us down anyway. They don't need us anymore."

"Oh? Why? Did they find something even more gruesome to kill people with?" Greta asked quickly. At that point she didn't care what the answer was. This wasn't her responsibility. She was done. She started to get up, still stunned.

"It turns out that they had other people working on it as well, not just us. Someone just came up with it faster," he told her.

Greta sat back down and practically snorted, "Who? Hitler's nephew?" It was meant as a joke, but neither of them laughed.

"No," he gulped.

"Who?" she asked again, but it wasn't a question, it was an order.

"Oddly, it was a child. An autistic boy," he answered, looking at Greta with regret.

"Who? Where?" she gasped, genuinely surprised.

"He was a student at the Weisenhoff School. A friend of

Bastian's, I believe. Kurt. He mentioned him when you brought him here. He's really quite brilliant, they've told me. They gave him the project about a month after they gave it to us, but with the help of the staff, he was able to solve it faster. Of course they needed your expertise in cleaning it up, but he made it. They tell me that it's probably the most flawless piece of work they've ever seen."

"Jesus. Does anyone have any kind of conscience? A kid for Christ's sake?" she asked in horror. She knew it was a mistake to send Bastian there.

"I don't want to tell you this, Greta, but I also have some other bad news." He looked at her nervously. "Kurt's parents were murdered this afternoon. Kurt is missing. Major Barnes, his wife, they're all missing."

Bastian!

"I have to go." Greta got up quickly, grabbing her coat. "I need to go check on Bastian."

"Wait!" Jack pleaded before she had the chance to get out the door, "The agents need to question you!"

"No. I'm going to check on my son. You answer their damn questions. You seem to have all of the answers. Consider this my resignation!" she snapped, not slowing down a bit. Bastian had been a huge pain lately, but he was her son and she loved him. If anything ever happened to him...

Greta ran to her car. She was going to Bastian's school. She needed to see for herself that he was okay.

What if they had taken him, as well? Panic seized her. She jumped into the driver's seat. She could barely put the keys in the ignition because her hands were shaking so badly.

Once she was finally able to start the car, she threw it

into reverse and narrowly missed a startled pedestrian. She gave a hasty wave of apology before speeding in reverse out of the parking spot.

No, she rationalized. Why would they take *him*? He didn't know anything about bombs. Geography and the populations of cities would hardly be considered valuable. Still, she drove quickly out of the lot, and didn't even bother to stop at the stop sign.

❖

Getting to the school in record time, Greta didn't even notice the absence of school buses, or that there were hardly any vehicles in the parking lot. She hurried inside, only then noticing the silent hallways and seemingly empty school.

Terror washed over her as she hurried down the hall to Bastian's classroom, only to find it dark and the door locked. She looked at her watch. Maybe she was she so wrapped up in the events at the lab that she forgot the time?

No, he should still be there.

Confused, Greta ran back down the hall towards the main office, and was relieved to see the school's director, Kim, just locking her door.

"Greta?" she asked, surprised when she saw her coming towards her. "Did Bastian forget something?"

"Forget something? What are you talking about? Where's Bastian?" Panic seized her once again.

"What do you mean? We called everyone this morning. When we didn't get any answer at your house, we left a message. When Bastian's grandmother arrived to get him, we naturally assumed that you'd gotten it."

She must be mistaken; there had to be a mix up, Greta thought with hope.

"Everyone was so upset after Miss Carol was found dead in her car this morning. No one can believe that she overdosed. No one even knew that she was taking anti-depressants. We called in a sub to help with the class, but all of the kids were so shaken up, and then with the news of poor Kurt, we thought it best to just to send everyone home early."

Greta's brain tried to process all of the information correctly, but it had become clear that she was missing key pieces of the story. She'd never gotten a message. She had no idea about Miss Carol or anything else until Jack told her about Kurt.

"Kim, Bastian doesn't have any grandparents. Miss Carol knew that. I thought you knew that. Please tell me that you made a mistake. Where is Bastian?" she asked quavering, on the verge of tears.

"Well, I don't know," Kim stammered, as she attempted to unlock her door again with fumbling fingers. "When I asked the substitute if everyone had gotten picked up, she informed me that Bastian was still waiting. Finally, a woman came and claimed she was his grandma. He was very excited to see her. He even called her mother, which I thought was odd, but everyone has different names for their grandparents!" she said defensively.

"Oh my God. That woman wasn't his grandmother. Did she use the sign out sheet?" she asked hopefully. There had to be an explanation.

"She would've had to. We make everyone who isn't a parent sign the students out. That's what I'm going to check," she faltered, finally getting the lock.

Grabbing the clipboard off the wall by her desk, she flipped through the pages until she found the day's sheet.

"Here it is," she cried, pointing to a shaky signature, scribbled in the midst of many other names.

Magdalena H.

Chapter Twenty-Two

K elly awoke after a night of strange and unsettling dreams. She knew that Helga gave some of them to her, to better cement her understanding of what they were up against.

She'd witnessed events that took place so long ago, the people she walked among in her sleep would all be dead.

In a way, it was somehow fantastical to be a spectator in a crowd gathered to hear Adolph Hitler speak.

While she didn't feel intimidated by him in that dream, the words he shouted out to the people were fraught with hate and violence. He was clearly demented. His jerky movements, the pacing, and his erratic eyes gave him the appearance of a caged animal. He was a skinny, wounded creature, with no hope of freedom.

Kelly found it enlightening to witness all of it firsthand. History books did not, nor could they have, accurately described the feeling among the people there.

The smell of sweat, the stench of death, the nervous excitement, and the horrible, grinding desperation was prevalent. It was in every corner of her dream. It washed over her, almost pulling her in. Kelly could almost see the fear rising up from the spectators.

If fear had a color, it could have been seen floating up and swirling in the air above them. It had a hum all its own.

It vibrated through every single one of those people.

Kelly would have seen it floating up from Adolph, as well. It would have been so bright that the people in the crowd wouldn't have been able to see around it.

It was that woman. Magdalena. She stood stoically next to Adolph as he spoke.

Her eyes were beautiful, but they were also daggers. Deep blue pools piercing a sea of black and white. They demanded notice. They demanded compliance. They willed the audience to follow and threatened harm to those who would defy.

Perhaps because she wasn't a resident of the era, merely a bystander of time, Kelly was able to see past the façade into someplace deeper. When she looked beyond Magdalena's aura, she saw shame. It cast a dark glow that entombed her whole body. It caused a loneliness within her that would never seek companionship. It made Kelly want to weep.

She understood then why Helga couldn't hurt her. She'd seen past her aura too.

It was obvious to Kelly that Magdalena had suffered a great deal. She wore her pain on the inside. Her aura hid it away and shielded it with hate so that no one would know. Whatever it was that she'd been through had altered her path forever.

Kelly noticed the faint lines, invisible to the others, stretching between the two. Something holding fast a connection that could not be cut. He was a puppet and she was the master. She could make him do whatever she wanted.

The last dream she remembered was a dream of flight. She used to welcome those dreams, when she was a little girl. That butterfly feeling in her belly, soaring over the treetops.

This one was different. It was a long journey, and in her dream she couldn't get home. When she looked down at her body, it was old and wrinkled. She was too tired to make it back home. Her wings were broken.

Shaking off the weirdness of the night, Kelly willed herself to get out of bed.

She had some thinking to do. Bastian and Greta would be expecting her, but there was no way she could go, knowing all that she did. If Bastian even suspected all that she had learned, someone could get hurt.

However, if she could ask him some questions, maybe he could tell her what was going to happen.

It was confusing. She still had a life. She still had a job, still had school, but none of it seemed very important now. It was all just trivial nonsense that didn't matter in the grand scheme of things. What was going on was far more important, and could not be ignored.

She'd been brought into something bigger, and until it was taken care of, she wouldn't be able to return to her normal life.

Until she was able to figure out why the people from the urns had returned, she'd have to focus her attention on that, and forget everything else.

Helga had asked her to be watchful. That was something she could start right then, she thought. She grabbed her laptop off her bedroom floor where she'd left it the day before. She went straight to Yahoo, as they always seemed to have the most current events, but nothing came up that seemed too alarming. Nothing had happened yet, as far as she could tell, and that was a good thing.

She would need to call Greta and tell her that she wouldn't be coming, and after that she would try to figure out the next step.

"Hello?" Greta answered on the first ring, sounding breathless and excitable.

"Hi Greta. It's Kelly." She didn't have the chance to say more.

"Kelly! Have you heard? I don't know what to do! They won't tell me anything. They told me to come back to the house and wait for someone to call or for Bastian to come home, but I have been up all night and no one is saying anything. I'm so scared!" Greta began to cry hard, making it impossible for Kelly to question her until she calmed.

Kelly couldn't understand what was going on. Bastian was gone?

"Greta, I haven't heard anything. Is Bastian missing?" Kelly asked incredulously.

"Haven't you seen the news? It's all over the local stations. Bastian was taken yesterday. Some woman went into his school and signed him out. She told them that she was his grandmother. They took Kurt too and killed his parents. An Amber Alert was issued, but no one has called. No one has seen them!" she cried.

I should have checked the local news, Kelly thought. For whatever reason, she'd decided that if something big were to happen, it wouldn't be local. So stupid!

"Oh my God, Greta! No, I hadn't heard! What are they doing to find him? Do you have any idea where they could've gone?" Kelly's reasons for asking didn't have anything to do with Bastian's welfare at the moment. If they'd taken Bastian and Kurt, then most likely they were needed for something.

Quickly putting two and two together, she knew that there would be no reason to take two autistic children unless they were going to use them for their cause. That was what Helga warned her about. The children were made to carry out what Magdalena and Adolph hadn't been able to. The men from the urns would guide them.

"I'll be right over, Greta, calm down. We'll figure this out," she told her, and trying not to panic, began cramming her feet into her shoes.

"Thank you, Kelly. I know that I haven't been very nice to you, but I really could use a friend right now. Someone who cares about Bastian as much as I do." Greta sniffled, on the verge of tears once again.

Not thinking clearly, Kelly tried calling Helga, but then remembered that she and the professor were probably already on the plane. Throwing her cell phone on the seat, she jumped in her car and sped on towards Greta's.

"I just don't know what to do." Greta met Kelly at the door. She reached out and caught her in a desperate hug, and held tight for support.

She was a mess, and Kelly couldn't blame her. Her son was missing, and though she knew how difficult their relationship had been lately, she also knew that Greta loved him very much.

Kelly went to the cupboard and gathered the things necessary to make tea. Greta sat with a defeated thump into one of the kitchen chairs and began repeating the same words over and over again, "Why Bastian? Why would they take Bastian? He's just a little boy."

Kelly poured the hot tea into mugs, set one before Greta, and then sat herself.

"Start from the beginning, Greta. Tell me everything that happened." Kelly didn't want to seem impatient, knowing how difficult it must've been for Greta, but the sooner Greta told her everything, the sooner she might be able to figure out what was going on. She needed to find them and stop whatever it was from happening.

Greta looked up, as though just remembering that Kelly was there, and began. "I got a call from work. I was supposed to have the day off. My boss told me that the lab had been broken into. I had to go and see what was taken. When I got there, my boss told me about Kurt, and I don't know, I panicked and went to Bastian's school, but they told me that his grandmother had picked him up, but you know, Kelly, Bastian doesn't have any grandparents, so I knew something was wrong," she blurted, beginning to cry again.

The whole thing was not making sense to Kelly. If the lab had been broken into, why would her boss tell her about one of Bastian's friends? It seemed unrelated.

"Greta, why would your boss tell you about Kurt? What would that have to do with anything? Tell me everything and try not to leave anything out. It could be important."

Though she looked confused, Greta began again, "I'd been working on a formula for a bomb. I couldn't get it right. The government was getting mad that it was taking so long. They'd been pushing me for weeks. That's why I had to get babysitters, that's why I couldn't be here with Bastian," Greta cried out, defensively.

"I know, I know." Kelly patted Greta's arm sympathetically. "Go on. It's okay."

Greta got up and took a tissue from the box on the bar,

and after blowing her nose noisily, began again. "The people who broke into the lab stole the main component. When I reminded my boss that it wouldn't work without the driver, he said that Kurt figured it out. Figured it out at that damn school. The Weisenhoff School. Kelly, did you know that they were getting those kids to help them make bombs and God knows what else? They were using those kids because they're all so smart. He told me that the teachers are all gone too, Kelly. I think they took my son. One of those people has Bastian, I know it," she accused miserably, as the tears began again.

Kelly was floored! No, she hadn't known any of that, but after what Helga had told her, it didn't surprise her. She was sure it had to be part of the plan.

Kelly shook her head in disbelief. There would be no way to explain all that was going on to Greta. She'd never be able to handle it.

"What I don't get is what they would want with Bastian. He was smart, but really only at cartography. He certainly couldn't have been any use at all. The only thing I can think of at all is that maybe Kurt asked to bring a friend. Maybe he wouldn't go along without his friend." She began sobbing in earnest. "I'm such a bad mother that I never even let Bastian have his friend over to play." Kelly got up and rushed over to give Greta a comforting hug.

"You're not a bad mother, Greta. I know how much trouble Bastian has been lately. It must be hard to have to work and raise a son all on your own. Please don't blame yourself," Kelly soothed.

When Greta calmed, again Kelly asked, "Is there anything else, anything at all that you can think of?"

"Not that I can think of. Well, I don't think so anyway. I

just feel so bad because Bastian and I had a fight yesterday morning. The last time I saw him I practically threw him onto the school bus. He wanted to bring his stupid paintings to school, but I wouldn't let him. He told me that he was going to need them, but they were too big…" Greta rattled on, but something Bastian declared began to come back to Kelly. 'I do have special power eyes. That's how I can see that I'm going to New York soon. How come I can see the map but you and my mom can't?'

Kelly remembered the day that he'd proudly shown her his painting. He insisted that the painting was a map. A map of New York City!

"Have you checked, by any chance, to see if those paintings are still here?" Kelly asked cautiously.

"I'm sure they're still here. Why wouldn't they be? I put him on the bus myself without them. It's probably a good thing that I didn't let him. Cora's son wanted one of them back, so I came back home to get it and…" Greta stopped and suddenly got up. She had an odd expression on her face. "I was mad that when I got home, the front door was open. I blamed it on Bastian…" She suddenly stopped talking and quickly headed down the hallway towards Bastian's room. Kelly followed.

"They're gone!" Greta cried in surprise.

"Greta, I know that you're probably not supposed to tell me this, but that bomb, the one you were working on, just how big is it? What was it for?"

"It's a bomb. What in the hell do you think it does?" she uttered, and then began to cry again, "I'm sorry. It's just that… Oh, Kelly you have to believe me that I didn't know! If I'd been told what it was that I had been working on, I never would have done it, I swear…but it's more than that.

It's…" Greta stopped herself, and, placing a horrified hand over her mouth, tried to stifle her sobs.

"Go on, Greta, this is important. What else can it do?"

Greta looked down at her feet ashamedly, "It's designed to kill Jews. To wipe out their race by making them sterile. Once that bomb goes off, the component inside will spread to all of the Jews," she spat out.

Oh my God, Kelly thought. This was worse than she thought. She was going to have to get to New York City and stop them before they could plant that bomb!

"I have to go Greta. I know you don't want to hear this again today, but you should stay here in case Bastian does come back," Kelly advised, as she hurried toward the door.

"Where are you going? What's going on? Do you know how to find my son?" Greta asked desperately.

"I'm not sure. I think I do, but I have to leave now," she announced, running out to her car.

"Kelly, please bring back my son. Bring Bastian back to me!" she begged.

Kelly paused, "I will try, Greta, but right now that's all I can promise."

CHAPTER TWENTY-THREE

K elly needed to think, and think fast. It was obvious what the officers from the urns needed Kurt for. As for Bastian, she still hadn't figured that out.

He could see a map in that painting when she and his mom couldn't. There had to be something there that only he could see. He'd been so sure it was New York City, insisted on it, and they'd taken it. What did they need it for?

If Kurt had been born knowing how to work with bombs, then it would make sense he'd been born to make bombs. Bastian, on the other hand, had apparently been born knowing geography and was a gifted cartographer. He also knew populations, race...Of course! He knew how to find the Jews, she thought, but then quickly dispelled her own thinking. The Jewish people were practically everywhere. They couldn't possibly plant bombs in every city on earth. However, if what Greta told her was true, and it somehow blew out something that spread, they wouldn't need to plant very many. A few well-placed bombs in New York City could do a lot of damage.

With all of the security though, especially around New York since 9/11, she doubted they would be able to get very far with a bunch of bombs. Someone would surely notice and report it. There were screenings at the airports, train stations and subways.

But what if they didn't have to carry the actual bombs? Only the chemicals that...

It dawned on her all at once. They needed Bastian just as much as they needed Kurt.

Bastian knew where to find the bombs that were already there! He had the map, Kelly thought suddenly, and he could read it!

The bombs were already in place, they just needed to put something inside them to make them work. Maybe a liquid chemical. But where? How would she ever be able to find them in a city she'd only ever been to once?

Suddenly, it was as if Kelly was awakening from the reality of what her world had been. Her eyes, then fully opened, could see the world as it actually was. It was terrifying.

Taking the veil down that had always shielded her eyes, it hit her all at once. She never suspected any of the autistic kids because she hadn't wanted to. They'd all been innocents to her, and no matter what she had heard on the news, it hadn't been in her reality to suspect them.

She shunned magic because it hadn't been real to her. It was real, of that she was sure. She witnessed it many times, but her brain made it into something else. Something she could handle.

And the language! How many times had she heard the *Tungri* language, but her brain had rejected it because it hadn't made sense to her reality?

Helga knew all of it because, as she told her, she was 'of' that, and Kelly was not.

She could finally see all of it because it was reality. The way the world really was.

Helga may have been mute all of those years, but Kelly

had been blind and that was far worse!

A pain like a jolt of electricity suddenly shot through Kelly's temple, so intense that she grabbed her head and pulled over to the side of the road.

"Call to your young man, Kelly. Call to him now," Helga's voice rang out in her ears as loud as if she had been sitting right next to her.

A vision rocked her into a sudden convulsion. In the dream eyes, she could see a busy city street full of people. There was a building up ahead of her. People were lined up, waiting to get in. She could see signs, but they were too blurry to read.

Someone caught her hand and held it. She looked up to see who it was...

Jason! Of course! She had the answer all along.

"He always keeps his part of the building a secret until opening day," she remembered Jason saying. The bomb had been planted in the building Jason helped to design! That didn't make sense either, though. Why would they need Bastian if that autistic guy already knew where they were? However, Bastian *was* missing. They must need him for something. There really wasn't any other explanation. Suddenly she realized the opening was that night. She quickly looked at her watch. She didn't have much time.

A sudden noise startled her. Someone was banging on the window of her car.

"Are you okay? Do you need a doctor?" A concerned young man was motioning for Kelly to roll down her window.

Fully coming out of her vision, she realized how she must look. She rolled down the window.

"No, I'm fine. Thank you." Kelly could see his disbelief.

"I really am fine, just a headache. Thank you. I have to

go," she told him as she put the car into gear and drove away, almost hitting the confused man.

She dialed Jason's number and was relieved to hear him answer.

"This is Jason." He sounded clipped, hurried.

"Hi Jason, this is Kelly…"

"Kelly, I've been hoping that you'd call, but, unfortunately, I don't have time to talk right this minute. I'm sorry. Can I call you back some other time?" Something was wrong. He didn't sound at all like his usual upbeat self. She wondered for a minute if she was too late. Maybe the bomb already detonated!

"Wait! Am I still invited to the grand opening party of your building, because I'm headed to the airport. I can't explain right now, but you have to stall the opening!" There was a few seconds pause, making Kelly think that he'd hung up.

"Of course you're still invited, but it already has been stalled. Haven't you been listening to the news? Someone set off a bomb in one of our other buildings this morning. It killed about a half dozen people and wounded a bunch of others."

"Jesus! Where?"

"It was a synagogue in New Jersey. We just finished the construction last summer. It was full of Jewish people that were protesting the opening of the Holocaust Museum."

Bastian! Kelly thought frantically.

"Who was killed Jason, do you have any names?" Kelly asked desperately.

"No, they haven't released the names yet. We got an anonymous call about an hour ago from some crazy lady at an airport in Vienna saying that there was a bomb in our building too. The police are doing a sweep now. It's a mess. There are thousands of people waiting outside for us to open. A ton of people came from really far away, so they're working as quickly as they can to clear the building so that we can still open. The mayor made a promise that it will be opening today."

Kelly was relieved to hear that Helga had made it to Vienna safely, and knowing how much courage it must have taken for her to make that call made her heart swell with pride.

"Jason, can you meet me at the airport? You have to take me into the part of the building that the autistic guy designed."

"Kelly, what's this about?"

"Please, Jason. I don't have time for this. Just say you'll meet me."

"I can't make any promises, but I'll try. It's a mad house here. They might not let me leave."

Kelly wound her way through the heavy Boston traffic. She finally reached the airport, and after finding a place to park, rushed in to buy her ticket to New York. Thankfully, she got the last ticket on a flight departing in less than an hour.

After buckling her seat belt, she couldn't stop her mind from racing with horrible possibilities.

Greta had said "paintings". Somewhere along the way, Bastian had acquired another map. If the one he'd shown her was New York City then the other one had to have been New Jersey.

Feeling sure that they still needed Bastian to find the other bomb, Kelly relaxed just a bit. He was still alive. He was okay. She just hoped that Helga was making progress on her end. She'd been right that they were going to need all the luck they could get!

❖

Kelly wanted to rush off the plane as soon as it landed, but everyone was in the way, blocking her, blissfully unaware of the horror unfolding around them. She saw a few people who were most likely Jewish, and were probably headed for the museum opening, but there was no way to warn them. They would never believe her, and would probably report her to the authorities if she even tried.

Finally, she was able to disembark. The first thing she saw after she rushed down the gangway were the posters. Posters everywhere telling people, IF YOU SEE SOMETHING, SAY SOMETHING. Remnants of 9/11. It was sad, really, that the world had become such a place. As bad as 9/11 had been, though, people still lived, married, and had babies. They were able to rise up from that day and persevere.

The bomb that sat somewhere in Jason's building had the capability of wiping out an entire race of people forever.

She thought briefly of saying something, reporting what she knew, but quickly decided against it. They would detain her, and if they didn't believe her story, she'd never make it on time to try and stop it herself.

She scanned the crowd looking for Jason, but there were so many people.

Thinking that he might be waiting at the luggage carousel for her, not knowing that she didn't have any luggage, she started heading that way when her phone began to buzz in her pocket.

"Jason? Where are you?" she shouted, trying to be heard over all of the people.

"I'm sorry Kelly, but they cleared the building and my boss won't let me leave. I have to be here for the ribbon cutting. They're going to start letting people in soon. Take a cab to seventh and Main and I'll find you."

Shit! How was she going to find him in all of those people? She had to get there before they started letting people in. She needed to find Bastian and the people who took him, and stop them before they reached that bomb.

"Jason, try to stall them some more! Do you understand me? This is no joke! There's a bomb in that building! I can't tell you how I know, but I'm sure of it. You have to stall them!"

"Kelly, there is no bomb. They went over the building with a fine-toothed comb, and they didn't find anything. It's safe. There are armed officers everywhere. It's okay, really."

"There *is* a bomb Jason, I'm telling you! It's hidden somewhere in the part of the building that your autistic friend built. Please! You have to trust me on that!" Kelly cried in frustration. The people around her began to stare open mouthed in alarm. She lowered her voice.

"Please, Jason, just listen to me," she begged.

She had to get out of there and find a taxi quick! She began racing out towards the curb.

Kelly felt as though she were in the middle of a nightmare. It was as if she was trying to dial 911, but couldn't get through.

"Kelly, I can't stall the opening. It's clear, I'm telling you. Look I have to go, they're calling me up now. I'll see you soon. There's a side entrance on East Street. Go to that one and I'll come and find you as soon as I can."

There was nothing else she could say. He didn't believe her. Kelly hung up the phone and hailed a cab. It took several frustrating minutes for her to be noticed, but finally one pulled up next to her. She quickly jumped in the back.

"East Street, near Seventh and Main!" she ordered the driver.

"Lady, ya gotta be crazy! That place is mobbed today. Opening some stupid museum there today. Gotta be thousands of people. Closest I can probably get you is Sixth Street. Ya gonna have to walk a couple of blocks, but I'll see what I can do," the driver chuckled in a thick New York drawl.

"Okay, okay, just hurry please!" Kelly begged him. There was nothing she could do but wait.

The driver, for his part, seemed adept at getting around the stopped traffic. He moved in and around the vehicles expertly. People honked at them as they sped by. He ignored the people who rolled down their car windows and shouted obscenities.

A feeling began to wash over Kelly, which by then, she'd begun to recognize. A vision was coming. Her body began to convulse slightly as it overtook her.

She could see Helga. She was standing in a large field. Next to her, there was a mound of freshly dug earth. The grass, long and still brown from the winter, wisped slightly in the light breeze. The vision was so clear that Kelly could see birds flying up, scattering with startled cries as they took flight into the gray skies above.

Helga looked so carefree. She smiled brightly at Kelly and waved. "You are good girl, my Kelly. Be happy. Always be happy." The realization hit Kelly.

"Why?" she asked. Tears formed in her eyes.

"To kill luck of one, to kill dreams, no matter how bad those dreams, is trade. You take the dream, the tree takes the life. Is way it is my Kelly. I fix my mistake from so long ago. Is my responsibility. I should have done dis long time ago, but I not brave like you. You are brave girl. I fix my mistake now. You go find the boy. You can save him now. I take bad thing away."

"NO!" Kelly protested. If she'd known what was going to happen, she never would have let her go!

"Goodbye, my Kelly. You live long, happy life. I see your happiness in my own vision." She waved one last time, smiling broadly, and then she was gone.

Kelly was overcome with sadness. Helga was gone and she wouldn't be coming back.

"Hey lady? You needa doc or somethin?"

The cab driver's voice pulled Kelly out of the vision, though she fought to stay in it to be with Helga. She was going to miss her so.

She could see the concern on the driver's face in the rear view mirror.

"No, I'm fine," Kelly told him, still feeling shaken. Even to herself she didn't sound very convincing.

"Yeah, well we're he'ya. Closest I could get ya. Go down that block, take a left, go down 'bout half a block and anothah left. You should staht seeing all the people. Follow 'em. That'll be thirty dollahs." Kelly pulled out some money and threw it at the driver, quickly opening the door to the cab and jumping out into the street. She knew that she didn't have time to grieve right then. There was too much at stake. The only way to honor her friend would be to find Bastian and stop that bomb from going off. That way, at least her death would mean something.

Kelly ran as fast as she could, following the directions of the cabbie until she could see the long lines of people. The buzzing and chatter among them was deafening. There had to be literally thousands of people. How was she ever going to find Bastian in all of that mess?

Looking up ahead, she could barely make out the entrance to the museum and could see that Jason was right. There were uniformed officers at the entrances. She counted ten officers, but she'd never be able to push her way through the crowd to get to them and warn them.

She looked around, trying to find a way around everyone, but there didn't seem to be a way. Children ran around legs, playing chase to amuse themselves during the wait. Their parents talked excitedly amongst each other. None of those people could guess what was about to happen to them…to their children.

Not finding a clear path through the main entrance, Kelly started making her way over to East Street, to the side entrance Jason mentioned. She tried calling him, but he didn't pick up.

Kelly skirted the edge of the crowd and had to walk through a diner and out the back door to get to the street. Finally, she could see what appeared to be the East Street entrance. There were no officers guarding that door, but she could see that it was closed. If Jason didn't answer his phone she'd have no way to get in!

She ran up the steep steps to the door and tried the handle but it was locked. She pounded on it, but doubted very much that anyone would be able to hear her with all of the noise.

"Miss! Hey Miss! Get away from that door!" she heard someone order. A man in uniform began rushing towards her from the courtyard. He looked angry. Kelly noticed that he had a sidearm on his belt, and wondered for a moment if he would try to shoot her.

"I need to get in. My boyfriend Jason asked me to meet him here. He designed this building. There's a bomb in the building. I have to find it!" Kelly blurted out, trying to explain. Even to herself, she sounded like a crazy woman.

Instead of looking alarmed however, the officer's face only registered anger.

"I think you'd better come with me," he ordered coldly. He reached out to grab her arm. Kelly noticed something about his eyes. They were not right. Something about the man was not right, and then she just knew. He was one of the men from the urns. They weren't protecting the people from harm, they were leading them in. Making sure that no one interfered.

Kelly jerked out of his grasp and began to run. She headed for the back of the building with him running after her. He was close, barking into his hand held radio an order to help catch her, but she was very fast.

Suddenly she heard a cheer rise up from the crowd out front. They were letting them in!

Her phone rang. It had to be Jason. He was done with the ribbon cutting.

"Jason, I'm here! Let me in!" she yelled, out of breath.

"Hold on. I'm coming. Where are you? Why are you out of breath?"

"One of the officers is chasing me. Go around to the back. I'll have to go in that way."

She saw a door up ahead open. Thank God! Jason peeked his head out and motioned Kelly to come that way.

She reached the door and stumbled in. Jason put a hand

on her shoulder to steady her.

"What in the hell is going on, Kelly? Calm down. I didn't see anyone chasing you, and there really is no bomb. There's nothing to worry about," he eyed her with confusion.

"There is, Jason! I'm not asking for you to do anything but trust me! I know it sounds crazy, but you have to take me to the part of the building that the autistic guy built. Please!" she begged.

"I can't. I didn't get a chance to tell you, but the guy that designed that part of the building died a few weeks ago in a car accident. My boss decided to honor his wishes to keep his part secret. They won't let anyone in yet, including me. The big reveal and dedication is not happening for another hour."

Just enough time to allow hundreds of people through the doors. So they really did need Bastian to find the bomb. Probably that one and any others they may have hidden in the city. Of course they would have a backup plan. When the bomb did go off, the people would surely flee and carry that awful crap out to the crowd on their clothes, Kelly thought. Everyone out there would be at risk.

"There has to be a way, Jason, come on! You helped to design the building, there has to be a way in."

"Maybe there is Kelly, but they've already checked that area of the building. There is no bomb, I keep telling you. They would've seen it, or the dogs would have sniffed it out. It was clean. They wouldn't have opened the building if they didn't think it was one hundred percent safe."

"The bomb is hidden. It's in the floor, or the wall, or somewhere. That guy, the guy that designed that part of the building designed it around the bomb. You have to believe me! The bomb that went off this morning in New

Jersey...He designed that part of the building too, I bet. Didn't he?"

Jason slowly nodded a confirmation. Kelly could almost see the wheels begin to turn in his mind. She was getting through!

"That's why he didn't want anyone to see his work during the construction. They'd see the devices before he could build up around them."

Kelly knew that she'd argued her point just enough. Jason shook his head, as if trying to grasp what she was saying, but took her hand and began leading her down a set of shiny, marble stairs.

"Come on. I think I know a way that we can get in."

"The bathroom?" Kelly asked in disbelief as he pulled her into the brand new facility on the basement level.

"There's a panel in the wall of the handicapped stall. I think we may be able to get in through that. Look, Kelly, if I get caught, I'm most likely going to get fired. Are you absolutely sure?"

"I'm sure, but you're right. If you get caught, you'll definitely get fired, and this isn't your problem. I think you should go back upstairs and keep an eye out for anyone trying to come down."

Jason seemed to struggle with her plan, "Kelly, if you're right, and there is a bomb, what are you going to do? You're going to need some help. I don't want you to get hurt."

"I'll be okay, really. I think I know what to do. This is my problem. I know you want some answers right now, and I promise that I'll give them to you when this is over. Just believing me and getting me in here was enough. I can't tell you how much that means to me. Go back up and try to act normal, but watch for anything suspicious."

Jason relented, "Okay, but I'm going to be waiting at the top of the stairs. If you're not back up in fifteen minutes, then I'm coming down with the police."

"Okay, but Jason...not any of the officers that were guarding the doors. They're all in on it. I think your boss may be in on it too."

CHAPTER TWENTY-FOUR

❖

K elly wrestled with the tabs holding the panel closed. They had been painted over, which made them stick securely to the new wall.

Finally, she pried the last one off and removed the panel. Placing it aside, she crouched through the opening to find herself in a small dark room.

It was hard to see until her eyes adjusted to the darkness. She used the wall as a guide, feeling her way towards a light that was shining through the bottom of a doorway across the room. As she neared, she could make out some voices talking low on the other side of the door.

"But I don't want to do anymore. I want go home. I want see my mommy!"

Bastian! Oh, thank God he was okay! Kelly hoped that Kurt was okay too. The poor kid had been through so much.

"Find the bomb, Bastian. I'm not asking you. It's an order and you will obey," a man's voice commanded angrily. It was familiar, but Kelly couldn't place it.

"No! I want go home! Take me home! You killed my friend!" Bastian cried.

Kelly's heart sank. She opened the door just a crack so she could try to gauge how many people she'd be up against, but there was a man standing in front of it, with his back turned towards her. She couldn't see much.

"Bastian, don't you want to make me happy? All little boys should want to make their mommies happy. If you find the bomb, I'll give you a nice new toy to play with," the voice tried to soothe. Tried to coax. It was a woman's voice!

"You're not my mommy! I thought you were my mommy but you lied to me! I'm not your little boy. He's gone. I don't hear him anymore."

"I don't understand what has happened to him. He's changed," the man accused angrily.

"I don't know, Dolphie, I just don't know, but we're running out of time. They'll be coming soon. You're going to have to make him, but don't hurt him. I'm going to keep this one. He's mine. He belongs to me."

The man moved away from the door, and as he did, the slight pull of wind it created opened the door a little further. Kelly didn't have time to pull away.

Bastian saw her. "Kelly! Help! I'm scared!" he cried.

He tried to run to Kelly but the woman reached down and wrapped her arms around him. He struggled against her, but she held tight.

Kelly recognized her right away. Magdalena. She was old, very, very old. Her skin was paper-thin. Kelly could see every tiny blue vein snaking along in contrast to her spotted but alabaster complexion. It was so odd how absolutely ordinary she looked. For all of her thunder, for all she'd done and been through, she could have been anyone's grandmother.

Her eyes, though, were still as bright as the day Kelly had seen her in the vision, and just as compelling. They revealed her.

The man grabbed hold of the door and threw it open.

"Bastian! Who is this?" he asked angrily. He reached in

and pulled Kelly out with a violent tug.

"Dolphie, call the others. Call them now. If this woman is here, there will be others," she ordered.

Only then did Kelly look up to see his face. It was Dr. Jackson from the hospital. She'd met with him many times at various case meetings. It was him in body, but was most definitely not him. She could see by his eyes that he was from the urns.

It may have been Dr. Jackson's body, but at that moment she was absolutely sure it was Adolph Hitler standing before her.

She should've been terrified. She was undoubtedly in the presence of the most hated and feared man of all time, but oddly, she wasn't at all scared. Kelly had seen through his mask, and it had shown her that he was nothing more than a frightened, pitiful soul. Even in death he hadn't been able to escape the grip that Magdalena had on him. She called him back and he would do what she wanted him to.

He ran off to do what he'd been ordered.

"Kelly! I want my mom!" Bastian wailed, trying in vain to wiggle out of Magdalena's grasp.

"Hold on Bastian. You'll be okay," Kelly soothed. She turned to face Magdalena. If she was going to get through to her, she'd have to speak her language.

"*Itz weildabalm, meip sie sunte. Es oist geit, die versinganheitz sur sihe.*" (*I know who you are. It's time to put the past to rest)*

Magdalena uttered a startled, confused cry. In her shock, she released her hold on Bastian for just a moment. It was enough. He bolted quickly behind Kelly for shelter and held onto her legs for protection.

Kelly could hear the footsteps of the others. The men

from the urns would be coming to try to finish what Magdalena had started all those years ago.

"You know nothing of me. How dare you speak my language?" Magdalena glared at Kelly. "Who taught you this language? MY language. You have no right!" she yelled, spitting her words in her rage. "I will not put the past to rest until every last one of them is dead! Bastian, come back over here and find the bomb. Find it quickly and I won't have to hurt you," she tried coaxing, lowering her voice into a soothing song.

Bastian stayed where he was, and clung more tightly. Kelly reached around herself and gave him a reassuring pat. "Stay here Bastian, no matter what she tells you," Kelly warned.

Kelly persisted despite Magdalena's protest. It was the only way. She began to speak in *Tungri* so that Magdalena would understand perfectly what she had to say. Her words were as clear as if she were speaking English.

"Helga taught me. Your wonderful cousin was my teacher and my friend. She has gone to kill your tree. Your power will die. She traded her life to save so many."

In any language, it was hard for Kelly to say those words. She hadn't had time to grieve. Helga was dead. She had killed Magdalena's tree, and the tree had taken her life. Kelly held back her tears.

She'd been right in what she had said. Magdalena's power was nearly gone, almost dead, but Kelly needed to stay focused. There was still danger there.

Magdalena's face registered anger and disbelief. Her eyes attempted to pierce Kelly. They would have done her some harm if they still could have, but it was mostly gone. It was a lost connection. Kelly knew that her aura must have begun to dim quite some time ago. She could see in the vision that her tree itself was gone. All that was left were the dried roots that Helga had dug out of the earth. She had been counting on using what little power she had left. Without the seed necessary to grow another tree, it was over. Kelly could see that resolution in the slump of Magdalena's shoulders.

The marching of footsteps became louder. They were just around the corner.

Kelly backed up slowly, being careful that Bastian didn't lose his grip. She pushed him into the room she had entered from and closed the door to keep him out of harms' way.

She turned to face Magdalena. She had to try to get her to see once and for all that this had to end.

"Listen to me, Magdalena. I will say this in my language. It's time to face your demons. What happened to you so long ago was a horrible thing. I don't know everything, but I know that Helga felt very sorry for you. She never wanted any harm to come to you. She let your son live because she knew that deep inside, you were not the person that you became. She knew how much you suffered, and didn't want you to have to suffer any more. She saw that you were more than that. No matter what you did, she still loved you."

Magdalena put her hands to her face and began to shake with silent sobs.

Kelly continued, "She saw your shame. I saw your shame. You have to know that what happened to you was not your fault, but what you have done to all of those people is. All of those people were as different as you and I, none of them thinking exactly alike. They were individuals. They felt pain and loss, just like you did. They were not the people who hurt you. You have destroyed the lives of millions to ease the pain of that horrible time in your life. How many lives will it take to make that pain go away? It has to stop now. Only then will you be at rest."

Magdalena reached out and placed a hand on Kelly's arm. The shock was painful.

"See," Magdalena commanded. Her vision began to fill Kelly's mind, but she fought to reject it. She took Magdalena's hand, and threw it away from herself.

Magdalena wanted to show Kelly what she'd been through. She wanted her to understand.

"Whatever you have been through, no matter how bad, it didn't give you the right to do what you did to all of those people. I don't want to see. I don't need to. I don't know you. You are right about that. What I do know is that you may have lived in your time, but you also live in my time. In my time, when something like that happens, even as horrible as it is, you get counseling. You get over it and try to make something good out of it all."

Suddenly Kelly felt herself flinging backwards. Thrown to the floor, she put an arm over her head to shield herself.

"Where is the boy? Where is the boy? They are coming! We have to hurry!" one from the urns cried. Kelly looked up to see a circle of twelve determined faces, all of them eager to please Magdalena, but she stood silent.

One of the men broke his formation and went in search of Bastian. Kelly was on his heels, but she was a fraction too late. He found him in the bathroom and snatched him violently, causing him to cry out. He reached for Kelly, but she could do nothing as he was thrown at Magdalena's feet. He was an offering.

"Tell him, my dear, tell him to find it. We can still do this. It's what you have always wanted." The form of Dr.

Jackson approached Magdalena with eager tenderness.

She looked up; her remorseful face still a mess of tears. She laid a gentle hand upon his cheek.

"My Dolphie. My poor, sweet Dolphie. The misery I must have caused you. I'm so sorry. You can't know how sorry I really am." She reached up to kiss his face one last time.

"I release you. Rest in the peace you have always deserved, my brother."

His eyes stared in stunned disbelief. Confused, but finally set free, Kelly watched as the fear and hate inside of them diminished until it was to be snuffed out forever.

Just like that, it was over. The men from the urns had returned to the dead.

Bastian got up, still whimpering, and scampered towards Kelly. He jumped into her lap, and she rocked him tightly in a hug and tried to soothe him.

Magdalena didn't try to get away. She would have to face her demons. There was nothing for her to do. She would have to endure many months of trials for her war crimes, Kelly was sure. Though it was widely thought that she'd been dead all of those years, she'd been left on the list of wanted for her crimes against humanity. She was, after all, the second most hated person in the world. She was Magdalena Hitler. The people gathered there that day for the opening of the museum would have something else to remember.

Kelly could hear the rush of people headed her way. She would have some explaining to do, if that was even possible, but then she was going to fulfill a promise.

❖

Kristy Gherlone

Greta stood anxiously at the gate waiting for Kelly and Bastian to arrive. She had rushed out of the house and to the airport as soon as she got the call. It broke her heart to hear about poor little Kurt. Surely, the things Bastian had witnessed would be with him for a long time. He would probably have many months of therapy ahead of him to get over the whole ordeal, but he was alive. No matter how he came back to her, she was going to give him the time and attention he needed. She'd do what she had to do. Not out of a sense of duty or responsibility, but because he was her son and she loved him. He could even call her Greta if he wanted to, she thought with a laugh. As long as she had him back, she would take him for what he was.

She watched as the stream of people exited the gangway. Scanning the crowd nervously, she heard him before she actually saw him. Her heart leapt into her throat with overwhelming relief. She could hear his sweet little voice chattering away to Kelly. She wouldn't be jealous anymore, she resolved silently. She owed Kelly everything she had for this.

Greta held her breath as they came around the corner to where she stood waiting. She didn't know what to expect. She would try hard to hold it together if he wouldn't let her hug him, though she desperately wanted to.

"Mommy!" Bastian cried, finally seeing Greta. He let go of Kelly's hand and rushed into her arms. Greta, overcome with joy, picked him up and held him tight. He snuggled his face into her hair and let her love him.

"Thank you so very much, Kelly. Thank you for bringing Bastian back to me," she whispered.

❖ 322 ❖

EPILOGUE

Two years later

Greta answered the phone just as she finished placing the last of the décor on the colorful cupcakes she'd made for Bastian's class. Her class. She had nervous butterflies in her belly thinking that at this time tomorrow, she would be getting into her wedding dress and walking down the aisle.

She'd found love, and in turn, a father for Bastian. He deserved that.

"Kelly! Are you guys still coming?"

"Coming? Pa-leeze! I'm the maid of honor. We wouldn't miss it. I'm officially on vacation, and I can't wait to see you all!" Kelly told Greta happily.

"You'd better be bringing that baby!" Greta warned jokingly. She reached down to rub her own not quite yet swollen belly and smiled secretively.

"Are you kidding? Nicholas would never let me go anywhere without him, the little fuss," she laughed.

"I know! Every time we talk, I can hear him hollering for your attention," Greta laughed. "He's stealing my best friend away from me!"

In truth, the time Kelly did have to spend away from him wasn't very much. She didn't really need to work, but as she told Jason, she would lose her sanity if she didn't. The money Helga had left her, with Professor Stein's blessing,

Kristy Gherlone

was more than enough to ensure she would never have to work again.

She stayed as busy as she wanted, taking various contracted roles as an interpreter. She loved it, but not as much as being a wife and mother. Of course, she still took on an occasional client. She would always be on the alert. Always listening for *Tungri.*"

"Hey, did you hear about Sophie Feinstein?" Greta asked.

"Yup! I'm so happy that she had a healthy baby. That antidote was a miracle. And to think that an autistic med student at Harvard came up with it! An extract from a tree root…a mandrake tree root." Kelly exclaimed. She, like the rest of the country, had been waiting for word on those poor people from New Jersey, and was glad they wouldn't suffer permanently.

"Are you headed off to class?" Kelly asked.

"Yup. I never thought it would happen, but I love being a teacher. I'm glad that the principal let Bastian be in my class this year. He still clings to me as if his life depends on it," she told Kelly with a chuckle. "Though he is pretty attached to Dan too. He's been calling him daddy for months now."

"Well, tell him hello for me! Actually, I'll tell him myself when I see him tonight."

"You've got it. He has so much to tell you. Just wait until you see how big he's gotten since the last time you guys were here. Which, by the way, has Nicholas outgrown any of those baby clothes yet?"

"Oh my God! No way…"

Kristy Gherlone